Chaos
At
Crescent City
Medical Center

JUDITH TOWNSEND ROCCHICCIOLI

ISBN-13: 978-1482009194

ISBN-10:1482009196

Enjoy!
thanks!
many
Julie R

DEDICATION

This novel is dedicated to the thousands of practicing nurses around the world who care endlessly for patients who are critically, terminally and chronically ill. The significance of their work, their tireless spirits and boundless knowledge of mankind, their experiential wisdom and the complex care they offer can never be quantified, nor can its impact be understood unless you are their patient.

ACKNOWLEDGMENTS

Seeing this novel in print will be the culmination of many years of dreaming and hard work. I could write 300 pages simply listing and thanking the people who have helped me pursue this dream. First of all, I would like to thank my huge circle of family, friends and former and current students for their support of my writing and their reassurances that *Chaos at Crescent City Medical Center* was a great novel and would be published. I would like to thank Dr. Sherry Sandkam of Richmond, VA who encouraged me many years ago to pursue my dream of writing and spent many hours reviewing my work. I would like to recognize and thank Dr. Anne Horrigan, an awesome emergency department nurse who was a technical advisor for me during the emergency department shoot-out, Dr. Julie Strunk, a faculty member at James Madison University who assisted me with the final editing of the novel and Captain Bill Lange (ret) of the Henrico County Fire Department who consulted with me about electrical fires and injuries. Additionally, I want to express my sincere gratitude to all of my wonderful friends who have encouraged me over the years. I would also like to thank my good friend Eric Blumensen for his encouragement and assistance throughout this process. With Eric's assistance and editing, this book is finally a reality.

JUDITH TOWNSEND ROCCHICCIOLI

CHAPTER 1

The pungent smell of Cajun spices permeated the February New Orleans air. With only one week before Carnival, the French Quarter was blazing with activity. Ornate iron balconies bowed under the weight of dozens of people, pressed together tightly for a better look at the street below. Being "up" on a balcony during Mardi Gras was prestigious, giving one an immense sense of power and control over the crowd below. You could get people in the streets to do just about anything for a Mardi Gras "throw" -- a string of plastic beads or an aluminum doubloon.

Raoul Dupree, a waiter at Tujague's Restaurant, was smoking outside the door of the European-styled bistro. His eyes were riveted on a gorgeous man hanging over a balcony a few doors down. The man was teasing a lovely but drunk young woman in the street. The man fingered a string of gold beads in front of her and repeated "show your tits" continuously. Others on the balcony picked up the chant, and it became louder and louder, almost deafening. The young woman kept reaching for the gold beads, just to have them snatched from her grasp each time. She looked around and smiled drunkenly and benignly at the large crowds gathered nearby and above on the balconies. The man was smiling at her, taunting her and luring her to grab the beads. The chant had become louder and frenzied. Crowds on the street and adjoining balconies were wildly excited and picked up the rhythm, hollering, clapping and stamping their feet. Finally, in the flick of an instant, the young woman pulled up her white T-shirt exposing her perfectly shaped breasts. The crowd went wild, clapping and shouting with approval. The woman grabbed her beads held them up for the crowd and quickly disappeared into an alley.

Raoul smiled to himself, shaking his head. Mardi Gras still amazed him. After a lifetime of Carnival seasons, he still wasn't used to the heavy partying, drunken and lewd behavior so common during the season. People would do anything for a Mardi Gras trinket. He shook his head and shrugged his frail shoulders as his eyes again located the handsome man just as a hand reached out and roughly grabbed his blonde hair and shoulder. Raoul startled and looked around quickly and saw the flushed face of the frowning Tujague's maitre d'/bouncer.

"Your boys in the private booth are getting anxious, Raoul. Better get your skinny ass up there and keep 'em happy. We don't want any of those sons of bitches on our bad side," said the burly maitre d' said as he gestured toward the door.

Raoul stamped out his cigarette butt, grimaced and ran up two flights of steps to a private dining room where three men sat smoking after a long lunch. Tujague's, the oldest restaurant in the French Quarter, had a reputation for privacy and discretion and was a meeting place for prominent New Orleanians engaged in all sorts of business legal and illegal. Privacy, circumspect service and seven-course prix fixe dinners made the restaurant a favorite.

The men were talking quietly as Raoul loitered outside the

dining room.   One glance at the group convinced him not to interrupt. He recognized one man, but he'd never seen the others and wondered how they were connected.   From what he'd observed, he didn't think they knew each other well and doubted if they'd ever been together before. They didn't seem to mix. After cocktails and several bottles of wine, the tone of their conversation had moved from strained politeness to menacing. The maitre d' had wasted no words when he'd told Raoul to stay out of the room except to serve.   Each time he'd entered the private booth conversation stopped.

The man Raoul recognized was Frederico Petrelli, better known as "Rico", reputedly a mob boss from Chicago who'd recently moved to New Orleans to oversee the "Dixie Mafia's" activities in the Riverboat and land gambling operations. Raoul knew Rico because he often dined at Tujague's and usually had his special waiter, Matthew. Unfortunately, Matthew was off today due to injuries he'd received last week.

Raoul kept his distance as he eyed the group and decided he never wanted to run up against Frederico. He was in his mid-fifties, balding and at least 40 pounds overweight. He had a long irregular scar on his right forearm, and dark beady eyes. He glared at his companions with distrust and impatience. His thick pursed lips moved back and forth over a wet cigar in his mouth. Frederico was a classic picture of a vicious Chicago mafia boss.

The second man was also distinctive but in a different manner than the gangster. This man was tall, with a swarthy complexion. His dark oiled hair was pulled back into a ponytail. He had a long face with an aquiline nose and thin lips that seemed to curl in a permanent smirk. His eyes were strange, the color somewhere between a blackish-yellow, and they gave the man a sinister appearance. It was impossible to tell his age. He could be anywhere between 30 and 60. His body was big, well-proportioned and in perfect shape. Raoul was pretty sure about this because he spent most of his time visually undressing men and he could easily imagine the man's six pack abs. His clothes were expensive, as was the gold medallion hanging around his neck. He wore dark trousers and a custom-designed dark shirt opened at the neck. He caressed a leather strap in his lap as if it were his lover as he alternately tapped his well-manicured nails against the hand-rubbed walnut table. His dark eyes moved side to side as he followed the conversation between the other two men. His eyes were unreadable and gave him a menacing and evil appearance. Raoul's attention was drawn again to the leather strap in the ponytailed man's lap as he continued to stroke the strap. The ponytailed stranger said little, instead following the conversation between Frederico and the third man. The ponytailed man gave Raoul the creeps, and Raoul rubbed away the chill bumps that had appeared on his arms. Raoul shuddered, thinking the man looked like the devil with those yellow-black eyes and dubbed him "the evil one".

The third man was less distinctive. Raoul wouldn't have paid much attention to him had his companions not been so macabre. The third man was about 40 years old with brown hair and an honest face. He spoke with a Midwest accent and seemed ordinary. The ordinary man was speaking when Frederico summoned Raoul into the dining room. Frederico rudely interrupted him.

"Give us sambukas all the way around. Also, a pot of espresso, and get the fuck out of here," Frederico barked at Raoul.

Raoul left quickly but heard the ordinary man say, don't

care what you do. I want Robert Bonnet ruined and dead. I don't know what your interests are in the Bonnets and the medical center, but I want the man dead. He killed my wife and baby three years ago. Kill him. He had a wild look in his eyes, and was shaking. He appeared unstable.

Raoul's ears picked up at the mention of Robert Bonnet. He knew Dr. Bonnet from the medical center where he worked as a volunteer on the AIDS floor. Dr. Bonnet had operated on his lover last year when no other surgeon had been willing to. Dr. Bonnet hadn't cared that Josh had AIDS and would probably die anyway but had pulled strings to give Josh a chance to get a new liver and live longer. He'd given Josh a lot of comfort before he had died. Hearing threats against Dr. Bonnet encouraged Raoul to take a risk, and he paused for a moment, eavesdropping outside the room.

Frederico glared at the third man with a bored expression and said harshly, "Shut up, choir boy. No time for emotions. They get in the way of business and cause mistakes. No mistakes, you hear?" The gangster's voice had become low and threatening as he glared at the ordinary man. "You make a mistake, you pay."

The ordinary man, frantic, stared at him. The evil one with the ponytail simply nodded his head, said "Salute" and raised his cup in a toast.

Rico continued to glare at the ordinary man and said "Get it choir boy, no mistakes. You know what to do."

The ordinary man nodded.

Raoul returned to the serving area, his heart thudding heavily in his chest.

JUDITH TOWNSEND ROCCHICCIOLI

CHAPTER 2

"You've got to handle this, dammit, Alex. You do treat Robert Bonnet differently from the other staff physicians. This is the third complaint we've received against him in less than six months. Something must be done. That, as lawyer for this medical center, is *your* responsibility."

Alexandra Lee Destephano sat on the edge of the sofa as she listened to her boss rant and rage. Don Montgomery was the chief executive officer at Crescent City Medical Center. Dissociating herself from his tirade, she glanced around the executive office. The office was stiff, formal, and uncomfortable and the décor mirrored the pretentious nature of Crescent City Medical Center's haughty CEO. If fact, there was a likeness between the man and the office. Don Montgomery was tall and stiff in his Versace suit and Louis Vuitton watch. His thinning brown hair framed his cold unsmiling, face.

Alex likened her boss to a fish, but she was brought back to reality as he closed the distance between them and entered her personal space. Alex rose from the sofa and backed away from him. Overlooking the sarcasm in her boss's voice, she prayed for patience and remembered the advice of her maternal grandmother, Kathryn Rosseau Lee of Virginia. Alex struggled for control and responded, "Why don't we take a few minutes to review these claims and see if we do have anything serious against the hospital? I am not convinced that we do." Alex watched the frown flicker across Don's impassive face.

The CEO stood up, walked to his office door, and opened it.

"I don't have time and that is not *my* job. I'm up to my ass in Obama Care bull shit regulations that are going to cost us millions, absolute millions, and I don't have time to discuss your ex-husband's inability to practice safe medicine. If you're going to play ball with the big boys, you'll just have to figure out how or get out."

Alex could feel anger seeping through her brain and tried hard not to roll her eyes as Don continued his self-aggrandizing, "Don't forget that *I* run this hospital. The financial success, image and future of this place are my responsibility. *I* have to second guess our competition and keep our market edge. No one here has any of the skills needed to assist me. Weren't for my leadership, the board of trustees would have voted for that Health Trust merger six months ago."

Alex was sick to death of Don's proclaimed "Savior Behavior" and wondered if he lived in a vacuum. She doubted he realized the efforts of the physicians, staff, and volunteers were part of the success of the world-class and prestigious Crescent City Medical Center. Don consistently took credit for all accomplishments at CCMC and cast blame on others when things went wrong. She sighed as the CEO continued eulogizing himself.

"If I didn't have a handle on internal and external sabotage we encounter daily, we'd be history. Only strong hospitals and medical centers with strong leadership will survive these times, but I can't do it all." Don paused his sermon for a moment and then shook his finger in her face.

"Now, take care of this problem immediately, dammit. I expect a report from you within twenty-four hours about how you're going to handle the malpractice claims against Robert

Bonnet."

Alex was angry at the CEO's disrespect and patronizing superiority but held her temper. "I'll meet with Dr. Bonnet and the staff involved this week."

As she left the office, her self-control barely intact, Alex wondered how many executives she was going to have to train. Don Montgomery was already the second CEO in her two-year tenure as in-house legal counsel for Crescent City Medical Center. She was beginning to wonder if she'd be able to stand it for another two years. Alex constantly wondered if she'd made the right decision in moving to New Orleans to practice hospital law. In all honesty, she wondered did she treat Robert Bonnet, her ex-husband, differently from other CCMC physicians. Sometimes feelings of uncertainty and guilt clouded her mind; she hoped it didn't cloud her professional judgment as well. Alex's thoughts returned to Robert as she left the executive offices and headed toward her own, continuing to think about Robert along the way.

Robert Henri Bonnet, M.D., was the chief of surgery at CCMC and a favored son of New Orleans. Alex knew that Robert was a skillful physician. They'd met over ten years ago at the University of Virginia in Charlottesville, when Robert was a resident in general surgery, and she was a doctoral student in clinical nursing. They dated less than a year before they married in a very small but circumspect ceremony at the UVA Chapel on the Lawn. Their union melded two of the most powerful families in the South -- the aristocratic Bonnets' of Louisiana and the powerful Lees' of Virginia.

Her musings led her through the opulent atrium of the world-famous hospital into the Hospital Café where she ordered a

Latte and continued to think about her failed marriage. The marriage to Robert had been perfect in the early years, and she still wondered when things had gone wrong. In truth, Alex rarely saw Robert at CCMC and knew little about his personal life. She was curious about Don's angst towards Robert. Her intuition suggested that something was involved but she wasn't sure what it was.

Alex reflected on her meeting with Don as she slowly sipped her coffee. Other physicians at CCMC presented greater legal risks than Robert. For instance, her greatest concern was the hospital's internationally famous vascular surgeon who allowed his physician's assistant to perform complex aspects of cardiac surgery. Another concern centered on CCMC's nationally known cancer physician whom Alex suspected of practicing active euthanasia. She considered these physicians much more dangerous than a few complaints about Robert.

Alex had considered her former relationship with Robert prior to accepting employment at CCMC. Their divorce had been final for four years, and their parting had been amicable. Much of their difficulty had centered on Alex's decision to go to law school and postpone having children until she established a law practice. Robert, a product of a traditional home, didn't like the idea of a professional wife who worked outside the home. Over the duration of their marriage, their individual lives took separate paths -- Robert's in medicine and Alex's in law. The decision to end the marriage was mutual although Alex believed two miscarriages, during her third year of law school, were the major reason Robert divorced her. Robert had wanted her to quit school at the onset of the second pregnancy, but Alex had refused, noting that she was healthy and too close to graduation. Robert had become extremely depressed at the loss of the second child and declared they'd grown too far apart to continue their marriage. He had moved out of their home shortly afterward and filed for divorce.

She'd been hurt by the separation and divorce but knew it would have been difficult to build a life with Robert. After the divorce and her graduation from UVA law school, she'd accepted an offer from a chain of Catholic hospitals in Houston.

Alex's tenure with the Catholic hospital group had provided her with experience and practice. Her nursing background added considerable depth to her ability to determine high risk and analyze potential malpractice cases.

Alex continued to mull over Don's curious request as she looked around the glass atrium. Why did Montgomery want her to fix Robert? Her intuition nagged at her and suggested there was more than was apparent in the CEO's behavior. She made a mental note to call Robert and speak with him soon.

As Alex entered her office suite, she noted that her secretary was late. Just as she finished checking email, her striking blonde-headed bomb shell Cajun secretary, Bridgett, almost six feet tall in red spiked heels, knocked on her door and came in.

"Happy Monday, Alex," Bridgett sang. "We've got a new unbelievable complaint for *the book*. You're gonna love it."

Alex looked up and smiled as she waited patiently waited for Bridgett to continue her story.

Bridgett combed her long blonde hair back with her fingers and grinned. "Well, patient's probably a nut bunny, but then what's

11

JUDITH TOWNSEND ROCCHICCIOLI

new?? Anyway, for the purposes of our book, she's got a great story."

Bridgett was dancing with excitement, dying to tell Alex about the new patient complaint. Her blue eyes sparked with the anticipation of her newest adventure in the legal advisor's office. Bridgett loved her job, and she was good at it. She could sell ice to Eskimos in December and had prevented many lawsuits at CCMC simply by listening and being supportive of families in crises.

Alex laughed. "Is it better than the guy who came in for the penile enlargement but refused to wear his weights?"

Bridgett burst into renewed laughter again. "Unbelievable. Yeah, that thing never did work, did it? The surgery would've worked if he'd worn his weights, right? I mean, you gotta pull that old thing up and out to make it larger, right?" Bridge dissolved once again into laughter.

Alex shrugged her shoulders and grinned, "Who knows? To be honest, I don't know much about penile implants, don't really want to but I do believe that obeying laws of physics would have made the surgery successful."

Bridgett, still laughing, thumbed through the book as she contemplated her answer. The Crescent City Medical Center book of *The Craziest Patients Ever* was a compilation of the most colorful, unusual and creative patient complaints known to the medical center. The addition of a new entry to the coveted notebook was a spectacular event made known only to a few individuals. Favorite entries to date included complaints from the penis man, another man who'd forgotten he'd agreed to have his foot amputated and complained later when he found it was missing, and the woman who had committed her husband to The

Pavilion, CCMC's psychiatric facility, and later sued the hospital for negligence after she signed him out against medical advice. And of course, there was the New Orleans Voodoo Queen who swore that the hospital had "taken" her magical powers after surgery. The suit had still not been dismissed and was being handled in the city court.

Bridgett continued to string Alex along, not telling her the new story until Alex erupted into a fix of impatience. "Tell me. Don't keep me waiting."

Bridgett hesitated a few more seconds. Finally she began,

"Well this one is straight out of the Emergency Department..."

"Yeah and....hurry up! You never know when we're gonna be interrupted around here," Alex said, as she scanned the outer office furtively.

"Well," Bridgett continued, "This man came into the ED and told the admitting clerk that he had to see a doctor right away because he couldn't talk..."

"Who was taking for him?"

"He was talking for himself."

Alex stared at Bridgett uncomprehending. "I don't get this. What am I missing? How could he not talk if he was talking?"

"That's probably a good question. Well, I guess the clerk didn't even pick up on it and sent him back him to see a doctor. Then they called in a throat specialist."

"Terrific," Alex said sarcastically, shaking her head and smiling. "We really have a bunch of rocket scientist clerks over there, don't we?"

"Yep," Bridgett replied, "but there is no new news there."

Alex nodded agreement, "Then what?"

"He saw a doctor, some new guy to the CCMC ED who kept insisting to the patient that he *could talk* until the patient just sort of went bonkers, screaming and yelling and holding his head."

"And then..?"

"The doctor left him alone and went out front, raging at the ED admitting clerks and then went to order a psych consult. About that time, the new throat surgeon came in and not knowing, saw the patient. Then a short time later the nurses heard a bunch of screaming and the sounds of stuff breaking coming from the guy's room. When they went to check, the patient had broken all the IV bottles and equipment he could find, pulled all of the equipment out of the wall and jumped up on the wall-mounted TV and swung back and forth on the TV while it was still on the wall. *The Price is Right* was on."

Alex looked at Bridgett, dumbfounded at the new story and at people in general. "What'd did the nurses do?"

"Called security but before they could get there, the man jumped down from swinging on the TV and ran out of the ED into the lobby where he turned all of the green plants over on the new oriental carpeting. If that wasn't enough, he turned the water fountain machine upside down on the carpet making an enormous mud slide."

Alex covered her mouth with her hand, "OMG, Don's gonna have a shit fit. He just had those carpets installed..."

"You haven't heard the end of it yet, Alex."

Alex stared at her secretary, her eyes huge, "What else?"

Bridgett was now reporting at full capacity, her long red nails clicking against the desk. "Well, he pulled down all of the framed art in the foyer too and smashed all of the glass all over the marble floor." Once again Bridgett dissolved into peals of laughter. "I heard Don almost had a heart attack when they called him."

"Wow. I bet he just about pooped his pants," thinking this must have occurred just after she had met with him.

"Probably. Anyway, the guy was apparently acting pretty crazy and people were afraid of him and ran away. When the area was clear, he ran over to the coffee kiosk and turned all of that over too. The newly opened marble foyer now looks like a black, gritty hell."

"And the art collection is smashed to smithereens. Good Lord, how long did it take CCMC security to get there?"

"All of this happened very quickly, probably 3 or 4 minutes at tops. The guy was fast! The staff is calling him the "Monkey Man" based on his ability to swing from the TV in the ED. He's also pretty good at slinging coffee and art." Bridgett was laughing so hard her big blonde curls were dancing and tears and mascara were streaming from her eyes. "We've got some great pictures from cell phones and digitals. Don is going to have a shit-fit."

"You got that right, if he hasn't already." The look of disbelief on Alex's face was mingled with humor. "Pretty incredible. He spent millions on that renovation."

Bridgett looked at Alex sideways. "Well, serves him right. Maybe he should spend that money on his staff and patients."

Alex nodded and asked, "Does Monkey Man have a regular doctor?"

Bridgett looked at Alex sheepishly, "Yep, Dr. Bonnet."

Alex raised her eyebrows and said sarcastically, "Huh, oh great. But why? Robert's a surgeon. Why would he have a medical patient? Well, I need to see him anyway."

"I think the guy is a charity case, from the clinic where Dr. Bonnet volunteers. Al," Bridgett began and then hesitated for a moment, "There are a lot of rumors about Dr. Bonnet among the nurses and the administrators. I know people aren't comfortable talking with you about him since he's your ex and all...."

"What kind of rumors?" Alex's voice was sharp, her former good mood gone. She knew Bridgett had good connections on the grapevine, particularly from her twin sister, Angela, a nurse in the operating room.

"Just that he's been irritable and unpredictable lately, and some of the nurses think he's been drinking when he makes rounds." Bridgett looked at Alex's face and was instantly sorry for repeating the rumor.

Alex's face darkened. "That's news to me. Keep me posted about our new complaint. Alex jerked her head toward the door, "I guess I better get to this pile of work." She tried to sound noncommittal, but Bridge could tell she was concerned.

Bridgett walked towards the outpatient surgery department and thought about the ongoing battles between Alex and Don Montgomery. Bridgett couldn't understand how someone couldn't get along with Alex. Alex was great, a regular person. She was patient and kind and a bunch of fun. Part of Alex's beauty was she didn't know she was beautiful. Besides that, she was really nice, a real down to earth person. Not snotty like that uppity female lawyer before her.

She hoped she hadn't upset Alex. She felt a pang of guilt for talking to Alex about Dr. B. She doubted Alex even thought of herself as exceptional. She never seemed to notice how people looked at her when she walked into a room. If anything, Bridgett thought, her boss seemed a little shy and unsure of herself. Guess it takes a long time to get over a bad marriage.

Besides, losing Dr. Bonnet would be hard. He was so good-looking and kind, a real hunk. Her cousin told her he ran a free surgery clinic in the bayou. A couple months ago her cousin told her he'd saved the arm of a little boy who had been bitten by an alligator. He didn't even charge the family. He was really good to the Cajun community. Bridgett flipped her blonde hair back and decided she didn't believe the rumors about the handsome Dr. Bonnet.

After Bridgett left, Alex sat at her desk and pondered her secretary's remarks about Robert. She valued her rapport with the nursing staff and was pleased that they, in spite of her law degree, still perceived her as one of them. Her relationship with them had come in handy more than once.

Alex reflected back to the times Robert had drunk more than she thought he should. She'd attributed it to the pressures of hospital life and hard work, although there were a few times when their own personal difficulties had seemed to cause bouts of heavy drinking, particularly after the miscarriages. She specifically recalled an episode concerning her refusal to quit school. It depressed her a bit to hear the rumors. Hope they're just rumors, she said to herself. I don't need this.

Several hours later Alex was immersed in a slip and fall case, when Bridgett buzzed her to say that Dr. Bonnet wanted to see her. Within moments Robert was in her office.

"Alex, how good to see you. How are things going?"

Alex looked up as she felt a blush creeping up her neck. At 42, Robert was an astonishingly attractive man. He was tall with sandy blonde hair and had the slight build of the New Orleans French population. His voice was deep and soft with a subtle Creole accent. His eyes were brown and expressive, kind eyes, she had always thought. Alex immediately stood and offered her hand. "Robert, how good to see you. It's been a while." Alex was stunned by her formality.

Robert's eyes appraised Alex critically. "It has. This hospital is so big; months go by before I see many of my colleagues. Alex, you look beautiful! New Orleans agrees with you. Tell me about your family. How are Grand and the Congressman? I read in the morning paper that he's here in New Orleans. Business?"

Alex felt a flush come over her again and she could feel the warmth as it moved all the way up and down her body. I can't believe that I'm feeling like this about seeing him. I must look like a teeny bopper to him. She was breathless and a little nervous as she responded. "Yes, Granddad's here. Some big political pow-wow, coalition building thing with Governor Raccine.

Grandmother's doing fine. She broke her hip last September, riding her horse. Fortunately, her fall didn't slow her down much. Still rides every day. She's still managing the family, the Washington house, and the horse farm."

In truth, Alex's grandmother, Kathryn Lee, was the strongest force in her life. Unlike her shy, reclusive daughter, she had an interminable strength, yet she was gracious and pragmatic. She had the patience of a saint and the soul of an angel. Grand had served as a role model for Alex all of her life and much of Alex's strength of character and integrity had been inherited from Kathryn. Her grandfather often joked that Alex had inherited her grandmother's bad points as well. Congressman Lee insisted that both women were the most stubborn and willful women on earth.

Robert smiled and said, "I miss seeing her. She's quite the lady. How's the Congressman?"

"The same. You know him -- still serving the conservative people of Virginia. He's actively drafting crime, drug, and immigration legislation. He's totally opposed to Obama Care and voted against it. He's convinced that it is going to ruin healthcare as we know it in this country. And, of course, he has his own ideas about health reform -- and they don't, as I'm sure you can imagine, complement those of the present administration."

"I can imagine," Robert replied wryly. "I'd think our views probably wouldn't match but would serve for some lively conversation. I miss seeing them. You seen your grandfather yet?"

"No. He's busy tonight. We're planning to get together tomorrow afternoon. He's taking the red-eye back to Virginia tomorrow night."

"Give him my best. Get to the farm much?"

Alex nodded as her blue eyes took on a faraway look as she visualized her grandparents' farm, "Wyndley," located half-way between Richmond and Washington D.C. in Hanover County, Virginia. After her parents had divorced when she was three years old, Alex had spent most of her childhood at Wyndley with her grandparents and her reclusive mother.

"No, I'm hoping to get up for a long weekend in April or May. Virginia's beautiful in the spring and Grand just purchased a new Arabian brood mare. Wyndley's becoming a well-known thoroughbred farm. I need to get back there more often. It grounds me and helps me sort through things and get them into perspective."

Robert nodded in understanding. "Yeah, I understand that. That's why I often go over to my summer home in Gulf Shores. I went last weekend and, as a matter of fact, I'm going this weekend for that very reason to escape Mardi Gras. The ocean, sun, and a few nights at the Floribama bar will allow me to relax."

Alex's thoughts immediately returned to the rumors of Robert's drinking. They'd spent many evenings "wasting away "in Gulf Shores, Alabama at the coveted Floribama Lounge, the legendary home of Jimmy Buffet where very few people left alert. Of course, the Floribama was gone now, washed away by Hurricane Katrina. "Be careful."

"Will do. By the way, Don Montgomery said you wanted to see me. What's up?"

Alex looked at him sharply, her paranoia kicking in. "That why you're here? When did you see Don?" Alex was suspicious.

"Last week at a medical staff meeting. He mentioned on the way out you wanted to see me. You never called, and today my morning OR schedule got canceled, so I just came by on the chance you'd be in.

Alex tingled with anger, and then suspicion set in. She felt ambushed.

"Did Don give you any idea about why we needed to meet?" Alex's voice was distrustful.

Robert picked up on the suspicious edge to Alex's voice. "No. Why? What's going on?"

Noting the flush in her check, his voice raised, "What! Alex, no games. We go back too far to play games with each other." His voice had a ring of concern in it.

Alex's intent was to be professional, and she chose her words carefully. "Don's concerned because we've received three complaints about you in less than six months. One will end up as a malpractice action. He thinks three complaints are too many for that period of time. Besides, Don really likes to micro-manage," she added quickly, shrugging her shoulders.

Robert ignored Alex's dig at Don Montgomery. He scowled at her and replied, his voice was reserved and formal. "I want to be clear here. I assume the action you're speaking of is the one where the elderly gentlemen with cancer developed a post-operative infection and died following colon surgery."

Alex nodded and Robert continued, "I warned the patient, the family, and the oncologist of this risk. He was a poor candidate because of his battered immune system; he was a sitting duck for a massive infection." Robert stopped for a moment and reflected. He shook his head sadly as he thought about the man's prolonged and painful death. "I'm not the only physician named. You should be able to defend that claim. After all, you are a UVA lawyer! What else?"

Alex flinched at Robert's sarcasm, and her own stress began to increase as she felt her heartbeat pick up. "Let me pull the files. I can't recall the other two off the top of my head." As she left her office, her gut tightened and the nausea began to mount. She had a sick feeling. Something's going on, she thought. What the hell is going on? He's freaked. This isn't the confidant, brilliant and self-assured surgeon I used to know. Alex took several minutes to compose herself and review the files before returning to her office.

Robert paced in Alex's office. As he waited for her to return, he could feel his own anxiety rising. He couldn't understand Montgomery's behavior towards him either, and, combined with the other things that were happening, he was feeling unnerved. He was constantly getting bumped from the OR schedule for no good reason. Several people he'd worked with for years were acting strangely, some were actually avoiding him, and he'd been greeted frostily this morning by another surgeon. Something was definitely stewing. But what? Robert shook his head but continued to think as he felt a darkness descend upon him.

Alex found Robert deep in thought when she returned. He looked at her expectantly, his voice reserved as he addressed her, "Well, what are they?"

Alex turned papers in the file. "In November you did an abdominalplasty and a breast augmentation on Elaine Morial

Logan. Now she's complained that her new belly button's disfigured, and her breasts are too large. She's also complained that you were short-tempered and angry with her when she came in for her follow-up visit. Several weeks ago her lawyer called and threatened a malpractice action because his client maintains she never knew that her 'new' breasts were silicon and could possibly cause cancer."

Robert face flushed with anger. "That's a pile of crap. What bullshit. We discussed the silicon controversy in great detail. Elaine Logan will never be satisfied with herself *or* her body. I didn't want to do the surgery anyway because I knew there'd be trouble, and her psychiatrist, Dr. Desmonde, agreed with me. All of this is noted in the medical record." Robert gestured angrily towards the file on Alex's desk.

"Why'd you do the surgery, Robert?" Alex gave him a curious look. She saw another flash of impatience as he responded, his voice disgusted and terse.

"It was political. I got a bunch of pressure from the hospital diversity committee. Apparently, she complained to some of the black physicians that I refused to operate on her because she was black. Of course that's BS as well. Consequently, the committee and Don insisted, pressured me to do the surgery. They wanted to avoid any negative publicity from the Morial Logan family."

Alex rolled her eyes, but she believed Robert's story. She continued, "Well, according to Don, Elaine Morial Logan is causing us considerable negative publicity in the black community. I don't need to remind you of her social standing or her network in New Orleans."

"Hell yes, I know their standing. I am *from* here, remember?"

Alex grimaced at his response. "Robert, be careful what you say. This woman and her family are potentially dangerous to us, both politically and economically. Her husband represents St. Bernard's Parish in the legislature. We've trying to get approval to build a new facility there. If her brother succeeds in his bid for mayor, CCMC will need him as a friend. We don't need the Morial and Logan families as enemies."

Robert shrugged it off, resigned, "Okay, Alex. Sorry. I still think you should be able to defend this. Where's the complaint now?"

"Well, it comes before the hospital risk and medical malpractice committee in two weeks. If Logan files, we'll settle out of court."

"That's bull-shit. You can't be serious. I've done nothing wrong." Robert, clearly angry, stopped for a moment. "If anything, I exercised extreme prudence by not even wanting to operate on this lady. I knew she was a problem. As far as I'm concerned, administration got me into this. They can damn well get me out. It's a set-up, and I'm furious about it. That's the last time I'll be their damn patsy. What else?" Anger was clear in Robert's voice as he slammed his fist on the table.

"The other complaint is an internal one lodged by several operating room nurses and techs who, at this point, must remain anonymous. They complained your behavior in the operating room is erratic and unsafe and that you are always short-tempered."

"This is preposterous. I have great rapport and working relationships with the OR staff. Who filed this? I don't believe it." Robert's face was suffused with anger.

"Robert, you know I can't tell you."

"Tell me what you can, please." He gave her his pitiful look she remembered from way back. She relented some.

"Well, mainly they complained of emotional and profane outbursts when you couldn't schedule your surgeries to meet your time constraints. You exhibited some, and I quote, 'acting out' behaviors. They also report that you yelled at them when a sterile field was set up incorrectly."

"Hell, yes, I was angry when they set the sterile field incorrectly the third time. That idiot, Bette Farve, keeps hiring these incompetent OR techs instead of RNs. Setting up the sterile field incorrectly delayed the surgery for forty-five minutes. Has anybody calculated what that cost the hospital in lost time and money? Besides, the patient had an additional forty-five minutes of anesthesia he didn't need -- that could have caused problems for him and us." Robert shook his head disgustedly. "What's the unsafe practice complaint?"

"It's unclear. Apparently one of your patients died during surgery and one OR staff member maintains the reason he died was because you incorrectly hooked him up to the heart-lung pump." Alex set the file down and looked hard at Robert.

His mouth flopped open. He was shocked. "That's absurd. I don't even do that, the cardiac techs do."

"This OR staffer says you rarely, if ever, check the settings on the pump. That's the unsafe practice complaint."

"Dammit, that's their job. They're licensed to do it." Robert stood and began pacing around Alex's office. "Something's wrong here. This is a witch hunt. Has to be. I don't understand it. I need to go, Alex, and think these things over. I'll talk to you later."

As Robert left her office, all his attention was focused on the barrage of complaints against him. He didn't see the tall dark-haired man with the swarthy complexion outside of Alex's office.

Alex decided to pack it in. It had been a really long day.

CHAPTER 3

Alex walked home from the medical center. She lived in the Riverbend area of the city, less than a mile from the hospital. Crescent City Medical Center was located on Prytania, between St. Charles Avenue and the river, in the shadow of Interstate 10. The location allowed easy access to its hundreds of patrons. Alex's home was a few blocks off St. Charles and she could, weather permitting, easily walk back and forth. The horrendous New Orleans traffic made walking preferable to driving and the exercise benefits were another boost.

As Alex reached home, she smiled at how well the restoration of her house had turned out. She'd decided to live in the Riverbend area of New Orleans because the neighborhood was convenient to work, and she loved the architecture. She'd purchased a large town house shortly after arriving in New Orleans, and divided it into two apartments, renting the lower flat. The house was built in 1875 and could be easily hailed as "Old New Orleans." Many of her favorite restaurants and shops were within walking distance.

As Alex reached her front courtyard, she was jarred out of her daydreaming as her cell phone began ringing. Searching for it in her purse, she opened the front door only to note the obviously loud ringing of her house phone. She immediately felt a pang of guilt as she heard the deep voice of Mitch Landry on the other end. She answered the phone and smiled as she heard Mitch's anxious voice on the other end of the line.

"Alex, you haven't forgotten our dinner plans have you? I've been calling and calling for an hour."

Alex smiled into the phone. "No, of course not. I'm sorry, I should have called you. I just walked in. It's been a long day, and, to be completely honest, I've been tied up all day. But, I'm starving, ready and willing. What's the plan?" Her voice was light-hearted.

Mitch checked his watch. "Well, it's now about six-thirty. Pick you up at eight? I've reservations at the Cafe Degas for eight-thirty."

"Sounds great. See you then."

As Alex hung up the phone, she felt guilty about forgetting her date with Mitch. Most people would die for a male companion like him. He was handsome, intelligent and well-connected. As an architectural historian and preservation consultant, he'd never be wealthy, but money seemed unimportant to him. Mitch was a pleasant escape from her day-to-day grind at the hospital and offered refreshing company. Besides, Alex smiled to herself, Mitch was very sexy, and she really liked him.

Her spirits brightened as she showered, dressed for her dinner date, and found herself mentally comparing Mitch with Robert. They were entirely different, she thought, in appearance and personality. Mitch was tall and dark with a muscular build. Robert was of slighter stature with much lighter coloring. Both men had a fervent passion for their work and both men were self-absorbed in their careers.

This is ridiculous, she chided herself. Why should I compare these two? My marriage to Robert has been over for years. It's crazy for me to even be thinking this way. Robert's completely out of my life. But, in all honesty, Alex had to wonder about her reaction to him today in her office. She heard the door bell ringing and saw Mitch standing between the two Grecian Columns in her courtyard. She answered the door, her heart beating rapidly.

Mitch looked devastatingly handsome as he stood in the door frame. He was perfect, too perfect Alex sometimes thought. He had on dark trousers and a white shirt open at the neck. He was in excellent physical shape and Alex knew he worked out most days. His wavy dark hair was combed back from his face. He was tall, dark, handsome and exciting.

Alex's heart began beating a little faster at the sight of him. Once again she wondered why Mitch, whom she'd been seeing exclusively for over four months, was reticent to start a physical relationship with her. At first, Alex had been relieved that Mitch hadn't pressured her into intimacy. Yet, several times she'd found she feeling vulnerable and rejected at the end of the evening. It was probably residual feelings that stemmed from her father's and Robert's rejections of her. More recently, Mitch seemed to be moving towards intimacy again, although his usually warm and inviting conversation often became stilted and aloof at the close of the evening.

Mitch's eyes lit up at the sight of Alex, and he appraised her admiringly. "You look great... That teal color of your dress sets off your eyes, and I like your hair down. You look so carefree and comfortable." Mitch groped for the proper words.

"I know, relaxed and casual. Bridgett tells me the same thing. I guess I must look like an old maid at the hospital. To quote my idiotic boss, 'I have to dance with the big boys, so appearance is important.'" Alex paused for a moment and inhaled the fragrance of the spring flowers. "These flowers are beautiful.

How about a glass of wine?"

"Sure. I told Andre at the Cafe we may be a little late. Do you have any of that Virginia Chardonnay we enjoy so much? I'm pretty impressed with Virginia wine."

"The Chardonnay is from Barboursville Vineyards, near my grandparents' farm. Help yourself. I also have some Brie, heated with honey and almonds, on the coffee table in the living room. I'll be in as soon as I arrange these flowers."

Mitch poured two glasses of the Chardonnay in Alex's wine glasses and gazed appreciably around her living room. The furnishings were impeccably beautiful, simple, and elegant, just like Alex. It's funny how people reflect their homes, Mitch mused, as he studied the lovely walnut library cabinet on the wall opposite the sofa. As his eyes continued to survey the room, Mitch again noted the architectural design of the flat. The heavily carved mantels and decorative woodwork in the living and dining rooms were left natural, and pale blue silk wallpaper pulled together the pastels in the living room.

Alex returned with the fresh flowers in a cut-glass vase which she placed on the dining room table. She seated herself on the sofa next to Mitch. After reaching for her wine and taking a sip, she asked, "How's your newest project going? Did you get your historical foundation funding for the Acadia Village Project?"

Mitch's face showed the animation he felt for his newest project. He'd been chosen to plan the preservation and restoration of a small settlement of historical structures in southwest Louisiana. He was delighted at the opportunity to finally pursue rural preservation. Since most of his work had been done in the French Quarter and in the Garden District, the opportunity to work on rural preservation would showcase his knowledge and ability in the areas of Creole and Arcadian architecture.

Mitch smiled and answered her question. "Yes. It's great. Next week I begin the Arcadian Village in Lafayette. Would you like to visit the project? It's a nineteenth-century Cajun settlement and it represents rural Louisiana." He continued, "Let's plan a weekend soon so you see the work as it unfolds." He looked at his watch.

Alex warmed at the possibility of a field trip to Mitch's architectural projects. "So I can have a full appreciation of your talents," Alex teased. "I would love to. When can we go?"

"Soon, but I haven't done anything yet." Mitch glanced again at his watch and said, "We had better get going. We don't want to keep Andre waiting too long. I'd hate to lose our table."

As they left her apartment and walked toward Mitch's car, Alex again savored the New Orleans night, and the fragrance of lilac and wisteria created an aura of romance. As Alex slipped her hand into Mitch's, she felt him stiffen slightly. She felt rebuffed and wondered why he continued to see her. He doesn't seem to have any sexual interest in me, so what's this all about, she thought to herself. She didn't understand his reticence. They seemed to go well together and had similar interests. He did seem to care for her and was warm and generous with his time and his gifts. Besides, she liked him better than any male companion she'd had since her divorce. That made it even harder to accept.

The ambiance at the Cafe Degas was perfect. Like many fine restaurants in New Orleans, it had an eclectic decor. There were no side walls, only louvered shutters in case of extreme cold or rain. The evening was almost warm enough for al fresco dining, but

Mitch, fearing the night would turn cool, ushered Alex to a table in the corner.

The cuisine at the cafe was excellent. After listening to the specials, Alex choose beef and Mitch selected crepes.

Their dinner conversation revolved around various topics.

"Your grandfather's in town. Read about it this morning in the paper. How's he doing?"

"Great. I talked with him earlier. He has a meeting tonight and he's leaving late tomorrow. We're having drinks tomorrow afternoon."

"Are he and your grandmother staying with you?"

"My grandmother isn't here. He's alone and staying at Palm Court. It's a quick trip. Some political brouhaha, I'm sure. He's especially good at those." Alex smiled, thinking of Adam Lee's particular talent of making people see things his way. "My grandmother swears the Congressman could make a leopard change his spots if given enough time."

Mitch picked up on her smile. "You're close to them, aren't you? Any chance I'll ever get to meet him?"

Alex, surprised, was taken back. "Umm,no. I doubt it, at least not this visit. He's tight for time. I'll introduce you to both of them later. They'll be here in June for another meeting." She could feel a warm flush come over her face. She felt a little guilty about denying him the chance to meet her grandfather. She hoped Mitch wasn't put off by her response.

Recognizing her embarrassment, Mitch reached for her

hand. "Sounds good to me. You ready for the Extravaganza Saturday night?"

Mitch had invited her to the costumed ball sponsored by the Krewe of Endymion. The Endymion Extravaganza was this weekend and was the largest and most lavish ball in New Orleans.

Alex had been anticipating the ball for weeks. She'd gone overboard in having Yvonne LaFleur design a sumptuous gown for her, justifying the purchase with the idea she could wear it again in a few years. Alex was hoping the Endymion Extravaganza would be the beginning of an intimate relationship between her and Mitch. They'd decided to stay overnight at the Fairmount Hotel, the night of the ball, and had plans to spend the weekend in the Quarter. She smiled in anticipation.

"Alex, am I boring you? What are you smiling about? You're in another world." Mitch's eyes were warm over the candlelight.

Alex was immediately apologetic. "Sorry. I was thinking about the Extravaganza and how much fun we're going to have. I'm looking forward to it. What were you saying, Mitch?"

"Nothing important. How about some cafe au lait and cheese cake? Buy the whole thing and you can take it home. I know how much you love it. It'll be the perfect ending to our meal." Alex nodded in agreement.

"How are things going at the hospital? You seem a little distracted tonight?"

"Busy. Health care's changing everywhere, and we are trying to prepare for Obama Care, which none of us truly understands. Nobody understands the health care bill. Not even Obama. The legislation is over 1,000 pages! There are all kinds of fears and concerns over health reform and the whole health care environment is fiercely competitive and focused on cheap care but good results. I know it's going to cost us millions and we will see significant job losses in health care providers, especially nurses, because reimbursement will decline. Most small to medium size hospitals are estimated to lose at least a million dollars a year in Medicare reimbursements." Alex noticed that Mitch was paying rapt attention and continued, "Obama Care includes $575 billion in cuts to Medicare to pay for a Medicaid expansion to provide health care for the poor, but these cuts are going to hurt those of us in acute care. The elderly are our most expensive and costly patient population. It's real competitive here, more than in most places, or at least that's what I hear from my colleagues. Look what's happened here in the past few weeks. American Hospital Corporation bought 80 percent of Tulane for $180 million. Then, they immediately merged with Health Quest and formed another huge conglomerate. Health Trust, as it's known, now owns twenty-five hospitals in Louisiana. It's going to be difficult for smaller hospitals to compete with these big boys." Alex paused for a second, thinking to herself and continued, "Health Trust even has international holdings, and, when you factor national health insurance programs into it, the times will be dangerous at best and the outcomes and quality of care uncertain, mostly like substandard to outcomes now. These huge conglomerates are buying up hospitals in Europe, specifically in England and Switzerland, and I understand they're even negotiating with hospitals in South America. Makes you wonder who'll still be in business in a few years with the fierce competition. It's a turbulent time for healthcare."

Mitch was listening closely and responded, "How many hospitals can they buy without it being a monopoly?"

Alex looked speculative. "All but one, I suppose. I'm not as worried about monopolies as I am about legal risks and cost-cutting to save money on patient care. Hospitals are struggling to survive. These mergers and buy-outs affect a hospital's credibility and image. Obama Care is going to make things even harder and more expensive. Look what's happened recently in Florida and in Boston, especially the hospital that gave 10 times the amount of chemotherapy drugs and killed the patient. These errors are tragic and have long term consequences. It'll take those hospitals years to recover from the negative publicity."

"Yeah. You would think a cancer center would know how to calculate the correct chemotherapy medicine. Those patients' families were really angry and the press had a field day with it. People pick hospitals because of their doctors, don't they?"

"Used to, but now they have to go where their insurance company will pay. Big business and insurance companies run health care now. They control health care and who gets it. Obama Care will only make it worse and more costly. Remember when hospitals first started advertising and using slogans like, 'the best care in town' or 'caring made visible' or 'the finest doctors in the country?'" Mitch nodded, and Alex continued.

"These slogans have come back to haunt us, becoming the basis for malpractice suits. Sometimes patients don't believe they got the best care or the finest doctors."

"Are these claims defensible?"

"Many are, some aren't, depending on the facts of the case.

Information systems make it possible for patients to search data bases kept on health care practitioners. For instance, a patient can find out whether a practitioner has ever been sued."

"Sounds like the medical information explosion to me. Pretty scary for doctors and nurses, I would imagine."

"It is. Patients can even learn how much money the physician earns. That adds even more fuel to the fires of malpractice actions. It's all part of the consumer rights movement." Alex was pensive as she stared into her water glass.

"You mean that if patients experience bad results from surgery or medical treatment, they can do their own research to build a malpractice claim?" Mitch looked surprised.

"Sure. Even more disturbing than the actual malpractice actions is the amount of publicity they receive, and how that publicity impacts the image and reputation of a hospital. I predict those hospitals in Boston and Florida will lose millions in revenues in the next couple of years. Times are tough. Many smaller and less powerful hospitals will be bought and closed by big corporations to decrease competition and costs. Others'll be forced out of business. We're already seeing that in New Orleans."

Mitch set his coffee cup down and pondered her remarks. "Many people think physicians make too much money anyway." He looked at Alex sheepishly. "Of course, people say the same thing about lawyers. You think the Obama Care will remedy any of these problems?"

Alex was quick to reply. "Nope. It will make it worse. CCMC is currently in pretty good shape financially because of our large international population. They represent a significant portion of our revenues."

"How do you think CCMC will do in the long run? You think anyone will buy them?" Mitch looked at her intently.

"Don't know. Someone tried a few months ago, but our board of trustees voted it down. They're adamant we remain independent. I know we're in for a long haul." Alex sighed, "I can't even predict what'll happen tomorrow. Another huge problem is the loss of Charity Hospital during Katrina. The city and hospital community has been struggling with how to care for Louisiana's poor, and disenfranchised population. It's gonna be a bumpy ride, no question about it."

Mitch stifled a yawn and looked as his watch. "It's getting late. Best be getting home. I don't want to keep you out too late." Mitch stood and helped her with her chair. Then the handsome couple walked hand-in-hand through the balmy New Orleans night.

At her door Mitch tentatively kissed Alex good night. "Call you soon. Sweet dreams."

"Thanks, Mitch. It was a lovely evening." Alex entered her flat and returned to the living room to clear away the wine glasses and cheese tray. After straightening the kitchen, she returned to the living room to close the French doors leading to the roofed balcony. She stepped outside again to enjoy the fragrant New Orleans night.

Once outside, she was surprised when she noticed Mitch on the opposite side of the street talking to a short stocky man with a cigar in him mouth. Strange, she thought to herself. It's after midnight. I'll have to ask him who that was. She watched the pair several minutes. After a few minutes the men parted ways, and Mitch headed towards his car.

***

Congressman Adam Patrick Lee sat impatiently in his room at the Palm Court Hotel. For the tenth time, he dialed Alex's number. No answer. Where in the hell is she, he thought to himself. It's almost midnight. Damn, I wish she didn't live here. This city's full of creeps and perverts. He had hated New Orleans for years, and was convinced that the city had robbed Alex's mother of her youth and her sanity. He still blamed New Orleans for her final, anguished mental break and the silence she had lived in for over 30 years.

Fucking nasty city, he thought as he impatiently redialed Alex's home phone. His hand still stung from where he'd cold-cocked some kid trying to pick his pocket several hours earlier. He's been right outside his hotel, for God's sake. The most expensive hotel in New Orleans, and it was worse that Washington DC. It was even worse than the pickpockets in Rome and Sicily, and they were supposed to be the worst on the planet. Was nothing sacred in this underwater swamp town? Congressman Lee had not been in favor of rebuilding the city after Katrina but had kept his thoughts to himself. Screw the levies. No amount of patching and reengineering could ever guarantee what could happen in a Category 5 hurricane. He shook his head as he remembered back to the travesties that had occurred in the Super Dome following the storm. Rape, violent assault, crack-cocaine and drug dealing not to mention suicide and disregard for the weak and elderly were all reported. What a hell hole the Super Dome was. Crime was out of control in America, and Adam Patrick Lee, before he went to his grave, was determined to do something about it, or at least make his mark in history trying to fix it.

His mind continued to wander and he reviewed the events of the day and his many visits to the Crescent City. Things had gone pretty well in most of his meetings, but something wasn't quite right in the Governor's office. Several of the Governor's aides had been short, practically rude, to him. Well... maybe not rude, maybe more embarrassed and uninformed. Didn't know a damn thing about how Governor Raccine was planning to use his influence with the Southern Governors to win the crime vote. Raccine had to have a plan. The Southern Governors were meeting next week.

What was up with Governor Raccine himself? Why was he unavailable for the Congressman? For God's sake, Adam Lee was one of the highest ranking Congressmen in DC. For years Raccine had been a wily, savvy politician, always in control of his issues and platforms. When Adam had finally met with him, Raccine seemed unsure of himself, sort of floundering all around the issues. Not even four bourbons had calmed him down, although his speech was a little slurred when he left. The governor had kept looking over his shoulder as if he expected someone to be there. Of course, his wife **was** sick with terminal cancer. But Adam thought it was more than that. Something was wrong. He could smell it. Fucking, dirty, nasty city.

Congressman Lee suspected that if Kathryn were that ill, he'd be screwed up too. He smiled to himself when he thought of his wife back in Virginia. He missed her. He'd never tell her, of course. But he knew she knew. He'd been a lucky man to find such a fine woman to stand by him. She was the best political wife a man could have, and she put up with his tangents, moods, idiosyncrasies, bouts of drinking and depression. He'd never make it without her. She was and had been his rudder in stormy seas for over 40 years. He knew that and suspected she did too.

He continued to muse about George Raccine. He'd known him for years. George was a real political machine. He'd brought respect and dignity to a state long famous for corrupt politics. Raccine had done a superb job working with Senator Bonnet and, for the first time in years, the economy of the state was growing.

Adam felt his impatience increasing and he dialed Alex's number for the umpteenth time. She answered in a sleepy voice on the second ring.

"Where the hell have you been, young lady? It's after midnight," he said, his voice gruff, but in a teasing tone.

Alex laughed at his tone. "Adam, need I remind you that I'm over thirty years old, educated, employed, and living on my own? I have no keeper?"

"Need I remind you that anytime I'm anywhere close you have a keeper? Where've you been?"

"Boy, you're bossy. For your information, I had a date with a most attractive man."

"Humph, who is he and what does he do. I'll check him out."

"That's precisely why I'm not telling. When and if it becomes important, you'll know." Alex detected the playfulness her grandfather's voice. She continued,

"Okay, Granddad. What's up? You didn't call to keep tabs on me."

"Hell I didn't. What's the story on Grace Raccine? She doing badly?"

Alex tried to remember if she'd heard anything recently about the first lady. "Not that I know of. She's still at CCMC, getting chemo, but is doing all right. Robert did her surgery a few months ago. Why?"

Adam hesitated. "Don't know. Nothing really. George seemed distracted. Not on the ball or something. He seems screwed up, unprepared, I guess. His aides don't know a damn thing about his plans for the Governor's conference. From what I picked up, the administration's going soft, sort of backing down on most important issues. This is a huge change in strategy. I need George's support to get my legislation through. You know if anything is coming down politically in Louisiana?"

"Nope. Not really. Hardly keep up with local politics here. CCMCs politics are all I can handle. I'll check around and let you know. Anything else, Adam?"

"Nope. We on for tomorrow?"

"You bet. See you at five."

"Love you, Alex. Nighty-night.

"Love you too, Granddad. Go to bed you impossible, irascible, crotchety old fool and don't call me back!"

Alex felt her heart swell with love for her grandfather as she hung up the phone. A teddy-bear in a lions coat she thought. Others would describe him as a wolf in sheep's clothing.

***

Mrs. Grace Raccine, the wife of the Governor of Louisiana, was resting comfortably in her VIP suite at CCMC when Kathy Smithson, the evening charge nurse, came in on rounds. Mrs. Raccine looked up from her book. "Hello, Dear, isn't it about time for you to go home?" She smiled gently at Kathy.

"I just wanted to see if there was anything else you needed before I left. Did you get your sleeping pill?"

"The nurse offered it to me, but I didn't take it. To tell you the truth, Kathy, I think that's what's been causing these horrible nightmares I've been having the past few nights. I could've gone home earlier if I'd had been resting better. Sleep always makes a difference in how you feel."

Kathy nodded in agreement. "You're still going home in pretty good time. It takes a long time to recover from abdominal surgery, and then, considering you had that terrible infection, you've done very well. I'll miss you when you leave." Kathy smiled.

Mrs. Raccine smiled back, touched Kathy's hand, and said, "I'll miss you too, dear. You and all the other nurses have been good to me. And, Dr. Bonnet's excellent. You know, Dr. Bonnet's father and my husband were childhood friends. I've known Robert since he was a tyke growing up on St. Charles. He and my late son were school chums, the best of friends." Mrs. Raccine paused for a moment, reminiscing and she continued. "You know, I've never been to CCMC before. Our family usually goes to Jefferson." Mrs. Raccine lay back against the covers, tired and weak. "I don't think I've ever had better nursing care, but I'm tired. I'm really tired. I know Dr. Bonnet said it would take time, but I need to feel better before they start the radiation."

Kathy smiled again at Mrs. Raccine and said, "You will. You'll start feeling better sooner than you think. Chemo is tough on you and makes you feel really tired. But, your blood work is looking better tonight. Get a good night's sleep to get a head start before you go home."

"Thanks, Kathy. I'll try. Have a good evening, at least what's left of it. See you tomorrow."

Mrs. Raccine was exhausted by the short conversation and laid back against her pillows. She was worried about her health, of course, but she was more worried about her husband. Something was up with George. He was not quite right these days. He'd been acting strangely for several months. She'd noticed secretive phone calls, cancelled meetings with trusted advisors, men hanging around the Governor's Mansion in Baton Rouge she didn't know as well as a lot of late night meetings in New Orleans. He was spending less and less time in Baton Rouge and more time here. Grace continued to consider things. George seemed to be pushing Andre Renou, his chief aide, aside and that was unusual. Those two had been joined at the hip for years and George never made decisions without getting Andre's take on the issue. She couldn't pin-point anything specific, but she knew something was bothering her husband. She continued to consider the strange happenings, but it just made her wearier. Finally, she fell asleep.

Kathy frowned as she left the room. Gastric cancer was bad enough as it was, but Mrs. Raccine's cancer had spread to her liver. She also had metastasis to her lungs which made her more tired and short of breath. It seemed so unfair for such a wonderful woman and community leader to be so cruelly ill. Kathy wondered if Mrs. Raccine's dreams were related to her diagnosis. She'd mentioned her dreams had snakes and evil things in them but Mrs. Raccine couldn't seem to remember much else. Mrs. Raccine was Creole and Creoles traditionally believed all dreams have meaning. Kathy wouldn't be surprised if Grace had brought a gris gris with her to the hospital to help her heal. Kathy left the hospital with a heavy heart for Grace Raccine.

At one-fifteen in the morning, the gentlemen in Room 626 had a heart attack, and the nurses were busy with him until after two-thirty. A nursing assistant documented at two o'clock that Mrs. Raccine was sleeping soundly with her side rails up. That was just an hour before all hell broke loose.

CHAPTER 4

Alex approached CCMC at seven-thirty on Tuesday morning and was dismayed to see TV trucks, camera crews, and reporters. A sinking feeling came over her, and she immediately felt her stomach knot. Nausea prevailed as she wondered what was wrong. What could have happened? It must be bad. Of course, she admonished herself, it could be something positive. Many great things happen at CCMC, but somehow she wasn't able to convince herself that something good had happened. Her gut told her the opposite. It was bad. Reporters never came out this early in New Orleans for anything, except to photograph the trash after Mardi Gras, unless it was something bad. Anything good could have waited until noon. She walked towards the administration offices with an overwhelming sense of dread.

The administration suite was in chaos. Two of the secretaries were trying to keep the press out of the suite, and the other two were on the phone. Alex wondered why everyone was in so early. One of the secretaries motioned her towards the conference room. As she entered, she noted Don Montgomery, Dr. John Ashley, the chief of medicine, Bette Farve, chief of nursing, and Elizabeth Tippett, the director of hospital-media relations sitting around the conference table. Don was speaking as she entered the room.

His voice was loud, blaming and arrogant. "Where the hell's Alex Destephano? *This* is when we need her. Where in the hell is she?" Don's face was red, his eyes blazing.

Elizabeth, a pretty young brunette, spoke calmly. "Don, we called her around six and didn't get an answer. It's only seven-thirty. I'm sure she'll be here soon. Relax a little. We need to focus on a press release. What are you going to say?"

The CEO glared at her. "I'm not saying a damn thing. That is *your* job. What is it about you people that you don't understand that I cannot do everything around here?"

Alex stood frozen at the door. Her voice was quiet. "I'm here. I was probably in the shower at six. What's going on?"

Her colleagues looked at her strangely, speechless, but obviously glad to see her. Elizabeth was the first to speak.

"We're not really sure what happened. At five this morning, the charge nurse on Six North was making final rounds on her patients. When she entered Mrs. Raccine's room, the room was in shambles, destroyed. Blood was all over the place."

"What! What about Mrs. Raccine?," Alex interrupted, fearing the worst.

Elizabeth continued, "Mrs. Raccine's alive, but in shock. She has no injury. Physically, she's stable, at least for now."

"What?" Alex looked dumbly at Elizabeth. "What about the blood? Where was she injured?"

"The blood's not Mrs. Raccine's."

"What?" Alex barked at Elizabeth. "I don't understand, then whose blood is it?... how did the blood get into the room?" Alex's voice was demanding.

Elizabeth held her arms up in a back-off gesture. "Alex, chill out and please let me finish. I'll tell you what we know, which isn't much. We think the blood belongs to a rooster found in the room with her. We also found a dead snake, cut in three pieces under her bed. We don't know the meaning." Elizabeth paused for a breath.

Alex could hardly believe what she was hearing. She was stunned and could feel the hair stand up on her arms. The hospital leaders started talking at once, shouting over each other in an effort to be heard, except for Alex, who was speechless. She watched as an administrative aide closed the conference room door from the peering eyes of news reporters.

"Quiet, quiet," Alex said firmly. "One at a time, please."

Finally the noise died down.

"Help me understand. What does this mean? What else have you done?" She looked around the room. "Have the police been notified? Does Governor Raccine know? How'd the press find out?"

Dr. Ashley, a fifty-some year old, silver-headed gentle-faced general practitioner who seemed a little calmer than the other administrators, attempted to answer Alex's barrage of questions.

"Alex, please keep in mind we don't know much. Yes, the police have been called. Captain Francois of the NOPD is currently questioning the staff on Six North."

Alex looked at her nemesis, Bette Farve, and asked her sharply, "Have you spoken to the nurses about what happened? Have you interviewed and prepared them for the police questioning? Did you impound the chart from the unit?"

Bette Farve, an angry, thin-faced stick of a woman, bristled at Alex's questions and responded sarcastically, "I talked with the night nurse briefly, but she was so traumatized that she didn't make much sense. It was a waste of my time." Bette hesitated for a moment and continued arrogantly, "If we'd been able to reach you, Ms. Destephano, perhaps we could've been more prepared for this." Bette's voice was cold and had a caustic edge to it.

Alex ignored the implication. She and the chief nursing officer rarely agreed on anything, and Alex frankly didn't like her. "We're preparing now. You need to get up there and provide psychological support for the nurses who cared for and observed Mrs. Raccine's situation for lack of a better word. You need to call psych and arrange for a post-traumatic stress counselor for the nurses. Please leave here now and report to Six North so we can know firsthand what is going on up there."

Alex knew she was invading the territory of the chief nursing executive, but didn't care. She detested Bette Farve and found her an inept nursing leader who neither cared about her staff, her patients, nor anything other than the prestige of her position and time off. Usually Alex had a little more patience with Bette, but it was unfathomable that Bette would be in a meeting with the administration when her staff was coping with a medical and political disaster and the police.

"I wasn't aware I worked for you, Ms. Destephano. As you know I report to Mr. Montgomery."

Alex glared at Bette, looked at Don and spoke directly to him, "To safeguard our legal position, Ms. Farve needs to be on Six North reviewing the situation and providing support for her staff. This is necessary for obvious reasons, especially for support of CCMC's potential liability. We can manage here without her. As soon as she assesses these things, she can report back to us. In fact, I'll be up there shortly to talk with the staff myself."

Don looked at Alex blankly and seemed unable to respond. He looked back at the floor.

Alex persisted, "Don, Ms. Farve needs to report to Six North. Now. I insist!"

After a brief silence, Don nodded his head, and Dr. Ashley addressed Betty directly, "Please go to Six North as Alex suggests. Any information you gather will help us handle this situation the best way we can."

Dr. Ashley continued to speak with Alex and the group after Bette left. "Captain Jack Francois will report to us shortly and give us his preliminary findings. And, to answer your final question, Alex, the Governor does know, and he's terribly upset, distraught even. We moved Mrs. Raccine to the other VIP suite and he's with her now. At this point, his concerns are only on his wife."

The room was quiet as each staff member reflected the situation and contemplated the hospital's situation. After a few moments, Don Montgomery's secretary, Latetia, entered. "Mr. Montgomery, the reporters are pressing for a statement. Are you ready?"

Don didn't respond, but continued to stare at the floor. Everyone was looking at him for direction, but he seemed incapable of speaking, much less of making a decision. He seemed to have checked out.

Alex glanced at Dr. Ashley and said, "Tell the press we'll

issue a statement at ten this morning. In the meantime, we'll continue to gather information and assess the situation." The other members of the executive team nodded their in agreement.

Alex spoke sharply. "Don, pull yourself together. We've got a major crisis here and need to deal with the media and the public."

There was still no response from the CEO who seemed unable to answer or understand.

Alex sighed and looked at the group, "Call an emergency meeting of the Hospital Board of Trustees. They can help us decide the best way to handle this. Are you with me on this, Don?" Alex stared at the CEO. He didn't answer, but did nod his head.

Elizabeth Tippett stood to leave the room to notify the board as Alex asked the group, "How did the press find out?"

Dr. Ashley shrugged his shoulders and replied, "Don't really know. We suspect a staff member on Six North called them. Otherwise, we have no idea."

"Actually, Dr. Ashley, that's not right. Someone made an anonymous call to the CCMC operator and told us to go check on Mrs. Raccine, that something had happened to her and she needed help," Elizabeth reported, "at least that's what the nurse told me earlier."

Alex could hardly believe her eyes. "What, someone called us? We didn't discover it on our own? This is incredible. That must mean that....."

"Exactly," Elizabeth interrupted, "Yes, that whoever is responsible called to let us know," Elizabeth finished the sentence for her.

"Who found Mrs. Raccine?"

"The night charge nurse reported that she was called by the hospital operator and told to check on Mrs. Raccine. The nurse did so and found Mrs. Raccine unresponsive and covered in blood at five-fifteen this morning. She immediately called hospital security, who called Bette, the administrator on call. After she called me, I contacted Dr. Bonnet. We all arrived about thirty minutes later. Then I called the police."

Alex's stomach knotted when she realized that Mrs. Raccine was Robert's patient. "Has Bonnet seen Mrs. Raccine since this happened?"

"Yes, he says she's stable, and has no physical injury, but is unresponsive, almost comatose. She hasn't moved or spoken since she was discovered. Her vital signs are stable, except for some heart problems." Dr. Ashley had a worried look on his face as he paused for a moment and continued, "The biggest concern here is her mental state, although we're monitoring her heart which could become a greater concern."

Alex stood up. "I'm going up to Six North and talk with the staff. If anyone needs me, call my cell. Let me know about the board meeting." Alex leaned over and whispered to Elizabeth. "See if you can get Don to pull himself together."

"Okay, Alex. How do you want to handle the press? We owe them something in less than two hours." Elizabeth looked desperate. "They didn't teach us how to handle these kinds of crises in journalism school," she smiled weakly.

"Elizabeth, nobody's prepared for anything like this. The best thing to do, at this point, is to admit there was an attack on the

Governor's wife and that she is stable. Tell them something while telling them nothing. You can do it. You know, the Texas two-step kind of thing... Draft it up and we'll talk about it later."

***

The Six North nursing unit was crackling with chaos and activity. Instead of the normal early morning baths, treatments and vital signs, there wasn't a nurse in sight. There were three uniformed NOPD police officers in the hall, and three others in the nursing station. Alex was greeted by Janelle Wells, nursing director of Six North. Her disheveled appearance and rapid speech indicated her stress.

"Things are bad. Six nursing assistants and hospital attendants have left the hospital, saying they were afraid to work here today. We've only two RNs. Angela's working days, and Susan is still here from a 12 hour night shift. She volunteered to stay over, but she's zonked emotionally and probably too tired and stressed to be useful." Janelle paused for a breath and continued as she waved her arms toward the policemen. "These guys in the police uniforms have got to go, or at least change their clothes. Patients are frantic, and their families are asking all sorts of questions. There are all kinds of rumors floating out there and some families are threatening to take patients to another hospital. I can't give care to these people with only two nurses. This is crazy." Janelle threw up her arms in dismay.

"Where's Bette?" Alex looked around for the nurse executive.

"In the examining room interrogating Susan who's so tired and upset she can hardly talk. Bette, B.F., the bitch, is brow-beating her to death." Janelle again threw up her arms in frustration.

Susan told the police everything she knows, there's nothing else to say. Bette told her that if she had been on her toes, this wouldn't have happened. What kind of bull shit is that?" Janelle's voice expressed her contempt for her boss.

Alex smiled as Janelle referred to Bette as B.F. She'd heard many interpretations of the initials by both nursing and medical staff, from big foot to butt face, and other less gracious interpretations. "What's Bette want from her?"

"Who knows? She's asking her over and over again why no one charted on Mrs. Raccine between two o-clock and five-fifteen this morning. Like, give me a break. Who gives a damn about the charting? Susan thinks she is blaming her for what happened."

Alex nodded but made no comment. "We'll worry about the documentation later. Call the nursing office and see how many of these patients can be transferred to other units. Have them call an agency and arrange for supplemental staffing to get us through the next few days."

Janelle's eyes dilated instantly, her fear evident. "Are you out of your mind?! I can't do this without Bette's approval. She'd fire me." Janelle paled at the thought.

"I'll handle Bette. Now, move before someone falls out of bed or leaves AMA," Alex said crisply.

Janelle hesitated, and then disappeared into her office to make the calls.

Alex walked down the hall. Robert Bonnet was walking toward her. He looked terrible.

"Robert, any change in Mrs. Raccine?"

"No, Alex. Things are the same. Physically, she was pretty stable but now her heart's acting up. She's traumatized. I don't know if she'll ever recover psychologically."

"A little early for such a dire prediction isn't it? Please keep that to yourself, " Alex said, putting on her lawyer hat. "How's the Governor taking this?"

"As well as he can. Hasn't said much and hasn't asked any questions. I don't think he's put things together, or realizes what's going on yet. I'm not sure I do." Robert sighed deeply. "Anyway, he was spared seeing his wife covered in blood and didn't see the dead rooster, snake, and black candle in her room."

"Black candle. I don't understand. What's this mean?" Alex looked confused.

Robert paused as his cell phone went off. Checking it he said, "Got to go. You'll know soon enough. Jack Francois is interviewing staff and security. He said he'd speak to all of us soon." He hurried toward the doctors' lounge to answer his phone.

"Where is Captain Francois? I'd like to meet him," Alex hollered after him.

"He and several other members of his troop are in the lounge."

Alex bravely opened the door of the staff lounge. As she observed Captain Francois, she wasn't impressed. He was a big man in his mid-fifties and a bit overweight and was balding. He had a steely look about him, an effect increased by his short salt and pepper hair. To top it all off, he was eating a jelly doughnut and drinking coffee. His tone was condescending as he continued to interview Susan. He was really pressing her, seeming intent on getting her to admit to things she didn't know. He was a little too Gestapo-like for Alex.

"Excuse me, Captain Francois --" Alex began.

"What the hell, excuse me, Missy," the captain barked at her. "I'm busy. I'm conducting a confidential police investigation. Get the hell out of here."

Alex remained in the doorway, more from shock than defiance. She didn't move.

Francois stood up and said in a mocking voice, "You deaf. Get out of here now or I'll have you escorted out ...on your ass," the captain said as he eyed her menacingly.

Alex, red-faced, composed herself and began, "Let me introduce myself. I'm Alexandra Destephano, the CCMC in-house legal counsel. I've got a right to be here --"

Captain Francois interrupted her, obviously unimpressed with Alex or her position. He lost his temper, and his face turned red. "I don't give a damn *who* you are! No one *needs* to be here. This young lady isn't under arrest. I told Ms. Farve I wanted to interview all staff, and she gave me her blanket permission. I was just being nice. I don't need anyone's consent. This is a crime scene, or don't you know that?" the policeman sneered, glaring at Alex. "You can leave," he gestured toward Susan. "I'll talk with this 'important lawyer lady' for a while, and I'll find you again later." Francois came across so angry and sarcastic that Alex braced herself for the worst.

Susan left quickly. Alex sat down next to the captain.

"Have any preliminary information you'd like to share with me?"

Captain Francois looked amused. "Oh, I've got lots of information, but I ain't ready to share it with nobody. I'm far from done. I'll have a short report for your board of trustees when they meet this afternoon." The captain stopped for a few minutes and surveyed Alex critically. "Incidentally, Andre Renou, the Governor's chief aide, would like to be present when the board of trustees meets. I trust you ain't worried about him being there?" He smirked at her.

Alex was astounded at the captain's barrage of sarcasm. "We'll be happy to have Mr. Renou present for the meeting but of course, if the board goes into executive session, he'll have to leave."

Francois gave Alex a deprecating look and said sarcastically, "You've got to be kidding. Who in the hell do you think you are? You really think you can throw out the Governor's right hand man? We'll see about that now, won't we? Anything else, Ms. Destephano?"

Alex continued bravely, "Could you arrange for the uniformed officers to leave? It's upsetting the patients and their families. If you need to continue surveillance, you could do it with plainclothes police officers."

"Surveillance with plainclothes officers. What kind of bull shit it that? Are you a policeman too, and a lawyer? I'll think about it. Now get out of here, now." The captain dismissed her with his behavior and returned his attention to his notes.

Alex quickly left. She was appalled at Francois' language and coarseness. Still smarting from his condescending behavior, Alex left and immediately ran into a red-faced and obviously pissed Bette Farve.

"Destephano, how dare you authorize the transfer of patients from this unit, or approve supplemental staffing, especially from an agency. Those are my decisions. Not yours. Who do you think you are?"

Alex looked straight at the nursing executive and said, "I am the hospital attorney. There's no staff to run this unit. How're you going to provide care with no nurses? As the legal counsel for this medical center, it is within my purview to evaluate risk potential. This unit and its complex medical patients present a high risk. Thirty patients and three nurses in a crisis situation predicts, rather guarantees, unsafe care. What you are doing is unsafe; now get out of my way."

Alex turned and walked away, feeling Bette's eyes as they bored into her back. She knew Bette was vengeful and would get her back. B.F. carried grudges, and Alex had previously been the victim of her vindictive behavior. It was usually pretty bad.

What the hell, Alex thought to herself. On her way to her office, Alex stopped in administration and found it still in chaos. Elizabeth was seated at the conference table.

"Has Don straightened out yet?"

Elizabeth shrugged her shoulders. "Nope, not really. How does this sound for the press? 'Early this morning, Mrs. Grace Raccine, First Lady of Louisiana, encountered an assault in her hospital room at Crescent City Medical Center. She is currently in stable condition, and resting in her room. Governor Raccine is with her. The hospital is investigating, and details will be forthcoming.'"

"Sounds good. Let it go." Alex wondered if the day could get any worse as she waved to Dr. Ashley on her way out.

CHAPTER 5

Alex found Bridgett strangely quiet when she finally reached her office at eleven o'clock. She had expected Bridgett to pellet her with a million questions. Even more, Alex had expected Bridgett to work her inside network and have the inside scoop about Mrs. Raccine. Bridgett was quiet and seemed unwilling to talk. She answered Alex's questions with a perfunctory "yes or no." Alex was surprised, even stunned by Bridgett's reticence and lack of interest in the events surrounding them.

"You okay, Bridge? You're mighty quiet."

Bridgett nodded without meeting her eyes, picking up the phone when it rang. "It's for you. Your grandfather. I'll put it through."

Alex closed the door of her office and pushed the button on her phone."

"Granddad, where are you?"

"In my hotel. What the hell's going on over there? What's happened to Grace Raccine?" Her grandfather's voice was loud, demanding.

"What did you hear?"

"TV said she had an accident in her hospital room and was in a coma. That true?"

Alex rolled her eyes. "Pretty much. It's actually a little worse. They found a dead rooster and a snake in the room with her early this morning. She was in shock and is unresponsive."

"What? What the hell! What's that mean? What the hell, this is one heathen damn city!"

"I don't know, Granddad. I have no idea. It's weird. I'll tell you more tonight when we get together, Okay?" At any other time, Alex would have admonished her grandfather's language.

"Yeah. Yeah, Okay. Be careful, Alex. Don't like this, especially this snake shit. This is one fucking low-life place. I want you back in Virginia. Don't understand you love for this hell-hole. Why would anyone do something like that to a sick and dying woman?"

"I don't know and I will be careful. Bye, Granddad." Alex hung up the phone, just as her cell phone rang again. She was already tired and it wasn't even noon.

Her grandfather hung up the phone and was soon deep in thought as he dressed for his lunch appointment. The events concerning Grace Raccine concerned him, mainly because he was fond of her and was disturbed by the brutality, or at least the symbolism of it. He shook his head as he left the hotel. Damn this city, he thought as he hailed a cab. Alex needs to move back home to Virginia. We've got plenty of hospitals there that need a good lawyer.

Alex returned to work and as she began to outline the events of the morning for the board of trustees, she became acutely aware that she didn't have the understanding or expertise to deal with the Raccine situation. She called John Marigny, an esteemed and politically-wise New Orleans lawyer, who handled most of the trial work for CCMC.

Alex explained the situation at the hospital, and John made

no comment, but agreed to meet with the board at one o'clock. Alex prodded John for an explanation of rooster and snake, but he remained silent.

***

The three men who had dined at Tujague's Friday night met for an early lunch at Bocco's on Tuesday at noon. Frederico, the mafia boss, glared at the evil-faced, ponytailed man and asked, "Things set for tomorrow, Salvadal?"

The ponytailed man stroked his leather strap and shifted in his seat and replied softly, "All set."

Frederico then turned his attention to the third man, the ordinary man, and asked roughly, "What do you know? Are things in place?"

The ordinary man nodded.

"No mistakes, you hear, none. People who work for me don't make mistakes or if they do, that don't live to make another one." Frederico glared at the man, his intent clear.

The ordinary man looked subdued. "Don't worry, Rico. Landry's a shoe in. He's weak. I have known him forever and he owes me. I have a meeting over there as soon as we eat."

Monte Salvadal fingered his ponytail, looked bored and wondered just how stupid his companions were. How'd he ever get hooked up with such bozos? His employer sure called this one wrong. Proved business people didn't know shit about crime and how to get things done. 'Course, the bozos were supposed to provide for his cover, keep the heat off him. Maybe it'd work. Who knows? But, in reality, he never depended on anybody. He always took care of things himself. Long as he had his friend here, he'd be okay. Salvadal smiled as he caressed the strap in his lap. His friend had never deserted him.

"Hey, asshole, you talking? Eating's supposed to be social." Frederico glared across the table at him, forking food in his mouth.

"Yeah, man. Talk. I'll listen." Salvadal started eating and wished that lunch was history.

Suddenly, the ordinary man got up and looked around frantically. "Got to go, got a meeting," the ordinary man said as he threw his napkin and a fifty dollar bill on the table. He ran out of Bocco's, not looking back at his companions.

"What's with the choir boy?"

Salvadal shrugged his shoulders and gave his plate his full attention and said, "Don't know, and don't give a shit."

***

At one o'clock, the board of trustees of Crescent City Medical Center convened in the main conference room. As Alex entered, she noticed two faces she didn't recognize. She seated herself between Elizabeth and John Ashley, and asked Dr. Ashley who they were.

"The man seated next to Don is Andre Renou, the chief aide for Governor Raccine. The other gentleman is a new member of the board. I'm not sure of his name, but I believe he's originally from the east coast but has lived in Texas until recently. He has tons of money in oil. Anyway, his strength on the board is supposedly his business acumen."

Alex studied the man, noting that he was young, mid-to-late thirties and pretty ordinary in appearance. Somehow he seemed vaguely familiar to her, but she couldn't seem to place him.

The tension in the well-appointed conference room was palpable as board members twisted and turned in their seats, uncertain of why they had been called in. Several members were at the coffee bar. They spoke to each other in low voices. They were not talking with the staff or administrators which seemed strange to Alex. Alex was always impressed by the collective power and wisdom represented by the trustees. They were pillars of the community and well acquainted with the nuances of New Orleans. She had appreciated their wisdom and the open discussions in previous meetings on how to best prepare for Obama Care.

Alex turned to John Ashley, "Is Don able to run this meeting?"

John shook his head and said, "Don't know, but I am if he isn't. He's taking this rather poorly, particularly the media fallout. Of course, we all are."

Alex thought John was merely being kind. Don was incoherent, and seemed unable to speak. It seemed to take an eternity for the next few minutes to pass. Alex glanced up and saw Dr. Bonnet enter. She was startled by the look of hatred and disgust that crossed the new board member's face. She could see the muscles tighten in his jaw as he clenched the table with his hands. It made her distinctly uncomfortable and even chilled her. She shrugged off a shiver. "John, maybe you'd better get started. Doesn't look like Don's going to."

Dr. Ashley stood up. "Thank you all for coming on such short notice. We've a difficult situation here and wanted to update you and get your insight and help. Before we begin, let's introduce ourselves since we have several new people. I'm John Ashley, the Chief of Medicine here at CCMC."

Alex and the other board members re-introduced themselves. Alex noted that the new board member's name was Kevin Anderson. She also observed the rapt look that Robert Bonnet gave him. The look was first confusion, followed by recognition and fear and uncertainty.

Andre Renou seemed pleasant enough and expressed his concerns, on behalf of Governor Raccine, related to the First Lady's condition. "The Governor is anguished and grieved over this situation. He's authorized me to offer any and all of his resources, including the State Bureau of Investigation and the State Police, to find out and explain what is happening here as soon as possible."

Mr. Gottfried LaSalle, an older member of the board of trustees spoke directly to Don Montgomery. "Mr. Montgomery, I don't know what has happened here. My secretary was told that there was a crisis over here and to come. Can you fill me in?"

Don seemed unable to speak and looked helplessly at John Ashley. Picking up on Don's cue, Dr. Ashley turned to Mr. LaSalle and said, "Sorry, Mr. LaSalle. I wasn't aware that you hadn't been briefed. Let me tell you what we know at this point in time. Later, Captain Francois will be updating us on his investigation."

Dr. Ashley, his gentle face tense, took a deep breath and began describing the bloody scene hoping he wouldn't traumatize the older members of the board. He shuddered inwardly, his stomach knotting as he began the gory tale. "At five-fifteen this morning, the night nurse on Six North was making rounds on her patients. When she entered Mrs. Raccine's room, she found the first lady covered in blood and unresponsive. After examining her, the nurses rang for help. Mrs. Raccine did not appear to be injured. Her room was in shambles, almost completely destroyed. The nurse immediately called hospital security and Bette Farve, the administrator on call, who notified me. I called the others as well as Dr. Bonnet, Mrs. Raccine's physician. We all arrived here at six. Someone, we don't know who, notified the press and they arrived shortly after we did." As John stopped for a breath, the board members looked at each other in confusion. Alex detected bewilderment on several board members' faces.

Lena Marquette said, "Dr. Ashley, I don't understand. If Mrs. Raccine wasn't injured, where'd the blood come from?"

Dr. Ashley took another deep breath. "There was a dead rooster in the room lying on Mrs. Raccine's chest. We found a mutilated snake under her bed and a black candle on her bedside table. Her windows had been shrouded with black cloth."

Mr. LaSalle looked confused, and then dismayed, the emotions playing across his face. His knuckles whitened as he clutched the conference table as the implications became clear to him. Ms. Marquette looked absolutely terrified. Kevin Anderson appeared incredulous, and Christina Baptiste, a younger board member, gasped for breath and ran from the room. Elizabeth, shocked by the behavior followed Mrs. Baptiste. After his initial response, Kevin Anderson's response was even more perplexing. He actually clasped his hands, gave a brief smile, and looked away. Alex was puzzled and thought he looked pleased at the story and then immediately chastised herself for her negative impression. I don't even know the man, she thought, but still, this is really weird.

Several moments of silence followed John Ashley's

revelation. As Alex continued to reflect on the responses to Dr. Ashley's announcement, she became uncomfortable, and then aware that a feeling of fear was permeating the room.

Kevin Anderson still appeared the least affected and spoke first, and appeared confused. "I don't know a great deal about Louisiana, since I came here from Texas several years ago. Anybody hear anything or see anyone entering Mrs. Raccine's room?"

Alex intervened, "No, once again, Mr. Anderson, our information is still sketchy, but the nursing staff report no unusual activity around Mrs. Raccine's room during the late night or early morning hours. Hospital security didn't report anything either."

Mr. LaSalle spoke up, his voice impatient. "Certainly someone was in her room, at some time, during the night. Don't you all write things down; you know things about how patients are doing?"

Alex quickly responded, "Of course we do. We document status and vital signs. Unfortunately, the Six North nursing unit was very busy last night. The RNs were tied up with a heart attack at the far end of the hall between one-forty-five and four-thirty. A nursing assistant, Bessie Comstock, charted at two am. that Mrs. Raccine was resting. The charge nurse reported that Bessie left sick shortly after four am. The charge nurse said Ms. Comstock was ashen and appeared very ill. The charge nurse asked about her patients, and Bessie reported that she had just made her four o'clock rounds, and that all the patients were sleeping. At that point, Bessie left."

"What did this staff member chart about Mrs. Raccine?" Mr. LaSalle asked.

Alex continued, hating to say the words, "Unfortunately, Bessie did her four am. charting on her patients up to Mrs. Raccine. Bessie made no 4 am. chart entry in Mrs. Raccine's medical record and there are no entries between two and five-fifteen." As she finished talking, Alex noted that Andre Renou was taking notes.

Elizabeth Tippett returned to the room, her face reflecting surprise. "Mrs. Baptiste has left the meeting. She said she can be of no use in this situation, and she'd see us at the April meeting."

Alex immediately thought that Mrs. Baptiste's behavior was unusual, odd even, but re-considered when she remembered her family was good friends with Grace Raccine.

Mr. Anderson spoke again, "How's Mrs. Raccine doing?"

Robert glanced nervously at Kevin Anderson and said, "Mrs. Raccine's stable, but unresponsive."

The group was startled when the door opened and Captain Francois entered the board room without knocking. Dr. Ashley suggested a short break prior to the captain's report. Alex turned to John Marigny.

"John, should we let all these people stay for Francois' report? He struck me as a little hostile, and I don't expect him to be supportive of the hospital."

"Alex, you'd best let them stay. These are the major decision-makers and public relations media for the hospital. They are well connected, and the general population will listen to what they say. Better they hear Francois' report directly." John paused while Alex digested his advice. Then he continued, "We need their support and understanding. Francois can be difficult, but basically he's honest, thorough, and knows his stuff."

Alex nodded. She knew John was right. It would be foolish to keep any secrets or pertinent information from the board members.

Francois ambled to the podium in the front of the room; his stocky frame and demeanor paralyzing the trustees. He stared at the group members individually for several seconds as if checking them out to see if any of them were the perp. The man's behavior was incredible. Francois addressed the board of trustees without a shred of dignity for the collective knowledge that was present in the room. He began his report in typical police fashion, his voice clipped and terse.

"You people are in for some bad luck now," he smirked. "You've really pissed off somebody in the worse kinds of way. Among other things, what we've got here is a case of criminal violence. The forensic people are still working the scene, but we have found no fingerprints or easy evidence. I'm pretty sure we aren't going to find anything else. What's interesting is that no one on the staff reports hearing or seeing anything unusual. Find that difficult to believe, as these things are usually pretty noisy."

Alex was struck at how well the police captain had been able to clean up his language. The gutter dialect she'd heard only several hours before was completely missing from his speech. She also studied his appearance in greater detail. His white shirt was clean and pressed, and his tie was in place. He could be attractive if he wasn't such an egotistical idiot, Alex thought to herself.

Perhaps under all the tough man police stuff was probably a nice man. She gave him her full attention.

John Marigny said, "What about the staff member that left sick? Has anyone from your department talked with her?"

Francois stared at him. "Nope. Sent a unit to her house around eight this morning. She never came home last night. We're watching her house but don't expect she'll be around for a while."

Kevin Anderson ventured another question. "Captain Francois, please, I'm new here. What does this stuff mean? I don't understand the rooster and snake stuff. What does it mean?"

The captain eyed Anderson as if he were from another world. He said, "Where're you from?"

Anderson didn't reply and Francois hesitated and then looked around the room, his eyes resting carefully on each board member. He continued sarcastically, "How many of the rest of you aren't from here, aren't Louisiana natives?"

Alex, John Ashley, Elizabeth, and Don gave each other a perplexed look and raised their hands.

The captain gave a short derisive laugh. "Well, folks, welcome to New Orleans. We've a little of everything here, you know, art, history, culture." Francois grinned wickedly.

Dr. Ashley was getting impatient. "Do you have any theories, any idea who these people are? Who would do this? Do you have any other reports like this? We're looking for answers, not a culture lesson. Please stay focused." Dr. Ashley was pretty angry with the captain and his laissez faire attitude.

Captain Francois looked lazily at Ashley. "Yeah, Doc, I got some theories. Want to hear 'em?"

Dr. Ashley was frustrated and asked angrily, "I'd just like to know if you have any idea about who did this or why."

Captain Francois gave Dr. Ashley a rude look. "It's simple. I'll give it to you straight." Francois straightened his posture and announced, his voice grim, "Grace Raccine's been 'fixed'. She's been Voodooed, Hoodooed, if you like, and so have all of you. Someone has placed a curse and hexed Crescent City Medical Center." With that, he turned and looked at the group.

The meeting broke into chaos; everyone was talking at once. Alex was shocked by the captain's disclosure. It was totally ridiculous that in 2012 someone could curse a world-class medical center. Finally, Dr. Ashley called for order.

Don Montgomery spoke for the first time, finally shocked out of his unresponsiveness. "This is the most ridiculous thing I have ever heard. Voodoo, black magic. This is one of the greatest technological and research-focused facilities in the country, *in the world*. Captain Francois, you are an idiot! How in the hell can you possibly suggest that the Governor's wife has been voodooed at Crescent City Medical Center?" Don's voice was an octave higher than usual, and seethed with disgust. "It's unthinkable that authorities could even suggest such a thing. This is total bull shit. Get the fuck out of my conference room."

Captain Francois stiffened. "You asked for my theory and I gave it to you." He walked straight toward the door of the conference room, parting the crowd as he left.

Dr. Ashley and Elizabeth were shocked by Don's outburst

but also doubted the possibility of voodoo. Alex was in a state of disbelief that the accusation had even been made. Maybe the police captain was an idiot.

Montgomery spoke again, "This has to be an act of corporate sabotage. Someone is trying to ruin us, shut us down. We are a *world class hospital and people are jealous.* Between Voodoo and the fucking Health Care Portability Act, aka Obama Care, they probably will destroy us."

Alex was stunned by Don's profanity and jabbed him in the side. She finally spoke, "I can't accept voodoo or black magic as the basis for what's happened."

Alex was attempting to sound reasonable when she realized that no one on the board of trustees from New Orleans had said anything or seemed to question or doubt what Francois had said. She looked around and said, "What do those of you from here think?"

A silence that seemed like an eternity followed. Finally, John Marigny spoke.

"Alex, Don, those of you who aren't from New Orleans. Here, like it or not, voodoo is a reality. There are plenty of people who practice voodoo as a religion, just like we practice Catholicism. Whether we choose to believe in it or not, it's a large part of our culture. We've got to consider it." There were still skeptical looks from board members who were not native New Orleanians, but they were pondering John Marigny's words.

Robert Bonnet spoke, "I have to agree with John. Before Katrina and the destruction of the medical archives at Charity Hospital, you could read full reports about patients who've been voodooed, or "hoodooed" as they call it. Nurses and physicians have been treating patients with these claims for years. Lots of patients would bring their gris-gris, or good luck charms, to the hospital with them for good luck or protection and keep it with them while they were hospitalized. It's the same all over the city. I've seen patients at Tulane, East Jefferson and LSU Health Sciences Center who have gris gris, or charms, at their bedside or in their bedside tables. We've even had nurses in the OR remove gris gris from patient's clenched fists after their general anesthesia. Hell, I have given permission for patient's to keep their gris gris with them during surgery."

Alex was incredulous at Robert's admission and flabbergasted to think that physicians in a world-class hospital would give credence to Voodoo. It was unthinkable to her, and she bristled at the thought of it. She glared angrily at Robert and attempted to interrupt him, but he silenced her with his hand.

Robert looked around and, noting the rapt attention of the Board members, continued, "There used to be tons of information, before Katrina, on metals, charms, coins, strings, and stones that patients' would insist on keeping with them when they were sick and hospitalized. There are also reports that support patients claims that if their gris-gris is away from them, they'll die and there are reports of patients actually dying when the charms were removed I don't know if any of those archives have survived, but I reviewed them as a medical student and actually completed some research that validated many of the reports."

Don went off in a fit of temper. "Bonnet, you mean to tell me that patients believe that if this shit is taken away from they'll die?"

Robert nodded and said, "Yes, and there are...were affidavits from professionals documenting that patients have died when their charms were removed. In fact, there are still many conjurers and voodoo priests all over the Louisiana. Voodoo is a religion here and a way of life for many people." Dr. Bonnet's voice was firm, but polite.

Don's tirade continued, as he sneered at the board members. "That's the stupidest, most idiotic thing I've heard. This is some crazy shit and now I'm convinced people in this town are ignorant."

Several board members stared at him, their faces showing anger and contempt at his denigration of their city.

Alex noted the stares and attempted to defuse the situation. She looked at Gottfried LaSalle whom she thought she knew very well. "Gottfried, surely you don't believe this?"

"Ms. Destephano, I know this is hard for you and the others. But, I'm well aware that voodoo is readily practiced in New Orleans. Dr. Bonnet is correct. I haven't learned much about it, because I'm smart enough to acknowledge its presence and also smart enough to stay away from it." Mr. LaSalle looked at Lena Marquette. "Anything on this subject you'd care to share with the others, Lena?"

Lena shifted uncomfortably in her seat and looked pained but said, "Many people have told me that my mother died from a curse placed on her by a Voodooienne, or voodoo Queen. My mother fired her for not taking good care of my little brother. She also refused to write the voodoo Queen any reference letters so she couldn't find a job anywhere in the city. Within three months, my mother was dead. She'd been a healthy, robust woman and had never been sick a day in her life. They did an autopsy but never determined the cause of death."

Elizabeth broke a long silence. "Do you believe it was a curse or voodoo magic that killed her?" Elizabeth was on the edge of her seat waiting for Lena's response.

Lena shrugged her shoulders and clasped her hands. "What's the difference? Dead is dead. No one was able to explain it. We found voodoo artifacts around the house during the time she was ill. Every time we found a new gris-gris, my mother became sicker. Finally, our gardener found a fish buried in the back yard. Following Voodoo custom, my father cut it open, and there was a slip of paper with my mother's name on it." Lena was becoming uncomfortable; her face was marked with red.

"What was the fish for?" Alex asked her voice astounded.

Lena continued her voice quiet. "Voodoo legend says that if you put someone's name inside of a fish and bury it in their back yard, that person will die. My mother was only 33 years old. She lost her mind and went insane at the end from terrible body pains that medicine couldn't diagnose or treat. She just got horrible stomach pains and died. None of the pain medicines worked and the doctors tried everything. Our priest did his best, but he said the black magic was too strong. So yes, Alex, I do believe in the power of voodoo. Its spell killed my mother when I was 11 years old and I have missed her all of my life." Lena sobbed quietly into a tissue.

Alex was feeling like all of this was a bad movie. It was surreal. There were smart, educated people, leaders in the city.

The aristocracy of New Orleans and they believed in these hideous spells. It was unbelievable. She looked at Andre Renou. "Mr. Renou, do you know of any reason why someone would place a curse on Mrs. Raccine?

Mr. Renou looked uncomfortable and perplexed. "No idea whatsoever."

Alex said, "Could it be a political maneuver, maybe a group angry with the Governor? A special interest group? Has he upset anyone lately?" Alex remembered her conversation with her grandfather and pressed the aide.

Renou replied, "No, not to my knowledge. Don't know. I don't think so, but I'll look into it. There is always some fringe group that is angry."

Alex searched Renou's face as well as the other faces at the table. She could hardly believe that Gottfried LaSalle, Lena Marquette, Robert Bonnet, and John Marigny actually supported the possibility that voodoo was responsible for the tragedy at CCMC. Also, Alex couldn't overlook the behavior of Christina Baptiste. Even Andre Renou had not questioned the possibility that voodoo could be the cause of the crime.

Dr. Ashley said, "Well, I guess we know why Ms. Baptiste left. Does anyone have suggestions for dealing with the situation? I have no experience in dealing with Voodoo."

Alex shrugged her shoulders and said, "Me neither. Let me work with our staff and John Marigny. I'll tell you, though; I'm not in favor of suggesting to the media that we've a voodoo incident at CCMC. Anyone disagree?"

"Yes, I disagree completely," said Mr. LaSalle.

Alex turned toward him as he continued to speak.

"Ms. Destephano, it makes no difference what you say to the media. If there's news that a rooster was involved in Mrs. Raccine's situation, all of New Orleans will know. I suggest that you be honest with them. And, another thing, Alex..." he began.

Alex attempted to give him her full attention, but her brain was moving at a million miles a minute,

"Yes, Gottfried,"

"This is important. Pay attention to what I am saying. This isn't over. This Voodoo curse now includes all of CCMC, patients and staff, doctors, nurses and therapists as well as all of us in this room. That's why Bessie, the nursing aide, left the hospital early this morning. That's probably why Christina left as well. To learn about the curse and give it credence and power is to accept the curse and all of us here have done that."

The silence in the room was deafening. The group just stared at each other. Finally Kevin Anderson looked at Gottfried LaSalle and asked, "What do we do?"

"I suggest you contact your parish priest. You administrators," Gottfried looked at the CCME staff, "should contact the Archdiocese of New Orleans as well as the departments of religious studies at our local Universities for further insight."

Alex was clearly subdued as were the other members of the board of trustees. "I will. Thanks, Gottfried, we will do that," Alex said, closing her legal pad.

Dr. Ashley stood, "I suppose we can stand adjourned. Don, anything else from you?"

Don shook his head, once again staring at the floor.

"In that case, thank you all for coming on short notice. We'll keep you posted."

On the way out of the conference room, Gottfried LaSalle whispered to Alex and Don. "You know that the voodoo is under the influence of someone else who apparently wants to damage this hospital. I doubt the Voodoos are acting on their own."

Alex gave him a strained smile. "Thanks, Mr. LaSalle. We'll keep it in mind. We'll keep you updated."

"Bad business, bad for business," LaSalle muttered on his way out.

Don glared at the remaining board members. "Yeah, this is just fucking great. These people are fucking lunatics. We'll be out of business in a year if this doesn't go away. Nobody in this heathen, God-forsaken town is coming to a cursed, Voodoos hospital."

***

Raoul DuPree, his heart thudding, leaned against a door jamb outside the coronary care unit. He'd seen the evil one and the ordinary man in the lobby and, on an impulse, followed them. He strained, his heart beating furiously, to hear their words behind the half-closed door in the empty patient room.

The ordinary man was speaking, his voice low.

"Board's freaked, particularly Bonnet. Eyes nearly popped out of his head when he saw me there. You ready to do him?"

The ponytailed man groaned, and once again inwardly cursed this stupid man and his boss who had sent him on this mission. "Patience, patience. All things in good time."

Raoul could hardly hear him; his voice was barely a whisper. He pressed his ear closer against the door.

The ordinary man's voice rose. "Dammit, I want it done. Don't mess with me, man. You got your money, a slick million." He slammed his fist against the wall.

Raoul jumped when he heard a thump in the room. Sounded like a chair being moved. He peered around the door and saw an overturned chair. The evil one held the younger man against the wall, his knee in his crotch, and the leather strap pressed against his neck. The ordinary man's eyes were wide with fright.

"Shut up, you fool. Don't rush me. No one rushes me. Never speak to me again" the evil one rasped as he threw the ordinary man against the bed.

Raoul moved away from the door towards the utility room. The evil one left the room and glanced at him on the way out.

Raoul was terrified and turned away from the ponytailed evil man. Hope he doesn't recognize me from the restaurant, he thought to himself. Glad I have on this isolation gown and mask. But, what should I do. Should I warn Dr. Bonnet? Raoul continued to struggle with his conscience and what was the right thing to do as he went into the next patient's room.

CHAPTER 6

Alex found a note from Bridgett when she returned to her office at three. She'd left for the day, saying she didn't feel well.

On Alex's desk was an early edition of *The Times Picayune*. The headlines were, in the biggest boldest type font Alex had ever seen, read: **"Grace Raccine Voodooed at Crescent City Medical Center: First Lady of Louisiana unresponsive."**

Alex read the account of the incident, amazed at the accuracy of the press regarding the incident. The press knew everything, and that unnerved her. As she was contemplating how this could have happened, her phone rang. Dreading the worse, she answered it and was surprised by Mitch's voice.

"Hey, I just saw the papers, so I'm surprised I got you. Bet you've had a rough day." His voice was warm and sensitive.

"Yeah, it's been pretty awful. Things are unbelievable."

"I'm sure. Feel up for some company this evening? I'll bring over dinner and we'll relax a little, unwind some." Mitch's voice sounded so concerned and kind, that Alex almost cried.

She paused to contemplate her options. She was seeing Granddad at four-thirty and she already physically and mentally exhausted. She was tempted to say no, but she hesitated to say that, once again unsure of their relationship. Besides, it would be good to see someone objective from outside the hospital.

"Sure Mitch, my place at seven. We need to make it an early night, though. Tomorrow could be as bad as today, and today was pure hell. Today took the cake. It couldn't have been much worse."

"Great. See you at seven." Mitch sounded pleased.

Mitch's phone call raised Alex's spirits significantly. She found herself looking forward to the evening.

***

At 5:00 p.m., while walking down Bourbon Street to his apartment, Frederico bought the evening edition of *The Times Picayune*. He was ecstatic as he read the CCMC article. When he reached his home, he made himself a drink and called Salvadal on the phone.

"You saw the paper?"

"Yeah. You must have a guardian angel, Petrelli." Salvadal smiled to himself and thought how stupid and what an asshole the Mafia boss was.

Frederico hung up and went back to the bar downstairs to celebrate.

Alex was physically beat and emotionally spent when she left CCMC at four in the afternoon. She decided to call Martin's Taxi to pick her up and take her the short distance to the Palm Court to meet her grandfather. As the big white Buick pulled to the hospital circle, Alex was pleased to see that Martin himself was picking her up.

"Hi, darling. Bad day, I bet. Saw the papers. Thought I'd hear from you so I kept myself open. That's some bad business at the medical center, real bad. My wife's cooking gumbo tonight, but it'll keep. Who's responsible for this stuff at the hospital?"

Alex still could not believe how fast native New Orleanians could speak, particularly those from the Ninth Ward with a dialect all its own. The entire verbal exchange with Martin took less than three seconds and covered three topics. Fortunately, Alex was just now getting used to the Cajun dialect and rapid speech and understood him...

She smiled at Martin. "You tell me. Some Voodoo Queen I guess. I need to go to Palm Court to meet my grandfather."

"We'll be there in 10. You OK?"

Alex pondered her next question carefully before asking it, probably because she was scared to, or didn't want to, hear Martin's answer.

"You're from this city, Martin. Do you believe in voodoo?"

Martin hesitated several moments before answering.

"Don't knows if I do, don't knows if I don't. I never paid voodoo no mind. Choose not to know about it. But there're some who believe in it mightily and they live by it and practice it every day, people you'd never think believe in it, rich people. Word has it there's lots of voodoo groups that meet every week, you know, like church."

"You've got to be kidding." Alex was appalled. By this time they were pulling out of the parking lot.

"Traffic's heavy. Yeah, yeah, darling, you wouldn't believe them who believe in the hoodoo. I hear that some of the best families in New Orleans, all up and down the Avenue do it, I mean, practice it. Don't know names though," Martin added quickly, seemingly afraid to be implicated.

"I'm just surprised it's so prevalent here. I know nothing about it but I can't imagine people believing in some archaic African religion in the twenty first century. It blows my mind. Besides, I thought it was just for tourists, you know, entertainment for tourists."

"You ain't from here. You couldn't know. It's New Orleans stuff. How's the Guv's wife?"

"She's holding her own. She'll be okay, hopefully" Alex said with forced brightness.

"Horrible thing. Ms. Raccine's a great lady, good to everybody. Can't imagine somebody 'fixin' her," Martin said, shaking his head.

"Fixing?" Alex said.

"You know, cursing her, hoodooing her, hexing her. She never hurt nobody, but she's helped a million people. Maybe somebody is trying to get back at the Governor—probably because he's not crooked enough for some folks."

Not everybody, Alex thought as they pulled up in front of the Palm Court. "Thanks for getting me. Go home to your gumbo."

"Want me to get you tomorrow, darling? Wouldn't mind at all. I'll pick up my first load at the airport and zip over your house by seven. You should save your energy. No telling what's coming." He gave her an ominous look as he opened her door.

Alex laughed and then replied, "Thanks, Martin. Nothing

could be worse than today. I'll call you."

"Get some rest, Alex. Nothing you can do when these things happen. What happens, happens. You can't do nothing about it!"

Alex felt anxious as she left the cab and her stomach knotted up. She'd never heard Martin say anything negative. He was the most positive, upbeat man she'd ever talked to. Maybe it's not over but certainly nothing this bad can happen again.

***

Alex paused to admire the beautifully decorated hotel lobby of the Palm Court Hotel as she searched for her grandfather. The marble floors were gleaming and the oriental rugs accented them perfectly. She spotted her grandfather sitting in the far corner of the lobby bar and checked him out briefly. He looked good. He was impeccably dressed in a dark blue business suit and his silver hair gleamed. He had what she supposed was a tumbler of Jack Daniels in his hand.

She approached him from behind, hugged him and placed a wet kiss on his cheek. The smell of bourbon and aftershave permeated her senses. It was comforting. Old Spice. Granddad had been wearing Old Spice since she could remember. The memory took her back to safer times and made her feel warm and safe.

As Adam Lee stood to return the hug, she said, "You look great, maybe a little too skinny." Alex couldn't resist and she hugged him again. He was such a rock of stability to her. She needed that today.

Adam held her tightly and said, "You're looking a little rough around the edges, girl. What the hell's going on at that damn hospital?"

"Wish I knew," Alex said, as she ended the hug.

"Want a drink? Looks like you could use one."

"White wine, pinot grigio, please."

Adam motioned for the waitress and ordered the wine as Alex settled herself on the sofa next to him.

"Well, what's the story at CCMC? Paper said Grace was still unresponsive."

"She is unresponsive. I checked before I left. It's a mess over there." Alex's eyes filled with tears as she continued, "It's just awful, Adam. Who could do this to Mrs. Raccine?"

"Don't know. What's with this voodoo shit? Paper said she'd been voodooed? Isn't that some sort of crazy, ancient, African crap?"

"Yeah, that's right. There's a curse against CCMC. Can you believe it? Even members of the board of trustees believe in voodoo, credible, educated people. The police think the same thing."

Adam stared as her wide-eyes, mulled this over and nursed his drink for a few minutes.

"Voodoo or not, somebody's behind it. Someone is after the hospital and/or Grace Raccine. The question is why. Why hurt Grace Raccine?"

Alex shrugged her shoulders. "Don't know. Maybe they are trying to get to the Governor, but it's bad press for the hospital no matter what the reason is. The place is a mess. Staff isn't reporting to work and patients are transferring to other hospitals. There's some sort of crazy archaic belief that if you acknowledge the curse then you become vulnerable to the curse and many people believe this and are trying to ignore or escape the Voodoo curse by staying at home."

"Humph, this sounds like bull shit to me! Sounds like some folks want some days off with pay. Shit, don't let the Jihadists know or they'll switch from terrorism to Voodoo!"

Alex cracked a smile at her grandfather's prediction and said, "In addition to everything else, our census dropped 38% today due to transfers and patients leaving against medical advice. Unfortunately, this will affect our bottom line if it continues, not to mention our reputation."

Adam nodded his head in agreement and signed deeply, "Bad for the hospital. Makes it seem unsafe. Good for George Raccine. Makes the public feel bad for him, sympathy, I would think. It could increase his chances of re-election or a senate bid."

Alex could feel chill bumps jumping out on her arms. "You don't think..."

Adam interrupted her, his voice brusque. "Don't know anything except that somebody's going to benefit from this, Alex. Question is who. Something's up with George. He's different, going soft on major issues, especially crime and illegal drugs. He keeps changing his mind on everything, waffling on major issues. It's like he preoccupied or something. I got little satisfaction from him when we talked yesterday."

Alex shook her head and was a little defensive when she said, "His wife has terminal cancer. He's probably upset about her. And now this voodoo stuff. I think Raccine's a good man. Not as popular as he was at first, but still well-liked here and the first lady is loved."

"Time will tell," he said. "In the meantime, is everything else okay?" He peered at her over his glasses.

"I guess," Alex replied. "We'll have to hope Mrs. Raccine recovers. Have you talked with grandmother today? I need to call her. Is everything okay at the farm?"

"Yeah. She's fine. I miss the old girl. I managed to get an earlier flight out this evening. Should arrive in Washington a little after nine with the time change. We've a late date." Adam winked at her, his eyes twinkling.

"I'll call her soon. I've got a date too. I need to go."

"Wait just a moment, young lady. A date with whom? Who is this man?"

"You'll meet him. When the time's right. It's not serious. He's a close friend. Very attractive. I like him a lot." Alex smiled at Adam who obviously wanted to know more. She stood to leave. "How's my mother? Is she doing OK?"

"The same. Never changes. Hug me, girl, and come home soon. Place's quiet without you. Alex, focus on getting out of this God-forsaken place."

"Will do, Granddad. Love you."

As Adam Lee watched Alex leave, his heart overflowed

with pride at her beauty and accomplishments. Chip off the old block, he thought to himself. I deserve her. Of course, her beauty came from her mother.

***

Alex barely had time to jump out of the shower and change clothes before Mitch was at the door. He appeared with a bottle of barrel-fermented special reserve Virginia chardonnay harvested and bottled at The Lake Anna Winery, a winery and vineyard not far from Alex's grandparents' estate in Hanover county. It was Alex's favorite wine.

"I've been saving this for a special occasion but knew you could use a boost. I'd saved it for the Extravaganza."

"Oh Mitch, you're wonderful, so thoughtful. It's perfect." Alex hugged him.

Mitch gave her a light kiss on the forehead and returned her hug. Once again he felt a pang of guilt that was paralyzing.

Mitch smiled warmly and continued speaking, "I also stopped at the French market and picked up some fresh-baked baguettes, some cheese and fruit. Put your feet up, and let me wait on you."

"Deal. Need any help?"

"I'll find everything. It may not be perfect, but it'll be good," Mitch replied on his way to the kitchen.

Alex sat in her favorite chair and mentally reviewed the events of the day. She still couldn't believe what had happened.

Mitch returned shortly with two crystal wine goblets and the bottle of chardonnay chilling in a silver wine bucket. A beautiful silver tray was piled high with bread, cheese and roasted almonds. Grapes, strawberries and apricots added color to the presentation.

"Mitch, it's beautiful. Such elegance," Alex was genuinely impressed. This man is perfect, she thought.

He placed the tray on the coffee table and went over to Alex's CD player and selected a compact disc. He then lit several candles. They made light conversation as they ate their dinner. The wine, food and music made Alex relax and drift through the meal. She closed her eyes for several seconds until the day's events jerked her back to reality.

"What do you make of the situation at CCMC?" she asked, remembering that Mitch had grown up in New Orleans.

He paused for a few minutes, as if collecting his thoughts and searching for the correct words. "Well, I really don't know what's happened, except what I read in the newspaper."

"The story in the *Times* was perfect. It was as if the reporter had discovered Mrs. Raccine. It was disarming in its accuracy."

"Sounds like a good newspaper reporter to me. Mrs. Raccine doing okay?" Mitch gazed at her intently.

Alex shrugged her shoulders. "She's stable, but hasn't moved or spoken since the attack. She had some heart trouble initially, but that seemed to have cleared late this afternoon. When I saw her, she seemed to be in a catatonic trance, almost. She was apparently very frightened and traumatized. She looked literally scared to death."

"I'd imagine so. I would think that being voodooed is pretty horrible, at least that's what I heard." He looked saddened, as he'd always liked Grace Raccine.

"You're a native. Do you believe in it?" Alex asked, once again almost fearing his answer.

"It's hogwash. Junk. It's just a way of scaring people. Of course I don't believe in it. Did you think I would?" said Mitch, noting the expression of relief cross Alex's face.

"I don't know. I learned today that some prominent New Orleans families do."

"Really, who?" Mitch replied and waited for more information.

"Well...." Alex hesitated.

"Don't tell me anything you're not comfortable with. Besides, I don't even know if I understand this stuff enough to be helpful. All I can really do is listen." Mitch picked up on her hesitation.

"It's not a matter of comfort; it's about confidentiality and ethics. In a nutshell, I found out that some board members do believe. They're all educated, prominent people. Guess I'm just not used to the culture here," Alex ended on a plaintive note.

"New Orleans does have its own culture, that's for sure. Any leads on who's responsible?" Mitch's face was intense as he waited for her answer.

Alex appreciated the objectivity she heard in Mitch's voice. "Not a one. The police captain is certainly not sharing anything. He grilled all the staff and presented himself at the board meeting as macho man, claiming voodoo and black magic as the reason for the attack on Mrs. Raccine. He's a real act. He had a toxic reaction to me, hate at first sight. Of course, I shared his feelings," Alex admitted.

"Who's the captain?" Mitch asked.

"Captain Francois, a real jerk."

"Oh, I know Jack. We went to school together. Your evaluation of him is correct. He seems like that initially."

Alex was stunned. "That's impossible. He looks like he's at least ten or fifteen years older than you."

"Hard living, I guess." Mitch's discussion of the captain was interrupted by the ringing of Alex's cell phone.

"Excuse me, Mitch, I better get that. Who knows, maybe it's the hospital with another voodoo attack." Alex smiled, feeling brash and a bit reckless from the wine.

Mitch continued sipping his wine and thinking over Alex's comments, and wished she had revealed more. He hadn't learned much.

He could hear Alex talking softly on the phone; her voice was the sound of rustling silk. Once again Mitch wished he could do things over again. He would never make the same mistakes. He'd never thought things would go this far.

"Of course, I'll see you. You probably need to talk. Come over in about thirty minutes," Mitch heard Alex say before she hung up the phone.

When she returned to the living room, Alex appeared a bit harried, piqued in fact.

"Trouble?"

"No, not really, at least I don't think so. That's Robert Bonnet. He asked if I'd see him for a few minutes later tonight. Do you mind?" Alex had a chagrinned look, and her face was streaked red. Was she blushing? Her face felt hot.

Mitch picked up on her embarrassment and reassured her. "No, no, of course not. Should I mind that you are dismissing me to spend some time with your ex-husband?" He smiled and winked at her. "Let me help you clean up. Is Bonnet involved in this stuff at CCMC?"

"Only insofar as Robert is Mrs. Raccine's surgeon," Alex replied cautiously. "Only normal that he should be upset, I suppose."

"I suppose," Mitch replied in a noncommittal tone.

As Mitch and Alex cleaned up together, Mitch said, "I know this voodoo stuff is foreign to you and probably seems ridiculous in many ways. Just know I'm here for you and will help you all I can. Call me anytime. I'm a good listener." Mitch smiled warmly at Alex and kissed her cheek.

"Thanks, Mitch. It means a lot."

"Well, let me get out of here before your company arrives.

I'm sure he wants to see you alone. He'd probably feel bad if he thought he'd interrupted your evening," Mitch replied while gathering his things.

As he leaned over to give Alex a good night kiss, something fell out of his pocket. Mitch retrieved it quickly.

"My new cell phone." Mitch explained hastily. "I have it for the Arcadian project." Then he gracefully lowered his head to Alex's engaging her in a long kiss. "Take care, call if you need anything."

After Mitch left her home, Alex touched her cheek, still flushed from the kiss. Well, she thought, maybe we're getting somewhere. He's such a nice guy. Any other date would wisecrack about entertaining your ex-husband this late at night. Mitch's just about as perfect a man as I've ever seen; she continued to think as she went into the bathroom to brush her teeth. Maybe he is just a little too perfect.

Ten minutes later Robert arrived at her door. He looked fatigued and disheveled. He had a tortured look in his eyes. His appearance was untidy and his clothes looked as though he'd slept in them.

Robert kissed her on the cheek as he came in, and she smelled bourbon on his breath. On well, not my problem and he can probably smell wine on mine.

Robert immediately began talking. "Thanks for seeing me. Hope I haven't interrupted your evening." Robert's eyes scanned the flat and saw its beautiful furnishings and neatness. "This place looks great. I recognize some of the antiques, though." Robert smiled carefully, his emotions clear on his face as he struggled to gain control.

"Suppose you do." Alex returned the smile, touching his arm for support. "Some of these things have been with me a long time. You know me, I find something I love, and I can never quite give it up."

As soon as the words were out of her mouth, she realized the implications of what she'd said. "The furniture of course," she added hastily, turning red with embarrassment, her heart beating frantically.

Robert grinned at her and replied, "I understand what you mean. I'm the same way. Anyway, the place is beautiful; the floors are in great shape. You did a lot of renovation?"

"Yes, a complete renovation. I lived in the warehouse district the first year I was here, while this house was being renovated. Can I offer you some brewed decaf and chocolate raspberry mousse pie?"

"My favorite, as you may remember. Yes, on both accounts." He accompanied Alex into the kitchen. Robert looked around and noted the silver tray and wine decanter in the dish drainer. He immediately felt guilty. "I'm so sorry, you must've had company."

He remembered walking past two men several houses down. One of them seemed familiar to him; probably someone he'd gone to school with but now wondered if one of them was Alex's beau. He felt a pang of jealously and was surprised by it.

Alex followed his gaze and simply said, "I had a friend over for dinner. We'd finished when you called. It's okay. Don't worry about it. Coffee is almost ready."

As they drank their coffee and ate their pie, Robert once again admired the beauty of the hand rubbed kitchen cabinets and the colors in the hand-painted tiles in the kitchen. He hesitated for a moment before he continued. "I didn't have anyone else to talk to. No one I could really trust. I trust you, and you know what happened. There's something strange going on, and I can't sort it all out. I'm hoping you can help me."

Alex intently gazed at Robert and said, "What do you think is wrong?"

As he searched for the best words, Alex watched him carefully, looking for signs of anxiety and discomfort. Robert replied, "I know you may think this is stupid and that I'm reading into things and perhaps I am. But, I feel as if someone is trying to hurt or destroy me. I don't know why. It's just a gut feeling."

"What makes you think so? Anything specific?"

"Some specifics, but nothing concrete to validate my feelings. I've had trouble with some business dealings. I've been pressured to sell some land, but I've refused. In and of itself, that's really not a big deal. I've been dating a woman for several months, and that relationship has been deteriorating. It's probably my fault. I just don't trust her anymore. Don't know why exactly. It's just a feeling. She's a real-estate broker, very successful, and she's been pressuring me to sell the same land. Of course, I realize she has a vested interest in the sale, but I have plenty of other property she could sell, and probably make more money. She brought me a generous offer on the property from some out of town venture capital group. I have a suspicion that someone must want to develop that last bit of river front with a casino or hotel because only an investment like that could pay off. I don't remember who the venture capitalists were. I turned it down. Anyway, since then I've gotten several threatening phone calls suggesting that bad things would happen to me or people I cared about if I didn't sell the land. Truth is, it's really not mine to sell. I own it jointly with my father. I know he won't sell, so I haven't even asked." Robert paused for a moment to think and then continued:

"I got another phone call at Gulf Shores this past weekend, sort of a 'sell or else' call. I hung up on them. Then, this morning I got to work and found out about Grace Raccine. I can't help but think that all of this is possibly tied together."

Alex interrupted him saying, "I hardly think someone attacked Grace Raccine because you wouldn't sell some land. Think about it. Whoever attacked her is certainly bad, very evil, but don't you think it's more likely a political maneuver?"

"Maybe, but remember that the Raccine's and my family have been friends for years. Grace is practically my second mother. Their son, Ron, was my best friend until he was killed five years ago in Afghanistan. Ron Raccine and I were practically brothers, and I virtually lived at the Raccine's house when I was growing up. I think they, whoever they are, they're trying to get at me, maybe through the Raccines. When I put all this together, particularly when I factor in what you told me yesterday about the malpractice actions and the internal complaints, I can't help but wonder if the events are related, you know, like a conspiracy." Robert paused and carefully watched Alex's reaction.

Alex shook her head but her response was pensive as she clicked through Robert's concerns. She remembered the tragic death of Ron Raccine. It was shortly after their divorce, and she had witnessed Robert's sadness. He was devastated. It seemed as if his world was crashing down. She had met Ron Raccine, a West Point graduate, several times, and had really liked and respected him, especially his patriotism when he easily could have been dismissed from entering an unpopular war.

"I don't know, Robert, I'm not sure. Some of these things are totally unrelated to the hospital. It just doesn't make sense. Anything else going on?"

"Just one more thing and it just happened a couple of hours ago. I got a phone call from a man. Said he had to warn me that someone wanted to kill me. Told me to be careful, that he thought they were planning to kill me very soon."

"What! That's awful. What else, did he say anything else? Did you call the police?" Alex could feel her heart thudding in her chest.

"Not really. Said he called to warn me because I'd been good to him. He said I'd helped him out in the past when no one else would."

"Who do you think it was?" Alex felt tingly all over while chill bumps popped up on her arms. She was scared and anxious for Robert.

"Don't have a clue. Could be a patient, or a family member. Could be some patient from the free clinic I run. I just don't know. He sounded young and scared." Robert repeatedly tapped his spoon against the table.

Alex shook her head. "This is frightening, extremely frightening. You should call the police."

"No, maybe later. I just wanted to tell someone. I'm going to wait a few days and see what turns up."

Alex's forehead was creased into frown lines as she considered Robert's story. "Do you believe in voodoo?"

He thought carefully before answering. "I believe in forces of good and evil. I think voodoo is simply a manifestation, an instrument of evil, but whether I believe in it or not is irrelevant at this point." Robert appeared sad. "Alex, I feel responsible for what happened to Grace Raccine. I think someone used her to get at me."

Alex sighed and spoke, "Robert, it's late and we're both tired. Neither of us is thinking very well or objectively. Let's talk later and try to figure this out. In the meantime, please please please be very careful. Please call me if you need help. Is Mrs. Raccine better?"

Robert nodded. "I will keep in touch and let you know. Grace was the same at nine tonight. I stopped by the hospital to make late rounds." Robert paused and added cautiously, "When I say okay, I mean okay physically. There's no improvement in her level of responsiveness; she's in a catatonic state."

Alex shook her head sadly. "Let's pray she improves," Then she smiled and yawned for her king-sized Euro mattress.

"It's getting late. I'll talk to you soon. Thanks for letting me come over. It means a lot to have a friend, someone I can trust." Robert looked grateful and smiled sheepishly. He reached out and hugged Alex, and she hugged him back.

As soon as Robert left, Alex remembered she'd forgotten to

ask him about the new board member. A small sense of fear swept over her, and she wondered if Kevin Anderson figured into Robert's troubles. The thought kept returning to her as she prepared for bed. Alex slept fitfully the entire night, with dreams of bloodied roosters, snakes, and angry realtors interrupting her night's rest.

CHAPTER 7

Alex walked to work the next morning. The day was crisp and beautiful, and the sun was shining brightly. New Orleans was lovely in February. The air was fresh and fragrant from the smell of lilacs, and the tulip trees were in full bloom. The walk also made Alex long for a simpler time, like springtime on the family farm in Virginia.

The walk was invigorating and gave Alex time to clear her head and figure out the best way to handle yesterday's events. She entered the hospital and was pleased that everything seemed normal. There'd only been one news truck in the parking lot. Good, she thought. Maybe we're old news.

The lights were out in her office. Bridgett wasn't in, but she usually came in around nine after she dropped her little boy at school. I've got a lot for her to do today, Alex thought. I hope she comes in. She checked her voice mail and there was an urgent message from the night nursing supervisor asking her to come to the nursing office right away. Alex left her office immediately and met Bette Farve on the way.

"Morning, Bette. Where're you headed."

Bette nodded stiffly at her and kept on walking. Alex ran after her.

"Bette, I had a message to report to the nursing office. What's happening?"

"More than you want to know about," Bette snapped, her rigid face displayed her anger and irritability. "Fifty percent of the nursing staff has called in sick, and we need an emergency staffing plan. Thought you may want to be included."

"Fifty percent? What the hell! What's going on?" Alex asked, alarmed, as visions of food poisoning, the Ebola virus and flesh eating bacteria ran through her mind. "Oh no, this couldn't be more of the voodoo stuff, could it?"

"Beats me. I don't have a clue." Bette rolled her eyes.

Alex wondered why Bette was being so accommodating when she usually did her best to make Alex appear unprepared and incompetent. "We've never had an absentee rate like this. Are the absences confined to specific units?"

"As best I can tell, they're spread throughout the house. I don't know what's going on. Probably just a bunch of lazy asses looking for a day off." Bette was sarcastic. Somehow that remark hadn't sounded so bad when her grandfather had said it yesterday.

Alex bit back a bitter retort. "They are probably afraid they'll 'catch' the voodoo curse. You talked to Don?"

"I left him a message. I'm going to meet with my assistant vice-presidents to review staff numbers. I guess these call-ins are related to yesterday?"

"Can I attend your meeting?" Alex expected Bette to say no.

"Yes, whatever plan we come up with will have to meet with your approval anyway, so we may as well get your advice early. Besides, I'm flying out of here tomorrow for New York. I have tickets to three plays and nothing's going to keep me from going."

Alex was amazed Bette was including her but suspected it was due to her upcoming vacation. "When do you meet?"

"Now. Let's go," Bette said.

***

The vice-presidents for nursing were drinking coffee and talking among themselves when Bette and Alex arrived.

The news wasn't good. There were currently 273 inpatients in the hospital at CCMC, not counting the patients housed on the research units. Critical care, medicine, and oncology were full. This represented a decreased census rate of 50% since yesterday.

The vice-president for surgery reported that eighty percent of her staff had called in sick. Ten percent of the critical care and emergency room staff had called in, but sixty percent of staff scheduled in medicine and oncology had also called in. The vice-presidents had already instructed the secretaries and staffing coordinators to call staff at home that were scheduled off and ask them to cover.

Alex said, "We need to close some units. Suggestions?"

Bette, her face as bright red as her dyed hair, shrieked at Alex. "You're crazy! We can't shut down units. Think about what that means to hospital revenues. We're having enough trouble keeping our market edge. I refuse to close units, and besides, Don would never allow it. God knows what Obama Care is going to do us and now you want to close beds."

"Bette, be reasonable. If there are no patients, there is no revenue. Besides, there's nothing else we can do. We can't run a six hundred bed hospital on fifty percent staff. Logically, that would suggest that we needed one hundred of our scheduled staff. We're setting ourselves up for trouble. Be practical. Our staff would run themselves ragged, and they'd be exhausted after two days. Fatigue itself would cause mistakes and accidents, and our quality outcomes would decrease."

Bette was furious and invaded Alex's personal space, her head inches from Alex's face. "I'm not closing units. Do you understand? We'll check out agency staff to get us through this." She moved away from Alex and glared at her VPs. "Anyone have any idea what is going on here?" She waited. "Come on, I know some of you know. Why are they calling in sick? This will count against them, their pay will be docked, and they will not be able to count it as a vacation day. Tell them that. I damn well guarantee it."

No one spoke. The tension in the room permeated the atmosphere. Bette was not defeated and said in a menacing voice, her nostrils flaring, "Some of you have good grapevine access; you must have some idea why we have this sudden rash of sick calls. Someone better speak up. Diane, what do you know?"

Diane shook her head. "I have no idea, Bette. Had a three day weekend and was out of town. I haven't even checked my units yet. Didn't even know about Mrs. Raccine until this morning when I came to work."

Diane Bradley, the assistant vice-president for critical care, stood up to Bette. Very little intimidated the veteran nurse. Diane continued speaking, "However, Alex is right. We need some contingency plans and we need to close units. I do suggest we develop several emergency staffing plans to get us through the next few days. Meanwhile, let's decide what to do today. We have patients on these units who have no nurse taking care of them. From what I can tell, the ICU and the emergency department are in pretty good shape. Medicine and surgery are a problem. I can lend some staff from critical care."

Alex smiled gratefully at Diane and could have kissed her. She was about to speak when her cell phone started to ring and the overhead hospital paging system began to STAT page her to administration.

"Got to go. Your suggestion is good, Diane." Turning to Bette, she said, "I'd like an opportunity to talk with you after you develop your plan. I'm free this afternoon. Good luck." Alex stood and smiled at the assistant VPs for nursing.

Betty hollered after her. "Just remember that I'm going away tomorrow. Any extra expenses here will be between you and Don," Bette warned on her way out.

"I'll take full responsibility," Alex said, and closed the door as she walked quickly towards the administrative suite.

On her way to administration, Alex ran into Elizabeth Tippet. "I've been paged to administration. How about you?"

"Same. Any idea what's happening?" Elizabeth said.

"Nope, but we'll know in a minute. How'd you sleep last night?"

"Not well at all. Had bad dreams all night. Do you have any more information about the voodoo? I can't believe we're in the twenty-first century, and people in this city believe in this crap. It's beyond me," Elizabeth sighed.

Alex nodded agreement and said, "Well, they do. Half of the staff called in today. Census is down over fifty percent from yesterday."

"That's great, that's just great. Don will be even more freaked," Elizabeth replied as she sarcastically shook her head.

As the two women entered the administration suite, they saw Don, John Ashley and Robert Bonnet seated at the conference table where they talked quietly. John and Robert stood as Alex and Elizabeth walked in. Don kept his seat.

Alex asked quickly, "What's going on?"

Robert spoke directly to Alex, "Mrs. Raccine's is in cardiac distress. I'm afraid she could go bad on us very quickly. I've called in the chief of cardiology and he's with her now. We'll be transferring her to the CCU." Robert was concerned and looked sad.

"How's she mentally?" Elizabeth said.

"Unchanged. The nurses report that she's moving about and grimacing. Although she remains unconscious, it looks as though she may be remembering something."

Alex said, "Well, that could be good news provided that when she wakes up she doesn't have a heart attack."

"Our fears exactly," Dr. Ashley replied. "Meanwhile, three newspapers have called for a press release, and unfortunately, the Associated Press picked up the story, and it ran in every major newspaper this morning. *The Washington Post, New York Times, Los Angeles Times, and Miami Herald* have correspondents who are eating breakfast in the hospital cafeteria."

"Did we offer them meal vouchers," Elizabeth glanced sideways at Don Montgomery. "We need to keep them as happy as possible and have another press conference. If these newspapers have sent representatives, you can bet all other major print media and news networks will send journalists, too."

Don's secretary, Latetia, appeared at the door. "Mr. Montgomery, we have *People* **Magazine** on the phone, and CNN just called and asked to speak with you. I told them you're in a meeting, so they said they'd be sending a correspondent and news team down. What are we supposed to say to these people? What are we supposed *to do* with them?" Latetia stood at the door, and refused to move until someone told her what to do.

After a brief silence, Elizabeth spoke up and said, "Tell anyone that calls that the hospital will be holding a press conference at five today. We'll take questions from reporters." She looked at Dr. Ashley and Don Montgomery. "We have to address their questions openly and honestly. Otherwise we'll get more negative publicity if it seems we are covering things up. We also need to get Governor Raccine to come. If he's supportive of us, it'll help us tremendously. Robert, you know the Governor. Will he participate?"

"I'll ask him. I'm sure he'll come if he can. If not, he'll send Andre Renou. I'll check it out and get back to you."

Elizabeth continued, "We have to draft something for the press and anticipate the questions the press will ask us. Can we do that now?"

Alex intervened. "I'm in favor of what you're suggesting, but first, there's another problem that takes priority." Alex looked around the table as she spoke. "I've just returned from a meeting in nursing administration. Our sick calls are up fifty percent today. Only half of the scheduled nursing staff have reported to work."

Don jumped up from the table and screamed at her. "Fifty percent of the staff called in sick? Who the hell's taking care of the patients? We can't run a hospital on half-staff. We'll be broke sooner than later. What a pile of shit all of this is! This is fricking insane!" Don's voice was loud, angry.

Alex continued, talking over Don's outrage. "The hardest hit areas are medicine and surgery. The ICU's are okay and so is the ED. So are the maternal-child areas. I asked Bette and her nursing managers to develop an emergency staffing plan and close several units to combine staff so we can offer safe care."

Don's face was beet red as he jumped up from his chair, "No, no, no, hell no. We will *not* close beds or units," he retorted angrily. "It's unthinkable! What'll this look like to the public, to our competitors who are probably laughing their asses off at us already? I still think all of this is corporate espionage. We will NOT close beds or the next thing you know, we'll have to close the damn hospital!"

Dr. Ashley said pleadingly, "Don, we have to close beds. We don't have any nursing staff to take care of these patients. Besides, it will save us money in the long run."

Don thought for a moment and said, "If we close half of our beds, we won't have an image, because we won't have a hospital. It's preposterous. Do you realize how much money each closed bed costs the hospital? A hit like this will kill us. I feel like I'm being blackmailed. You have to find something better to do," Don said as he pounded his fist on the table.

Alex couldn't believe he was reacting this way. He was like a child in a rage. What an imbecile. "Don, we have to do this. We don't have a choice." She was beginning to think that Don and Bette were joined at the hip. "We have to combine resources. We have a lot of patients and need full staff for heaven's sake. The ratios are low anyway, barely adequate in some areas and hardly meet national standards. That's always been a huge risk for us. We need a plan designed to maximize resources as best we can and to keep as many beds open as possible. I'll ask Bette to call Louisiana State University and Loyola and offer overtime to all nursing students. Meanwhile, we'll call Tulane and see if they can help us out with morning care. We'll also check with the agencies for extra help. We'll never get these patients back in here for care if we don't handle this situation correctly. John, can you arrange to have our inpatient admissions redirected? We probably should consider directing the emergency department patients to other hospitals and distribute the ED staff to cover the house."

John nodded in agreement. "Yes, Alex, of course. I think you're on target. I'll call a meeting of the medical staff this afternoon. We can also reschedule elective surgery for the next few days. If possible, I'd like to keep the emergency department open since we're the major trauma center in New Orleans."

John was surprisingly calm in assessing the situation and Alex was grateful for his ability to work under pressure. She nodded her support for keeping the ED open.

Don remained red-faced and sullen.

John glanced around the table and asked, "Anyone know why we've had all of these sick calls? Is it associated with yesterday?"

Alex said, "That question came up at the nursing meeting. No one had any explanation for the deluge of sick calls."

Robert looked up and shaking his head said quietly, "Yeah. I know why. It's very simple, if you think about it. It is about yesterday."

All of them stared at him, looking perplexed. "Speak, Bonnet," Montgomery roared.

"Voodoo legend says that if you accept the curse, that is, if you accept the voodoo, then you assume the curse. In this case, people who believe in voodoo would assume the curse by reporting to work. Even people who don't believe in curses are scared. That's why the police can't find Bessie Comstock, the nursing assistant, and they won't find her anytime soon. She's most likely left town, trying to escape what happened in Mrs. Raccine's room. I had several physicians tell me this morning that they're admitting their patients to other hospitals. Simply put, the staff and the physicians are afraid to admit here and won't because they will most likely lose patients."

"What did you say?" Don roared. "They are admitting to other hospitals? I want those damn, fucking doctor traitors taken off our medical staff list. They no longer have privileges here, Bonnet. You tell them that."

No one responded to Don, so Robert continued, "Basically, I think we're lucky to have half of the staff here. I'm surprised that many reported."

Elizabeth looked at Robert. "Dr. Bonnet, how long do you expect this to continue? How long will people stay out of work?"

Don answered before Robert could speak. "They'll either get their asses back here tomorrow, or they're fucking fired!" In a fit of temper, Don left the room. The rest of the executive team looked at each other.

Elizabeth shrugged her shoulders and finally spoke, "I don't know if it's worse when he doesn't speak at all, or when he screams at us. Either way, he's pretty useless."

Dr. Ashley nodded his head in agreement. "You're right. He certainly isn't helping at all. Where does he think he's going to hire staff? If what Robert says is right, no one'll work here. Robert, how long before this blows over?"

"Don't know. It'll depend in part on how well Mrs. Raccine recovers. The other part will depend on how well we handle the situation. Firing people won't help."

"Don't worry. I'll talk with Don a little later. Let's get to work. I've got to go. I've got patients to see." Dr. Ashley spoke authoritatively.

***

The executive team worked until almost noon on the press conference and staffing plan. Shortly before then, Alex toured the medicine and surgery units and found that things were going surprisingly well. Sixteen first-year nursing students from LSU were giving baths and making beds. Also, Delgado Community College had sent over ten nursing students. Alex was pleased at the cooperation between the local university, colleges, and hospital. The nursing vice-presidents reported that an additional twelve nursing students were coming in for the evening shift. Bette was nowhere to be found.

* * *

Alex grabbed a bite for lunch in the cafeteria and returned to her office a little after one. Bridgett was in but looked unwell.

"Bridge, how you feeling?"

"Much better, thanks. How're things going," Bridgett had a strained look on her face and she was quiet, a total contrast to her normally vivacious self.

"Better than I would have anticipated early this morning," Alex replied. "What's the rumor mill saying about the Raccine case and voodoo?"

"The usual, what you'd expect." There was no eye contact and Bridget looked at her computer screen.

"Bridgett, what's going on? You know everything that goes on in this place. You are my grapevine! What gives? You've been awfully quiet lately. Is anything happening with you I need to know about?" Alex gave her secretary a hard look.

Bridgett's voice was hesitant. "No. Not at all. Just didn't feel well yesterday. I knew you'd be out most of the day, so I left about two." Bridgett had kept her eyes on her computer screen the entire time she was talking to Alex.

"Bridge, you're acting weird. Look at me."

Bridgett looked up from her computer. "Alex, I don't want to talk about the Raccine case or the staff shortages. As a matter of fact, I'm thinking about resigning. Darryl wants me to stay at home with the baby."

Alex stood, looking at her in amazement as she finally realized what was wrong. Bridgett was Cajun and was scared. Bridgett believed in voodoo and was afraid that, by reporting to work, she'd assume the curse.

"OK, I get it. I understand what's happening here. Take some time off, all you need to, but don't resign. I need you too badly. Take the time you need, and we'll talk later."

"Thanks, Al. Thank you for understanding. I'll stay awhile today and finish up. Then I'll decide what to do." Bridgett looked relieved as she continued to type.

Alex went into her office, decided to take a stress break and phoned Mitch. He was in, but his voice sounded strange, cold. He told her he was busy and couldn't talk, saying he had to get downtown. It was an unusual and tense -- the tersest conversation she had ever had with Mitch and Alex was baffled.

***

The ponytailed stranger, Monte Salvadal, stood across the street from the busy CCMC emergency department. Hordes of people entered and left through the glass doors. Business was looking good for CCMC—at least for now. He smiled to himself.

After several minutes Salvadal became impatient. The evil one hated to hire people, preferring to do all his own work. At least that way all would go smoothly. He saw Frederico smoking a cigar across the street. The gangster waved his hat in greeting, but the evil man ignored him. He detested the stocky man and his gangster tactics. He just wanted to get the fuck out of New Orleans. He hated this town.

111

CHAPTER 8

Sandy Pilschner, RN Nurse Manager of the CCMC Emergency Department was working on a staffing plan in her office. Her boss, Diane Bradley, was meeting with her to determine if the emergency department could send several nurses to Surgery to help out over the next few days.

Sandy said gratefully, "Thank goodness it isn't the weekend! With the shootings in this town, we're always running. We'd be up the creek if it were Friday. We had six shootings last Saturday night."

Before Diane could reply, both nurses heard several strange crackling sounds coming from the patient care area of the emergency department. They also heard loud voices.

"Sounds like an equipment malfunction. I'll go check it." Diane immediately left, and with a sense of foreboding, Sandy quickly followed.

As Sandy and Diane entered the open area of the emergency department, two reception clerks were screaming. They could hear gunfire in the patient reception area. Before anyone could act, a masked gunman, carrying a machine gun, entered the open area of the emergency department and began shooting. An ER physician immediately lunged towards him but was shot. Blood spurted everywhere. The physician, Dr. Ron Davis, fell to the floor, with half of his head missing.

The gunman swung around, still firing. Bullets dismantled the patient care area and oxygen and carbon dioxide tanks released gas that caused a cloud of gas vapor in the area.

"Down on the floor, all of you," the gunman screamed. Before the staff could hit the floor, a second gunman appeared. He began pulling open patient privacy curtains and shooting up the patient care areas. He laughed at the terrified patients. Glass cylinders and IV bottles exploded with the gunshots. A burning smell permeated the ED area from two computer work stations that had been destroyed by gunfire. A large shard of glass hit the second gunman in the forehead, and caused a burst of blood from a superficial head wound. The shooter went wild, screaming, "I've been hit, I've been hit. I'm bleeding. Where's the son-of-a-bitch who shot me!" The gunman, blood pouring from his head wound, turned his gun on the staff members, crouching and crying on the floor. Another burst of weapon fire hit an emergency department staff nurse from behind as she lay crouched behind a supply cart. She slumped forward.

Diane heard the telltale beep of a cardiac monitor in bed four, that symbolized the beginning of a heart attack. She stood helpless for what seemed like hours as the monitor screen displayed a dangerously rapid heart rate. Finally, the line of the monitor was flat, signifying a cardiac arrest. Diane, without thinking, intuitively moved toward the patient and cut on the cardiac defibrillator.

The first gunman screamed at Sandy. "Get me the drugs! Get me the drugs, bitch! Now! Now, dammit! Move!"

Sandy got up and began moving towards the narcotics cabinet but realized that she had no key to the locked bin. She immediately began throwing vials of saline, sterile water, needles, and plastic bags of intravenous fluids at the gunman.

The gunman looked at the vials and screamed at Sandy,

"Don't give me this shit. Open that goddamn cart and cabinet and give me the drugs, now. A nurse, crouched behind a bed, slid Sandy her set of narcotic keys. As Sandy picked them up, the gunman moved closer to her. Sandy could literally smell sweat, body odor and gunpowder as he leaned over her shoulder and looked at the locked narcotics bin. He was within a foot of Diane. The second gunman had momentarily stopped shooting and, temporarily unable to see, was frantically wiping blood out of his eyes.

As Sandy struggled to unlock the narcotics bin, Diane turned the cardiac defibrillator up to 360 joules and moved closer to the gunman. The shooter, intent on getting the drugs, didn't notice her. Within a second, Diane touched him with the paddles sending the electricity surging through his body. The gunman turned toward Diane, and dropped the automatic weapon on the floor as the electricity surged through his body. He tried to reach out to grab her, but his arms flailed, and he fell. Diane again struck him with the paddles, and the man immediately had a grand mal seizure. He fell to the floor; his body writhing with volts of current, his limbs and torso in spasm. Foam covered his face. Finally he lay still, except for a few involuntary jerking movements.

The second gunman, momentarily able to see, realized his partner was down, ran to him, and bent over him for a moment. Then he made a piercing animal-like noise, and turned his weapon on Diane, emptying several rounds into her body. Diane fell forward onto the dead gunman's body.

The second gunman ran from the emergency department, and collided with a third man with a ponytail. "Out, out, let's go. Get the fuck out of here. Johnnie's dead." The gunman and the man with the ponytail ran out of the side emergency department door. The gunman shed his mask, ran towards St. Charles Street, and disappeared into hundreds of costumed revelers.

***

At three-thirty, Alex was completing her review of the hospital emergency staffing plan and preparing to go to administration to finalize the plans for the five o'clock press conference when Bridgett screamed and burst into her office.

"Alex, Alex, security just called. There's been a shooting in the emergency department. Come quick."

Alex and Bridgett ran to the stairs and took the three flights to the ground floor. By the time they reached the emergency department, they could hear telepage announcing a code red and a code blue in the ED. Alex's heart stood still, and she could barely breathe. She was paralyzed with fear. Hospital security was clearing out patients, families and bystanders. All available physicians were called to the emergency department. A code orange was announced. Alex's stomach reeled at Code Orange, the disaster code. She was struck by the memory of the only other code orange she'd been a part of. It had occurred shortly after her graduation from nursing school when she was a staff nurse at the Washington Hospital Center. She'd been part of the rescue team that had pulled dozens of bodies out of the Potomac River after an airplane had crashed shortly after takeoff from Reagan National. Oh, please God, don't let this be as bad as that, she prayed.

Bridgett and Alex ran past security into the patient care area of the emergency department. Alex gripped the door frame to keep from fainting and Bridgett doubled over, vomiting. Blood was everywhere. The floors were sticky from spilled intravenous fluids. A metallic smell of blood, gunpowder, smoke and sweat permeated the area. The noise, while quiet, was chilling as patients and staff cried softly to themselves. Several staff members remained in shock and crouched in corners of the patient care area. All seemed paralyzed in place and everything seemed to be moving in slow motion. Dr. Davis's body was prostrate on the floor; his face revealing the horror of his death. A make-shift medical team was bending over the body of a nurse. Alex couldn't tell who it was, so she moved to the side to see.

"Oh no. Oh no," Alex cried when she recognized Diane. Her knees buckled. She looked around for Bridgett, then saw her being lead off by a paramedic. Alex vaguely noticed a fine spray of black powder all over the Emergency Department's brightly polished floor, sticking quickly to the spilled glucose fluids.

"Is she alive? Is Diane alive?" No one was paying any attention to Alex. The medical team were busy intubating Diane and several nurses were starting IV fluids. She heard a physician she didn't recognize call for 10 units of O negative packed cells. Other members were stanching the flow of blood from Diane's abdomen.

"Get her up to the OR STAT! Maybe we'll be able to save her if the internal damage isn't too bad," the same physician was saying to the team. "Take her out through the back. This place is going to be crawling with cops and press any minute. Dr. Bonnet's waiting in the OR. If she's got any chance at all, it's with Bonnet."

Diane was placed on a stretcher and rushed from the emergency department. Then Alex noticed the body of the dead gunman and the slumped body of another emergency department nurse she didn't know.

Within moments, the entire emergency department was

covered with New Orleans police. The crime team retrieved the machine gun and began dusting it for fingerprints. Other policemen were rolling the entire area in yellow crime tape, taking photographs, videotaping the scene, and removing emergency department staff from the patient care area.

The noise level in the emergency department became louder, almost deafening and the smell of sweat, vomit, and gunpowder become intolerable. There was a low hum of agonized human sounds coupled with static voices of police radios. People were yelling at each other for help, and the trauma team were crashing intravenous bottles together and racing for equipment, in an attempt to treat other injured people.

Alex noticed Don who appeared to be in a trance. His face was vacant and his eyes were unseeing. She grabbed his arm. "Let's go to Sandy's office and pull ourselves together."

Don willingly, like a child, allowed Alex to lead him out of the emergency department area. Within seconds they were joined by Elizabeth and Dr. Ashley.

Alex realized that even Dr. Ashley was too traumatized to speak. Elizabeth found her voice and spoke first. "What the hell is happening?" Before anyone could answer, Sandy Pilschner appeared.

Alex hugged her and said, "Sandy, tell us what happened?"

Sandy's eyes looked wild, her pupils dilated. She braced herself; she was visibly shaking. "I'll try. I don't know. It happened so fast. Diane and I were in here reviewing staffing. We heard a crackling sound, some pops and then loud noise. We ran to the patient care area just as a man with a gun was entering the room. He made us lie down on the floor. I don't know, I think they were after drugs."

Dr. Ashley said gently, "What about Dr. Davis?"

Sandy continued her story, "Ron charged the gunman and tried to take the gun away, but the gunman shot him. Then another man with a gun came in. He started shooting up the place. A piece of glass cut his face, and he was so mad he started shooting at us on the floor, and I think he hit Sheila. Then he asked me for drugs and he moved close to watch me open the narcotics cabinet. Then Diane moved over and shocked him with the defibrillator. He came at her, but missed and she shocked him again. I think he's dead. Then his friend shot her. Is Diane okay? I'm so worried about her. There was a lot of blood." Sandy started crying uncontrollably, then stopped, her eyes again attempting to focus.

Elizabeth touched her shoulder and spoke to Sandy gently. "Diane's in surgery. Dr. Bonnet is operating on her. We hope she'll be okay. Bonnet's the best, you know." Elizabeth was positive, but Sandy, in her shock and grief, just cried, her shoulders shaking with her tears.

After a few minutes, Elizabeth led her out of the office and took her over to the Psychiatric Pavilion where Dr. Monique Desmonde, the head psychiatrist in Crescent City Medical's Psych Pavilion, was setting up a post-traumatic stress treatment area.

Alex and Don were still standing in Sandy's office when Dr. Ashley suggested they again check the patient care area and go upstairs to the administrative offices.

It was easy to locate Captain Francois in the inpatient area. He was barking orders at the uniformed cops. Alex urged Don and

John from the area. I just can't deal with Francois now, she thought. Her attempts were in vain. He quickly saw them and walked over.

He had a tight smile on his face as he started talking. "Well, we meet again. More excitement at your world class hospital. What the hell. It looks like your Emergency department has an emergency."

Was Francois actually mocking them? Alex was too numb to tell.

She was speechless with indignation. "Captain Francois, really. You've no right to act this way."

Dr. Ashley interrupted her. "Francois, it's tragic here. You tone and manner of speaking to us is inappropriate. Please just help us and don't harass." John's tone was quiet, but authoritative.

Francois laughed at the chief of medicine. "Could've been worse you know." The Captain stared at Alex and added, "Well, miss lawyer lady, do I have permission to interview your staff or what?" Francois laughed at his own macabre humor.

Alex, though appalled, ignored his behavior. "Do what you need to do, gently. These people are traumatized. Would you object if one of our staff psychiatrists was with them?" Alex was surprised at how strong her voice was.

The captain looked at her with a grudging respect. "No problem, lady. Send the shrink to administration. That's where I thought I'd start the interviews. Plan to set up a command post there. Any objections?" Francois looked at Don who shook his head.

After they left the emergency department, John said, "That man's impossible. I only hope he knows what he is doing."

***

Alex, John and Don returned to the nursing suite. Don told Bette's secretary to have Latetia come over from administration. Alex asked where Bette was.

"Oh", her secretary said, "she's gone for the day. She said she came in at five this morning. She left a little after two to get ready to go on her trip."

Alex was furious that Bette had left. "Call her at home and tell her to get here. And beep Elizabeth Tippet and tell her where we are." Alex's voice was stern, and she was so angry she was shaking.

The three sat in silence until Elizabeth appeared. "I've given a statement to the press. I canceled the press conference at five o'clock and issued a statement that there'd been a shooting in the emergency department. I neither confirmed nor denied any deaths. I told them we'd have another statement later this evening when we had more details."

Alex was glad Elizabeth was there. The two men had regressed into a zombie-like state. "Thanks, Liz. Good work. Did the press seem satisfied?" Alex asked.

Elizabeth looked strangely at Alex. "You know, it's just too weird. They knew. The press knew there was a death. They knew Dr. Davis's name. They even knew Diane was in surgery. How'd they get their information? They knew as much or more than I did at the time. How do you explain this?"

120

She looked searchingly at her three colleagues. Neither man responded, both contemplating what had happened.

Alex said, "I don't know. I don't understand, and it worries me. Did they know that a gunman had died?"

"No. I don't think so. I know CCMC has a hell of a grapevine. But I talked with them within forty minutes of the shootings. Everyone in the emergency department was in a state of shock. No one could've talked to them that quickly. Hospital security had already blocked off the area."

"Perhaps a patient left and told them?"

"Impossible or at least I don't think so," Elizabeth interrupted emphatically. "No patients knew that anyone had died, or been shot, much less a doctor by the name of Ron Davis. It reminds me of the accuracy of the news accounts in the *Times Picayune* yesterday. The story was perfect. I couldn't have given a better account myself. Someone from this hospital gave out the information, or someone who knew it was going to happen reported it quickly." Elizabeth's voice was suspicious.

"Could be, I guess," Alex said, not picking up on her insinuation. "But anyone could've told. We have a great grapevine in this place. Elizabeth, did you know a nurse had been shot and killed during the shootings?"

"Other than Diane?"

"Yes," Alex replied. "Her name is Sheila. I don't know her. I think somebody said that she was new."

"So we have a dead doctor, a dead nurse and another nurse in surgery?" Liz asked.

Alex nodded. "Yes, and a dead gunman and at least one dead patient. Do you know how the gunman died?"

"No, how?" Elizabeth was reeling from the knowledge of another death.

"Diane Bradley shocked him with the cardiac defibrillator."

Elizabeth was speechless.

Alex continued, "She shocked him, she electrocuted him."

Elizabeth said simply, "Good. He deserved it."

"Yes, he did. I hope everyone sees it that way."

***

Outside, Mitch stood and shook in the phone booth near the hospital. He'd followed their instructions to the letter. He'd called the press and the police. He hated them, but most of all he hated himself.

.

CHAPTER 9

The day was never ending. It wasn't easy working in a cursed hospital. Between the media blitzes, the reruns of the ED shootings on the news, and the pundits telling the world about the Voodoo curse at Crescent City Medical Center, no one was getting any work done. Alex only hoped that the patients were getting cared for.

By seven-thirty that evening, the hospital leaders had been joined by Bette Farve and several other physicians. Elizabeth had left shortly before to hold a brief press conference.

"Any word on Diane, John?" Alex was sure she had asked the same question every 20 minutes or so.

Dr. Ashley shook his head. "I just checked with the OR and Dr. Bonnet's doing a total bowel resection. Robert says her injuries are bad. The bullets from these automatic weapons explode when they enter the body and make a terrible mess. Most people don't survive this long. Diane has extensive liver damage and lots of bleeding. She's already received 12 units of blood and Bonnet predicts she'll need twice that by morning. Hospital's put out a call for O negative blood."

"Anyone talked with her family?" Alex asked.

Bette replied. "I talked with one of the nurses in surgery. Her husband's here and very upset, and her parents are driving in from Alabama."

Dr. Ashley nodded at Bette. "Good," he said. He turned to Alex and added, "Alex, will you go over with me to see her husband? I want to offer my personal concern. Don, you should go with us on behalf of administration. I suppose you've been, Bette?"

"Why, no I haven't. I've only been here a little while. I've been busy," she replied.

Everyone stared at her, their eyes showing their disbelief at her behavior. Alex was dumbfounded. "You need to go with us. You're her direct superior. Besides, Diane's behavior is heroic. She saved the lives of staff and patients. You must go!"

Bette looked scorchingly at Alex. "Ms. Destephano, I set my own priorities!"

Dr. Monique Desmonde, the CCMC chief of psychiatry, looked weary as she entered the executive suite. Between offering support to the hospital staff that was present, she was constantly being harassed by the media. Monique gave Bette a disgusted look and said, "Have you seen or talked to Sheila Monroe's family? They're local. I've already seen them, and they're traumatized. I can assure you that once their grief subsides, her father is going to be angry. I suggest you go see them and offer them anything you can to avoid a lawsuit. I also suggest you meet with your emergency department staff and your surgery people and help them work through some of the trauma they've encountered the past two days. I met with the Surgery staff today. They've got a lot to work though. The emergency department staff is even more traumatized and will need considerable help."

"I'll have you know, Dr. Desmonde, that I have no experience in psychiatry. I don't do psychobabble. My role is to run a nursing service. You are the psychiatrist, you do it. Besides, I'm going on vacation tomorrow afternoon and have important things to tie up."

"Ms. Farve, how can you run a nursing service when half your staff is out sick, fearing voodoo hexes, and the other part is either dead, dying, or grieving? Your job is to support your staff! Now get the hell out there and do it!" Dr. Desmonde got up from her chair and opened the door for Bette.

Bette immediately left.

Monique looked at Don Montgomery and spoke directly. "That woman is worthless and incompetent. Why on earth do you keep her? Her management style is founded on control and fear. Her staff neither like nor trust her. From what I can see, she certainly isn't representative of the philosophy of nursing that prevails here at CCMC. It's unforgivable that she hasn't seen the victims' families or spent time with her staff. It's a damn good thing she is leaving tomorrow, or I'd probably kill her." Dr. Desmonde looked around the room, and she saw that all heads at the conference table were nodding in agreement, except for Don. Alex suppressed a smile, and wanted to give Monique a standing ovation.

Don answered in an irritated voice. "Thanks for your comments, Dr. Desmonde. We've more important things to discuss than the leadership of nursing at CCMC." He looked at his watch. "Elizabeth is giving a press statement confirming the deaths. She'll also be confirming that Diane Bradley is in surgery and that CCMC knows of no motive for the emergency department shootings."

"Have we heard anything from the police?" Dr. Desmonde asked.

"No," Dr. Ashley replied, "but I expect we'll be seeing

Captain Francois soon. How was he treating the staff he was interviewing?"

Dr. Ashley looked so fatigued and weary that Alex was concerned for him. He wasn't a spring chicken, and he was carrying most of the administrative burden at CCMC.

"Actually, he was fairly good, at least as good as Jack can be. He's pretty hard-nosed, but he knows these people have been under tremendous stress. At several points he was actually gentle," Dr. Desmonde responded.

"Glad to hear that," Alex said. "Yesterday, he seemed to be pretty rough with one of them. Monique, it sounds like you know him. Any inside information we should have?"

Dr. Desmonde laughed, her long dark curls shook and her eyes crinkled at the corners when she smiled. "Well.....I can't tell you everything but I've known Jack Francois since we were kids. We grew up together, lived in the same neighborhood and our parents were friends. We even had a few dates in high school."

Alex was speechless for a moment, unable to believe the revelation. She was fit to be tied. She had great respect for Monique Desmonde. "What, you dated him. Yuk, OMG."

Monique ignored Alex and continued, "What I do know is that he's tough, a straight-shooter, and honest. His bark is much worse than his bite. I'm glad he's assigned to us. Not all New Orleans' cops are as honest or first-rate. And Alex, he's really not so bad."

Alex was surprised and pleased by Monique's favorable review of Jack Francois. She made a mental note that Monique probably knew Mitch, too, since he'd also gone to school with the police captain.

As Monique finished speaking, Liz returned from the press conference. Her cheeks were highly flushed and her eyes were bright. "We are big news. The media loves the idea of a 'Cursed World-Class Hospital.' Every major newspaper and national publication is represented. After I read the statement, I took several questions from reporters."

Alex said, "How'd it go?"

"Pretty well. They wanted to know what safety precautions we're taking to prevent this from happening again, and they wanted to know if CCMC was a safe place to come for medical care. One reporter even asked if the staff were afraid to come to work. Of course, I told him no. Only one question really bothered me."

"What was that?" Dr. Ashley asked, his face reflecting worry.

"One journalist asked me if the emergency department shootings were the work of the voodoo curse." Elizabeth was interrupted by Don.

He howled at her, "What the hell'd you say?"

Elizabeth looked angrily at Don. "I denied it, of course. I told them, based on the preliminary evidence, the emergency department shootings were the result of gunmen after narcotics."

Alex turned to Elizabeth. "That seemed to satisfy him?"

Elizabeth shook her head and said, "I couldn't tell. He

mentioned twice that he had it on good authority that the incident was related to the Raccine case and involved a voodoo curse directed at Crescent City Medical Center."

Dr. Ashley said, "Where was this journalist from?"

"I don't know. Local, I think. He didn't identify himself. He had a Cajun accent."

"So what'd you say to him?" Don confronted Elizabeth.

Elizabeth gave him an irritated look and said, "I denied the rumor and attributed it to gunmen after drugs. I told you. Do you forget I'm on your side? Did you even listen to what I said?"

"Side, who the hell is worried about sides? I'm worried about staying in business. Stop whining about who's on who's side." Don turned and left the room.

The group in the conference room began talking with and over each other but stopped when Captain Francois entered.

He looked smug as he eyed the group around the table. His look and voice were condescending. His eyes rested on Alex. "CCMC's in trouble again. Big news. You're the lead story on the local and national news networks. You guys just don't take care of the sick and suffering, you create them."

Confused, Dr. Desmonde looked at Jack Francois and said, "Jack, please, we're under considerable pressure here. We're all feeling a lot of stress. Finished your investigation? What have you turned up?"

The captain gave Monique a short look and said, "I've some preliminary information. First of all, we've had to call in the Drug

Enforcement Agency and the Bureau of Alcohol, Tobacco and Firearms. It's standard procedure. The dead gunman has been identified and he's a known drug dealer, user, and snitch. He's got a rap sheet three feet long. The emergency department nurses say the second gunman, the one with the glass head injury, had dreadlocks and spoke with a foreign accent, Jamaican or some sort of Caribbean lilt. Don't know who he is yet. We're trying to pick up prints, but doubt we'll get any good ones. There seems to be some question of whether there was even a third man. My men are asking questions. The emergency department staff only report seeing two gunmen. Anybody here know about the third man?" Everyone shook their head.

"Do you think any of our staff could identify the second gunman, the one with the dreadlocks?" Dr. Desmonde asked.

"Possibly. Place on his head where the glass hit him is the giveaway. It's gonna be hard to ID him with a ski mask. We'll get men on the street to check with the dead man's friends. We should turn up something.

"Well," replied Dr. Ashley as he continued to look troubled, "at least this is normal, or as normal as these things go. I guess there is really no normal emergency department shoot-out." Dr. Ashley stumbled over his words.

Francois stared at Ashley and replied sarcastically, "Well, Doc, what do you mean normal? There ain't no such thing as a normal crime. They're all different in lots of ways."

Dr. Ashley looked pensive. "I guess I mean this was a typical drug crime, only they disrupted the running of a hospital and killed two, possibly three, staff members before they got away."

Francois looked around. "There ain't nothing normal about this crime. Public ain't gonna think it's normal either. Ain't gonna help your public relations."

Dr. Ashley's patience was wearing thin, and he was furious with Captain Francois. "Captain, what I'm trying to say is that this situation, as horrible as it is, seems more open-and-shut than the case involving Mrs. Raccine. Don't you think it'll be easier to solve?"

"I don't know. Hard to say. Tracking down these slime balls is rough. We may get lucky though. We'll do our best." He turned to face the others and demanded, "How come nobody saw the third gunman? I think he was there, acting as look-out. Think the staff is holding back some?"

"I doubt it." Alex spoke firmly. "Everyone here at CCMC wants this craziness to end." As soon as she said this, Alex realized how stupid it sounded.

Francois stared at her, dumbfounded, "What planet are you on, Missy. That's the stupidest thing I have ever heard."

Don returned and interrupted Alex. "If we step up security, this shouldn't affect our patient admissions or staffing, as long as people know CCMC is a safe place to come for medical care. I think we should make the very best of this. Elizabeth, we should portray Diane, Sheila, and Ron as medical heroes. Start working on it. Anybody owe you any favors at *The Times Picayune*? Capitalize on what's happened here and use it to our benefit."

Elizabeth was shocked. After a few seconds she said, "No. I won't. It's a bit early to begin this type of media blitz. Let's wait and see what else turns up. For god's sake Don, this entire approach makes me sick. I won't do it. I suggest we simply use the media to reinforce that good and safe medical care is available at CCMC. Nothing else."

"You *will* do it," Don said stood up and placed his face directly in hers, and gritted his teeth. "You'll do it tomorrow. We need to get away from this voodoo shit. Understand?"

Dr. Desmonde noticed that Captain Francois was twitching in his seat. She looked at him and said, "Jack, is there anything else you want to say?"

Francoise stared at Don. "You know, you make me sick. You're an asshole. You are supposed to run this place. I can't believe you'd exploit the lives of staff and colleagues to meet your bottom line. You're despicable and disgusting, Montgomery." The captain's voice was quiet. No one disagreed with him.

There was a long silence. Don Montgomery and Captain Francois glared at each other.

Finally, Alex spoke. "Captain Francois, please understand our position. We're grieved and horrified by what's happened here in the last two days. I think John and Don were trying to say that the hospital is grateful that what happened today isn't related to voodoo activity or a curse against this medical center. "

Francois abruptly interrupted her. "Well, Miss Lawyer lady, I hate to pop your bubble, but these shootings are voodoo. See this?" Jack Francois withdrew two evidence bags from his briefcase and tossed them on the conference table. Inside the first bag was a strange doll made of sticks, scraps of fabric, and pins. The second bag contained black powder.

No one spoke and an overwhelming sense of fear and dread permeated the room. Dr. Ashley covered his face with his hands.

The captain continued. "This doll's a gris, representative of something, or someone here at CCMC. The gris was on the dead man. The second bag of black powder is a greater concern, a huge concern actually. The powder is a combination of gun powder, ashes, and cayenne pepper. The voodoos call it war powder. They use it to declare war on people or places or families. It's clear to me that a Voodooist has declared war on Crescent City Medical Center. I'll keep you posted." He looked at the stunned group, his face in a smirk. "So… still feeling comfortable with this crime?" Then he turned and abruptly left, slamming the door behind him.

Don Montgomery also left the room abruptly and was followed by several physicians and nurses. Only Alex, Elizabeth, John, and Monique remained.

Alex spoke first, "I hardly believe this. It seems as if someone is working hard to hurt us. Why? John, is there anything coming out of the physician group that could account for this?"

"I doubt it. I know some of them are admitting patients elsewhere and have expressed concern, but none of them could be responsible."

"Monique, you think it could be the work of an angry patient? Maybe somebody pissed at us for some obscure reason? I'm looking for anything that could help us understand."

"Don't know, Alex. It's possible. Many mentally ill patients are very bright and manipulative and carry grudges as well. Of course, so are other patients. I'll talk to the other psychiatrists and our patient relations people tomorrow, but I don't recall anything from our team meetings that would suggest this. I try to stay in the loop with these kinds of things."

Elizabeth asked, "Do you think that the journalist knew voodoo was involved with the ED shootout? How could he? We just found out. Whole thing's crazy, ludicrous, screwed up. The public seems to know more than we do and I don't see how that could happen."

Alex replied, "I know, and that bothers me. It looks suspicious but it's a logical assumption to make based on what happened to Mrs. Raccine. It doesn't mean he knew anything."

Elizabeth pondered Alex's response. "Well, I do agree it's logical, but that seems too pat, too convenient. I've got really bad vibes about this. It's almost like someone here, on the inside, is giving them information. Who would do that?"

"We all have bad vibes but I don't know of anyone in my area that would be a spy or mole. It is something to consider though," Dr. Desmonde responded as she stood to leave. "It's late. I'm making final rounds and heading home. See you all tomorrow."

"I'm leaving, too. I'll be in early to see patients. That is if we have any left tomorrow," Dr. Ashley said morosely as he stood to leave. He nodded to Elizabeth and Alex.

Elizabeth turned to Alex. "Do you think someone inside the hospital could be feeding information to the media?"

Alex shrugged and answered, "You know, it's certainly possible but I don't know how to start to search them out. It makes me sick to think this."

Elizabeth nodded in agreement and said, "I meet with the press again at eight in the morning. Can you go? That way we can field questions and look for "suspicious journalists" and also see who is attending from the medical center. Maybe I'm paranoid but....all of this is just too well packaged for me." Elizabeth looked sheepish.

Alex was thoughtful. "Good idea. I'll see you at seven-thirty and we'll talk about it. Let me call the operating room before we leave."

Alex's face was grim when she returned from making the call. Elizabeth had already compiled a list of potential questions from the press. She handed a photocopy to Alex. "Take this with you for reading material tonight. Mull it over in your dreams. Feel free to add or delete. What about Diane?"

Alex shook her head and said, "It's really bad. They're still operating. The charge nurse said it's a nightmare up there. Diane's vital signs are erratic, and they've had to stop surgery twice to stabilize her. She's just so fragile and unstable. Dr. Bonnet's dead on his feet but refuses to stop. It'll probably take a couple more hours."

"Think she'll make it, Al?"

"I don't know. She's been in surgery for hours. I know Robert's doing his best. If she makes it through the surgery, a lot will depend on the next few days. Its touch and go, I'd say. I'm hopeful but not optimistic," Alex said shaking her head.

"It's so unfair. None of this should have happened. I don't

understand. I think I'm going to cry." Elizabeth reached for a tissue.

"Let's go, Liz. We can't cry yet. We've got a lot more to go through before this is over. It's pretty clear that most of the decision-making is up to us. Want to share a cab ride with me and Martin?"

"Sure, sounds good, but let's get through this final press conference first."

CHAPTER 10

At five o'clock the next morning, Alex was abruptly awakened by someone pounding on her door. Grabbing her robe, she opened her door to a disheveled and tired-looking Robert.

She concealed her surprise at his presence and said, "Robert, how are you? How's Diane?" Alex was genuinely glad to see him even though he was grey with fatigue and worry.

"She made it through the surgery, but it was rough. We about lost her three times. Still very unstable. To tell you the truth, I don't think she's going to make it. If she does, it'll be a miracle," Robert sighed. "Her injuries were just too comprehensive, too vast and widespread."

Alex put her hand on his shoulder, and then gave his a hug to comfort him. It just seemed like the natural thing to do.

He took a long breath and continued, "She's in the ICU - unconscious and on a vent. I can't begin to imagine her pain. She was really shot up, full of bullet injuries. Her internal injuries and bleeding were massive. I did a liver resection. She also has a compound fracture of her right arm, and I suspect she'll have permanent nerve damage if she recovers."

Alex was searching for the best words. "Well, you never know. Diane is young and strong, and she is motivated, so maybe she'll make it. We both know many people we write off live and do great. How's Mrs. Raccine?" Alex touched Robert's cheek, to offer comfort.

"The same. No different. Don't know about her, either. She

should be alert by now." He paused and continued on a brighter note. "Think I'll apply for a job as golf pro at the Club. Couldn't be more stressful than the medical center these last few days."

Alex smiled and nodded. "A golf pro, huh. I think you may be better suited as a chef!" Hard to believe it's only been three days since this started. It seems like an eternity. Come into the kitchen, I'll make some coffee. Grab the paper on your way in," Alex added, as she nodded towards the newspaper in her courtyard.

Robert and Alex drank decaf in Alex's kitchen while she told Robert about Captain Francois' findings. Robert hadn't heard any of it, and his face showed his dismay. When Alex told him the suspicion of voodoo, Robert shook his head.

"There's more here than meets the eye. Has to be. There's got to be some sort of plot against us. I'll have to admit, Alex, this voodoo stuff can be very nasty."

"No doubt about this. It is nasty." Alex said as she watched the emotions cross Robert's face. Finally, a look of realization appeared, followed by a dread. Robert stood to leave. "Got to go. Just remembered something important."

"What's wrong? You look as if you know something. Does something make sense to you?"

"No, nothing, at least nothing I can prove. I'll let you know." Robert checked his watch. "I have a 7:00 a.m. case." Robert stood, looking at Alex.

Alex's voice implored him. "If you know something, tell me. Two heads'll be better than one."

Robert shook his head. "It's probably nothing, no sense adding fuel to the fire. It's just a few loose ends I need to follow-up. I'll talk with you tonight after I've checked some things out."

"Is this related at all to the things we discussed last night?"

"Maybe, well... no not really. I really must go."

Alex walked over to Robert's side of the table and noticed the morning edition of *The Times Picayune* that had fallen off his lap as he had stood to go. Her eyes were riveted to the headline. For the first time in the four years Alex had lived in New Orleans, the newspaper headline was four lines deep: **"Voodoo War on CCMC, Shoot-Out Kills Three, First Lady Unconscious, CEO Claims Conspiracy:"**

The text under the headlines contained graphic, detailed descriptions of the events of the previous day, so detailed Alex and Robert couldn't believe the accuracy. Alex was beginning to agree with Liz that something was rotten and wondered how journalists were able to acquire such factual information. She decided to hold Don accountable. He was the only administrator unstable enough to have leaked information. At some point, Don must've told the reporter someone was conspiring against the hospital. Besides, she liked blaming Don.

"This is really strange. Elizabeth didn't tell any of this at the press conference yesterday. She didn't know it. We didn't know most of it until after nine last night. How do these people get their information?"

Robert replied wryly, "The article reeks with disclaimers of 'an unofficial source' or 'an eyewitness report'. Seems they have a pretty good investigative reporter with an inside track to somebody. Don must've talked with them at some point. Think he told them?"

"He's my choice, but I wouldn't think so. Of course, Don's not predictable these days. Regardless, it's going to give Don and John a heart attack, so don't venture too far from CCMC. What's today's date anyway? This week's been a year long!"

"It's February 22, 2012. Things are going to pick up and get better. They have to. Keep your chin up. I need you to keep me running. Besides, the way I hear it, you're practically running the hospital."

Alex smiled and said, "Thanks, that's not entirely accurate but it does feel like that. We're all trying to pull together."

"From what I've seen of Montgomery, he's been virtually useless."

"No argument from me there."

"I've gotta go. Talk with you tonight."

Alex had another cup of coffee after Robert left and re-read the news accounts. She was pretty sure there was a leak in the upper ranks of the hospital. Alex shrugged her shoulders, cleaned up the kitchen, and headed for the shower.

Her phone was ringing as she emerged from the shower. It was Don's secretary, telling her to hurry in for a seven-thirty meeting. Latetia assured her no more trouble had occurred. After she hung up the phone, Alex called for a cab. By the time she'd finished dressing, Martin was waiting for her at the curb. His straight dark hair was held in place by some sort of oily substance. Although Martin referred to himself as a Cajun coonass, Alex had often wondered if he had a bit of Native American Indian in him as well. His oddly colored eyes were often noted among New Orleans Cajuns.

There was concern all over Martin's darkly complexioned face as he held the door open for Alex. "Looking good, Alex. I'd suspected you'd be worn right down to a crocodile skeleton by now. These days been bad for you?"

Alex laughed as his description. "You're so refreshing. You're the only person in three days who hasn't wanted something, so it means a lot. Yes, it's been hard lately."

"I guess it's pretty bad there at the hospital. My first load, they told me that they was leaving town two days early 'cause of the voodoo. They're from Texas and said they was scared. They visited that voodoo museum down in the Quarter and got their pants scared off. Museum folk told 'em the worst was yet to come. I took them to the airport first thing this morning." Said they couldn't wait to get outta here."

"The museum told them more was coming? What else did they say?"

"That's about it. They just ranted and raved that this city wasn't Christian, was a heathen' hell hole. Said they couldn't spend money in such a heathen place. Sorry I didn't ask them any questions. They gave me double my money just to get 'em out quick. They ain't the only ones. Airport was jammed, lotsa people leavin' and we are booked for the day with airport trips"

"That's okay. Where's the voodoo museum? Do you think they really know anything?"

"Doubt it. Mostly sells souvenirs, power, Gris and things like that. I guess they're more in it for the money-making than real voodoo people. I take lot of folks there, tourists. Most like it, though it's sort of spooky. Want to go sometime?"

"Where is it, the museum?"

"There's several in the city but the most common one is down in the Quarter on Rue Domaine. It ain't too far."

"Think they'd know anything about what's going on at CCMC?"

"Don't know, though you never can tell. I'll take you if you want, but I'm not too sure it'll be good for you. Nasty stuff to mix with."

"Not now. I've got a big meeting. Lots going on."

"We be pulling in the hospital five minutes. Sit tight." Martin accelerated and the big white cab pulled recklessly in and out of traffic.

Alex gave Martin a big tip. She continued to think about the voodoo museum as she walked to her office.

She had just enough time to lay down her purse and listen to her voice mail before making her way to administration. The most important calls were from Mitch, who'd left four messages. He'd apparently been calling since late yesterday afternoon and left his last message several minutes before. Alex wondered why he hadn't phoned her at home last night, but made a mental note to call him the first chance she got.

When Alex entered the board room, she was startled to see

Governor Raccine and Andre Renou sitting at the conference table. Don, Robert, John, and Elizabeth were also there. Her stomach knotted as she anticipated the worse. Robert had obviously postponed his surgery. She was afraid something terrible had happened to Grace Raccine and immediately looked toward Robert who appeared as uncertain as she and the others. Don was busy sucking up to the governor but Raccine could look less interested. He appeared worn-down, but intense.

Don opened the meeting by saying, "Governor Raccine has asked that we meet this morning to discuss what's happened in the past few days. I believe you know everyone here. Governor Raccine, the floor's yours."

Alex was amazed at how charming Don could be. He was a regular Jekyll and Hyde. She knew he could be a silver-tongued devil and was awed by his ability to turn on his charm. She was also pleased that he was behaving. Well, she thought to herself, if he doesn't behave himself in front of the Governor, I guess he won't behave himself in front of anyone. Don's not a complete idiot. He knows we need state money to stay in business.

Governor Raccine, admittedly Creole, was a curly headed, white haired, seasoned politician who had the square-faced good looks of many elected officials. Her grandfather had mentioned to her several times that beneath that polish and veneer was the strength, steel, and tenacity of a cobra ready to strike for what he wanted.

Alex smiled at the governor as he began to speak quietly, "I'm here for several reasons. First of all, I want to thank you for the care you've given Grace. The expertise of the nurses and Dr. Bonnet has been much appreciated, but that has been marred by the situation several nights ago. It was unpredictable and tragic, but I'm sure that my wife will recover in good time with the continued support of Dr. Bonnet and our family."

As Governor Raccine paused for several moments, his gaze moved to each hospital executive's face. He continued, "My second reason for calling you together is not quite so simple. I realize this medical center is one of the finest in the world and certainly, one of the finest in New Orleans…"

Alex could feel her skin begin to prickle up like something bad was coming. 'One of the finest' was an indicator.

The governor continued, "I can't tell you how dismayed I am that things are so unsettled. There's nothing that you could've done to prevent these tragedies or curse, or whatever it is. I'm confident you'll be able to recover from the damage that has been caused by these events."

Alex thought a big one's coming here. She hastily glanced at her colleagues and noticed the Governor had their rapt attention, except for Don. He was smiling, probably still basking in the "caring expertise of the staff and best medical center in the world," line and didn't have a clue of what was coming. Alex could feel her heartbeat picking up, and felt a little short of breath. She glanced at Robert, whose eyes met hers. He knows something's wrong too, she thought.

The Governor continued. "In the meantime, I've received some distressing news from my Secretary of Tourism. Two major conventions scheduled here canceled their reservations because they consider the city 'cursed' and many hotels are reporting cancellations, up to sixty percent for this weekend. The reasons are clearly and directly related to the voodoo curse against Crescent

City Medical Center that has been headline news on every national and cable television news program in the country as well as in the print media."

Don replied, "This is ridiculous...the curse is ridiculous. CCMC's not to blame for this."

"Mr. Montgomery, I must remind you again that it is the disaster here at CCMC that has made national news. Media attention has been directed at the hospital and at New Orleans in general. Did you know that my personal tragedy is colorfully detailed on the front cover of **People** magazine this week? There is even a picture of Grace unconscious in her hospital bed with that horrible look on her face!" The Governor surveyed the group around him noting the incredulous looks of everyone around the table. Everyone was shocked at his announcement. The Governor, trembling with either rage or anxiety repeated his announcement. "Yes, CCMC's on the front cover of **People** and a very graphic and detailed description of what happened to Grace at this hospital is the lead story in the issue that's to be released at noon today."

No one in the room responded. No one knew what to say.

"I detest this kind of publicity for many reasons...a major reason being the revenues we count on to run the state that comes from tourism. You all know that we are just now beginning to recover from Katrina, both financially and from an image standpoint. Everyone still remembers the horrors that occurred during the storm at the Superdome. The reputation of New Orleans has been, shall we say, in the gutter, for years since Katrina. Now it is happening again. Consequently, I believe that the events surrounding the hospital are causing the city an additional image problem and drastically affecting tourist revenues. I want you to close Crescent City Medical Center for an undetermined length of time, at least for the next few weeks, so that we can begin to rebuild our tourist industry, which is the bread and butter of this state."

The silence in the room was deafening. Each person was weighing the implications of closing the hospital.

Dr. Ashley spoke first. "Governor, Isn't there another way? We've a number of patients awaiting transplants...we have surgeries scheduled. We have loyal patients who'd be uncomfortable going to other hospitals."

The Governor looked at the physician and replied in a quiet voice. "I'm aware of what you're saying, and I'm aware that you have many international patients. These people can be treated at Tulane, Ocher or Jefferson. I'm sure your physicians will be willing to send patients to those facilities. I'm sure we can direct most of your nursing staff to those agencies. I see this measure as short term. Your patients will see the same staff, hopefully, and only the location will be different."

Don interjected in a calm voice, "I simply can't close this medical center. I need to talk to our trustees and move in the direction that they suggest. If we close our doors, it's doubtful we'll ever recuperate financially, or recover public confidence. It would take us months, maybe years to reopen considering the bureaucratic red tape we could encounter. Closing would be admitting defeat. It would cost hundreds of employees their jobs and incomes. I can't and I will not make such an arbitrary decision." Don's voice was firm.

"Gather the board and tell them what I've proposed. I'll contact each of them as well. There's no other way to do things differently. I understand that war powder was a part of the last incident. Because of this, I'm not convinced that the trouble has ended here for Crescent City. I'm sorry for the inconvenience this causes you."

Alex finally spoke. "Can we talk about this a little further?"

The governor nodded and Alex continued "There're several things that come to mind. First of all, isn't it possible that the trouble is over? Isn't it likely all this'll blow over in a few days? As soon as there's something else for the media to jump on, they'll forget we ever had a black magic scare here at CCMC."

Governor Raccine shook his head negatively and responded, "Alex, I can't answer that question, since I've no idea what the future will bring. I can't predict national or local events. Sure, if some national agenda demands attention, then New Orleans and the voodoo war won't be featured on the national news in every town in America. We don't have that guarantee. Remember, it was just yesterday that the voodoos declared war on CCMC. Whoever is behind it has an ax to grind and I, for one, don't think it's over. It couldn't have come at a worse time for the city. You had another question?"

"Closing the hospital gives strength to the people responsible for the scare. It's a victory for them. At the risk of sounding impertinent, Governor Raccine, would you have closed the courthouse if it had been shot up by a group of voodooists, or terrorists? If we bend to this kind of pressure and fear, what'll these people do next?" Alex finished, expecting to be chastised by Governor Raccine.

After a considerable silence, Raccine responded, "Ms. Destephano, your points are well taken. In my mind, the voodooists are terrorists, they are just homegrown. However, the gravity of the crimes that have been committed here are considerable. People come to hospitals expecting a safe environment, to feel better, to be free of pain and mental stress. At this point, CCMC cannot guarantee these things and it is more likely that others will be hurt."

Alex persisted, "We've stepped up our security. The police are cooperating, and you offered us access to the state police. We accept."

Governor Raccine pondered Alex's words.

She continued, "The Drug Enforcement Agency and Bureau of Alcohol, Tobacco, and Firearms are involved already. They'll be providing additional security, too."

Governor Raccine thought for a moment, then spoke. "I get your point. Nevertheless, much of what you say is true. We don't want to suggest that voodoo has this kind of power in New Orleans. In view of your argument, I'll issue a five-day reprieve until Sunday, unless there's further evidence of cult-related violence. If there is, you will close your doors immediately, just as soon as patients can be transferred to others health care centers."

A feeling of relief flooded the room.

Raccine continued, "Be advised that I know CCMC operates as a private hospital and I'm aware that your charter is unique, but you can easily be closed, either by me, or by a vote from the state legislature. Mr. Renou will coordinate the State Police investigators and security."

"Thanks, Governor. We appreciate your help," Dr. Bonnet

said.

The governor nodded. "There's one more thing. With Dr. Bonnet's agreement, I'll be transferring Mrs. Raccine to East Jefferson Medical Center. Thank you for your time." The governor immediately left the board Room with Andre Renou on his heels.

Dr. Ashley looked at Alex and said, "Well, you pulled us out for a while. Hope our trouble's over and things settle down. He'll close us down if anything else happens."

Don exploded. "The SOB doesn't have the power to close us down. It's incredible that he even considered it!"

"Shut-up Don! Get a grip and sit the hell down," Robert said. "He's the governor and his party's in power. He can do any damn thing he wants. Don't forget that forty percent of our patient base is indigent care, and indigent care is completely funded by the State. With Charity being destroyed in Katrina, this hospital will be in the red in two weeks without state revenues."

Donald Montgomery said, "Shit, that forty percent is only about twenty-seven percent of our gross revenues. This thing's political. Something we don't know has caused this. He's getting pressure from somewhere. Maybe someone agreed to take the curse off his wife or something. I've never heard of a governor attempting to close a hospital. It's ludicrous!" Don quieted down for a moment, and then continued. "Besides, it probably won't make a damn bit of difference anyway. Our inpatient census has dropped again. We're losing thousands and thousands each day. We'll be bankrupt in three weeks if this keeps up."

Elizabeth stood up. "I've heard enough of this. Let's be positive and focus on security, safety, and the media. Thanks to Alex we have five days to clear this up. Let's use our time to work together productively."

Alex took the cue and spoke. "Elizabeth's right. I'll be glad to work with the State Police, along with our director of security. John, can you talk with the doctors? I'll ask Monique Desmonde to work on nursing security with me since Bette Farve leaves today to go on vacation." Alex stopped for a moment and looked at Don. "What do you think of this plan? You should have Latetia schedule a meeting of the board as soon as possible to tell them the governor's concerns."

"Do what you want to. Damn *People* magazine. That's what he's pissed about. I'm calling a head hunter so I can get out of this crazy, fucking, Voodoo town!" Don threw up his hands and left the room.

John Ashley looked at Robert Bonnet and said gently, "You know, Robert, the Governor's given us a vote of no confidence by transferring Grace."

Robert nodded his head. "Yes, I know, he absolutely has. But, if I were in his shoes, I'd probably transferred her two days ago. Are you aware that three of the general surgeons have canceled their surgeries at CCMC and rescheduled them over at Jefferson?

"I heard," John said tiredly. "I expect some internists and general practitioners will also divert their patient admissions as well. Anyway, let's savor our small victory and get to work to try and keep this place open past next Monday."

They all nodded to each other, and then departed to their separate offices.

CHAPTER 11

Alex returned to her office and called Mitch. She wanted to talk with someone completely uninvolved with CCMC. When she got him on the phone, she didn't tell him anything about the meeting with the governor, saying only that the situation was worsening.

After she made plans to meet him for dinner at eight that evening, Alex sat at her desk and mulled over the Governor's ultimatum. As much as she hated to admit it, Don did have a point. It seemed strange that the Governor had even considered, much less planned to close the medical center. Such behavior was unprecedented. The more she thought about it, the more Alex was convinced of the possibility that CCMC was involved in some type of political power struggle. She considered calling her grandfather to get his advice on the situation, but decided to wait. Just then, Bridgett buzzed her from the outer office.

"Can you talk to Elizabeth? She wants you to meet with the press in about forty-five minutes."

"Put her through, better still, ask her to come over."

As Alex was glancing through Elizabeth's list of anticipated questions from the press, she remembered Martin's conversation about the voodoo museum. She again wondered if the museum had any knowledge of the events at CCMC. Alex made the decision to visit the museum after work.

Elizabeth arrived a bit out of breath within five minutes.

Her long dark hair hung loose in wavy curls giving her a more vulnerable look than she possessed most days. "I told the press we'd meet with them at nine-thirty and apologized for the delay. There's a whole horde of them out. It's amazing. I think every news media, even from the more rural parts of Kansas are out there. What do you think of the statement? We can present it and take fifteen minutes of questions."

"Scared?" Alex said in a rueful voice.

"Of course, aren't you?"

"Hell yes! You don't look it," Alex said as she read Elizabeth's statement. "You look really calm, cool and collected." Alex nodded her head, approvingly. The statement was simple and straight forward. It acknowledged that two gunmen, apparently searching for drugs, had entered the emergency department the afternoon before. It also confirmed the deaths, and ended with the assurance that CCMC was operating at full capacity, with tightened security, and remained the only world-class hospital in Louisiana.

"Looks good. The most important thing we have to do is get across to them, and the public, that CCMC is a safe place to get medical care. If we can convince people of that, perhaps we'll be able to increase our inpatient admissions and outpatient visits. How many questions do you think we'll get? I don't have a feel for this sort of thing."

"More than we want to answer based on my experience. You look over the list I made last night?" Elizabeth asked.

"Yeah, I think you're pretty much on target. Of course, who knows? So far, the media seems to be one step ahead of us. Let's ask each reporter to identify themselves and their affiliation before they ask their question. Why don't you answer each question initially, and then I'll add necessary comments."

"Good," Liz said. "Did you see *The Times Picayune* this morning?

"Robert and I read the article a little after six this morning when we were having coffee. We couldn't believe the accuracy of the news story" Alex continued as she noticed the look of surprise on Elizabeth's face.

Elizabeth was silent.

"Liz, what's up? You looked surprised, even shocked. You know something I don't?"

Elizabeth remained quiet, and Alex realized that Elizabeth had totally misunderstood her visit with Robert early that morning.

Alex hastened to set the record straight. "Elizabeth...Robert just stopped by to give me a report on Diane and find out what'd happened at the meeting. He was on his way to the hospital. That was it, really. There is nothing else."

"Of course. You don't need to explain, it's really okay." Elizabeth was blushing.

"Elizabeth, Robert may be my ex-husband, but he's also my friend. We're good friends, and that's all. There's nothing else going on, I swear." Alex gave Liz a hard look. "Understand? I don't want any rumors going around."

Liz held up her arm but she looked hurt that Alex could think she would spread rumors. "Say no more. I understand. I am trustworthy." Changing the subject Elizabeth continued, "What else should we expect from the press, particularly in the way of questions?"

"I don't know, but I have something else I want to talk to you about. This morning, Martin told me about some people who'd visited the voodoo museum last night. Apparently they were told the voodoo war wasn't over. I don't know what that means, but I'm thinking about going down there after work. Want to come?"

"To a voodoo museum?"

"Yes, Martin said he'd take me anytime. It may be a blind lead, but it's the only lead we have at this point. I'm going to follow it up."

"Can we go out for drinks afterward? I have to have something to look forward to after a trip to the voodoo museum?"

"Sure. Sounds great. You game?"

"Help me through this press conference, and I'll go anywhere with you." Laughing, Alex and Liz left Alex's office.

Bridgett looked at them like they were crazy as they passed her desk. "What's so funny? Please tell me. There's not much to laugh about in this place anymore." Bridgett looked at her watch. "It's only a little after nine, and I feel like I've been here all day. By the way, Alex, since you obviously aren't going to tell me what is so funny, I'm setting up a board of trustees meeting for tomorrow morning at 9:00. Consider yourself informed. Attendance is mandatory."

Alex was happy to see a bit of the sparkle back in Bridgett's big blue eyes. "You got it, Bridge. If we're still alive after this press conference, I'll bring the doughnuts," Alex replied, and, still laughing, the women made their way to the hospital auditorium. Bridgett shook her head, and smiled at the retreating backs of the two women. She thought what a beautiful and powerful combination they were. Both women were tall and each dressed in dark colored business suits. Both Alex with her long hair in an elegant French twist and Liz with her dark curls appeared in control and self-assured. They'll wow the media out, Bridgett thought. This place is gonna make it after all. She smiled and returned to her computer happy that she had decided to bite the bullet and return to CCME to "fight" the voodoo curse.

Alex and Elizabeth appeared calm and confident as they approached the press. There were hundreds of print media reps, and the entire parking lot was filled with TV news vans and camera crews.

Elizabeth whispered fiercely, "Wow, can you believe this Alex? I don't think Obama brings out this many news vans. Are you ready?"

"Yep, we'll be great." Alex squeezed her hand.

It was chaotic, and the confusion was intense. People were shouting and pushed forward to get near the two CCMC employees. Most of the initial questions from the reporters were directed at the emergency department disaster. Alex and Elizabeth were able to field the questions skillfully, constantly reinforcing the safety and excellent medical care at CCMC.

Then one reporter who introduced himself as Steve Parker from the *Miami Sentinel* said,

"I have it on good authority that the emergency department shootout was voodoo related. Can you verify this?"

Elizabeth responded without hesitation. "The New Orleans Police Department has established a connection between the dead gunman and voodoo. We have little information on these findings and the cause remains under investigation. Contact the NOPD for further information but I don't know if they are releasing any evidence."

Liz pointed to an attractive blonde reporter on the front row.

"I'm Susan Roshen from the *Washington Post*. Do you think there's a plot to destroy Crescent City Medical Center?"

Alex thought for a moment. "A plot? I don't think so. We're certainly encountering some unfortunate events but we have no knowledge or evidence of a plot and don't know a reason why anyone would plot against Crescent City Medical Center."

The journalist continued, undeterred. "Please, Ms. Destephano. Let's get real. Health care is one of the most lucrative and competitive businesses in America. It's also the fastest growing business. No one knows or has a clue about what Obama's Health Care Portability Act will do to medical centers who stand alone, are independent and not members of huge health care organizations or conglomerates. Your viability is significant. Corporations will go to any length to keep their market share at any expense. Why should health care be any different? Don't you think someone is out to destroy you, or at least destroy your image in preparation for a quick take-over?"

Alex grappled with the question, and then replied, "Ms.

Roshen, I don't know how to answer your question. I can assure you the hospital's executive management, the board of trustees, the New Orleans Police Department and federal authorities will be investigating every possible reason for what has happened here. I can assure you that there are currently no negotiations with any outside organizations about an acquisition or merger. CCMC is financially solvent and intends to remain independent."

A voice from the back of the crowd said clearly, as if spoken through a microphone. "You people are crazy. You think you are such smart asses. I heard Governor Raccine is going to close CCMC just as soon as he can. He thinks this place is cursed and bad for New Orleans. When's the hospital scheduled to close?"

The silence was deafening.

Finally Alex spoke. "Sorry, sir. I didn't get your name. Could you repeat it?"

"I'm from the *Dayton Daily News* in Ohio. I heard the governor's going to close the hospital. When's your closure date?"

The voice was clear, distinct, and persistent. The reporters were listening intently and scribbling notes.

Alex smiled, although she felt breathless. "I assure you we have no date of any hospital closure. We do not plan to close. It is business as usual here at CCMC. Crescent City Medical Center is open for business. Governor Raccine has voiced concern about the recent events here, as he should, and has offered the assistance of the Louisiana State Police in an effort to quell any further incidents."

Elizabeth moved to close the press conference. "Thank you

for your time and patience. We'll keep you posted on further findings, but we're confident things are back to normal at CCMC."

Elizabeth and Alex left the auditorium. Neither spoke as they climbed four flights of steps.

When they reached Alex's office, Elizabeth collapsed in a chair and said quickly,

"What the hell. How did anyone know that? Where's the leak? There must be a leak? We've only known for two hours."

Alex shook her head and said, "I don't know. Must be a rumor in the Governor's Office or someone here must have heard. I can't imagine anyone on the executive committee talking to reporters. It couldn't be our Board of Trustees. They don't even know yet. I'll let Don and the others know. I'm more and more suspicious that someone's plotting against this place. Maybe we are cursed!"

"Well," said Elizabeth, as she brightened a bit. "Maybe we'll find out more at the voodoo museum. I've got to go return calls. See you at four."

As Alex returned to her desk, she had a fleeting thought that perhaps Don could be sabotaging his own medical center, and then considering that idea far-fetched, she discarded it.

As the minutes clicked by, Alex continued to ponder the idea of an internal leak. It seemed as though someone was deliberately and maliciously out to get them. But who? She knew the New Orleans healthcare market pretty well but couldn't imagine other health care systems who would want to hurt them. CCMC had picked up most of the indigent care in New Orleans, a patient population that the uptown hospitals didn't want to care for. The hospital's Psychiatric Pavilion also housed some of the most dangerously mentally ill patients in the state, another unpopular vulnerable population. What CCMC did have that other local medical centers did not was a huge international self-pay population that other hospitals coveted. They also had the best physicians and surgeons in the New Orleans area. The idea of corporate sabotage was becoming a fixed possibility in her mind. Her thoughts returned to that idea throughout the afternoon. She even began to wonder if the hospital conference room was bugged. She decided the executive team should meet somewhere else, at least until this stuff was over. Bridgett came to the door.

"Martin's on the phone. He wants to know if you're going to go to that place you discussed this morning."

"Yes, ask him to pick me up at five. Call Elizabeth and tell her to meet me here just before." Alex didn't dare tell Bridgett that she was visiting the Voodoo Museum in the French Quarter. That would have sent Bridgett way over the edge.

CHAPTER 12

Martin was telling terrible Cajun jokes to Elizabeth and Alex as he darted in and out of the rush hour traffic. Alex couldn't wait to get out of the cab. She tried, without success, to get Martin to talk about other topics but he was resistant. He didn't seem to want to talk about the events at CCMC. Alex suspected he was more intimidated by voodoo than he admitted.

Elizabeth, tired of the jokes, tried changing the subject as well. She was more successful than Alex. "Martin, have you ever known anyone who practiced voodoo." I can't imagine anyone could believe in that stuff in 2012."

Martin's tone became serious. "Don't make fun of it, Elizabeth. It's life here in New Orleans. It's our culture. I ain't gonna throw you no stuff. Voodoo's big in this city. I've known plenty of voodoos. There are still lots of white witches all up and down the Avenue in the Garden District. Rich white women conspiring with their servants to do harm to each other. Voodoo means 'spirit of god' so these folks are thinkin' they are practicing their religion, just like you do in church. Back in the time of Marie Laveau, it's said she had power in every house and every wealthy white family in town. They say that Marie knew everybody's secrets and that's how she got so rich and powerful because she hexed and cursed them when she was angry. Then they hired her and paid her big money to remove the curses. She was mighty powerful."

"Who was Marie Laveau?" Alex and Elizabeth said simultaneously.

"Marie was the Queen of the Voodoos here in Nawlins' for over eighty years. I can remember my grandmamma talking about her. She said Marie was as beautiful as a woman can be; even when she was old and she always wore hoop earrings. People would bow down and worship Queen Marie when she walked through Congo Square. She was the most powerful Voodooist in New Orleans, maybe even in the world. They say her ghost still walks once each year on St. John's Eve. She is buried over in St. Louis Cemetery 1. I can take you there if you like."

"How did she know all the rich people? What did she do so she knew all the powerful people?" Elizabeth asked.

"She was a hairdresser. She fixed all the rich ladies' hair and learned all of their secrets. Some say she was a maid, a house servant. She would charm the husbands and make them cheat on their wives with her. Don't know that I believes all of that. I don't think so." Martin stopped for a few moments to think and shook his head negatively. "Rumors says there were really two Marie Laveau's. The second was her daughter who took her place when she died. Some say the second Marie was even more beautiful and powerful than her mother. They say her powers of evil could kill and hurt folk forever, and that she had more potent magic potions and gris than anybody. She communed with the devil every night and killed anyone she thought was her enemy or was getting too powerful. Some say she killed her own mother out of jealously, the first Marie Laveau." Martin paused, and waited to make a left turn.

"What else? This is pretty interesting," Elizabeth was intrigued. It was much more interesting than Cajun jokes and stories.

Martin loved having the attention of the two lovely women

and continued, "Well, she could charm snakes and spread curses. My grandmamma had a friend that crossed the second Queen Marie. My grandmother swears that Marie stole, and sacrificed, my grandmamma's friend's baby. She sacrificed the baby at a voodoo gathering out at Bayou St. John. Others say Marie kept the baby's skeleton in her parlor, as a reminder to any woman who ever crossed her again. Queen Marie was a powerful Voodooist, and peoples were scared of her. Some say she was full of love, too but I don't know. I just know what I hear."

Alex was a bit miffed at Martin. Wasn't it only yesterday that he'd told her he didn't know much about Voodoo? What was all of this about?

"Tell me more about it." Elizabeth was sitting on the edge of her seat. "How'd your grandmother's friend know her baby was taken by the voodoos? What happened to the baby?"

Martin considered her questions for a moment, and knew he had to placate Alex and Elizabeth without scaring them. A look at Alex's face in his rear view mirror alerted him she was unhappy. "I don't rightly know, but I guess that she fed it to a snake. Course, if the snake ate it, then there wouldn't be no bones, would there? So I guess I really don't know. "

Alex had enough. She was livid. "Stop it Martin. This is crap. No more of this. I am sick of voodoo stories. Just get us there."

Elizabeth was surprised at Alex's angry reaction and gave her a sideways glance. Martin looked hurt and no one spoke until the cab pulled up in front of the voodoo museum. Elizabeth then attempted some feeble chatter with Martin to try and ease his obviously hurt feelings. Martin was responding in monosyllables, still stinging from Alex's criticism. Alex was feeling guilty about her outburst.

"Want me to wait, Alex?" Martin said as the ladies were exiting the cab. "Be glad to."

"Would you, Martin? I'm really sorry I was so abrupt. Will you forgive me?" Alex said meekly.

Martin didn't respond. "I'll be back shortly. I may have to move the cab. Take care. Don't get in no trouble. Museum's about a half a block down." Martin smiled weakly as he pulled from the curb.

It was just turning dark as Alex and Elizabeth walked the half block to the museum. Hordes of tourists, some costumed and some obviously drunk passed the women. A juggler had attracted a large crowd of people. Typical French Quarter partying, thought Alex as they were walking down the block. If this keeps up, Fat Tuesday would be sensational; no matter what the governor said, or his minister or secretary of tourism or whatever he was predicted.

"Business looks good. The streets are packed," Elizabeth noted wryly. "Doesn't look like the voodoo scare has decreased tourism to me. Maybe you ought to go call the governor and ask him to come with us." Alex nodded in agreement as they stopped outside the museum.

It was located in an old building on the south side of Dumaine. The museum was long and deep, as were most buildings in the Quarter. As Elizabeth and Alex entered the shop, both were humbled by what was inside. The museum was narrow and eerie, an effect increased by the candles burning throughout the building. It also smelled really funny, sort of like burning hair and mold. Various accoutrements of evil hung on the walls. There were half-burned skeletons, animal heads, stuffed snakes, effigies of humans, animals and other items neither Alex nor Liz recognized. Against one wall were frightening instruments that could easily be instruments of torture. Alex had no idea. Glass cases lined the other walls and were filled with various charms and magical powders. Alex saw love powder and boss-fixing powder, but no black war powder.

Although the atmosphere was ominous, it wasn't nearly as threatening as the figure in the very back of the room. Dressed completely in black, she slowly turned to face the women. Elizabeth grabbed Alex's arm and dug her nails into her wrist. Alex was also unnerved and took several seconds to pull herself together. Then, using sheer force she pushed Elizabeth towards the figure in the back of the room. Alex's brain was racing with thoughts and the whole thing was scary, surreal. OMG, this was much worse than I had expected. She pinched herself to make sure she wasn't dreaming. What have I gotten myself into? My grandfather would disown me if he knew I had done this. How stupid I am. Maybe my judgment is crappy.

Alex and Elizabeth continued to walk very slowly and make their way to the darkly clad woman. Alex doubted she'd be able to talk to her. Her tongue felt thick, furry, and paralyzed. Her mouth was dry. She seemed to have lost all the saliva in her mouth. The walk seemed endless. As they got closer, Alex noted with some relief that it was her attire that made her so frightening. Her face was dead white and was surrounded by a halo of long, black hair. Her lips were also black and in her hands was a live snake which the woman was stroking. She continued to stroke the snake as she watched Alex and Elizabeth approach. Alex was transfixed by the darting tongue of the snake, although the woman's face and countenance didn't change. A CD of drum music made it even spookier. The woman's eyes never blinked or never left Alex's and Elizabeth's faces. In Alex's opinion, the woman didn't look happy to see either of them. OMG, doesn't this person ever blink? Everyone blinks at some point. Alex could feel her heart jumping.

Finally, Alex and Elizabeth faced the women and stood in front of the counter. None of them spoke. The women just looked at each other. Alex could hear the bounding of each of her body pulses. Elizabeth was immobile, paralyzed with fear. After a silence that seemed like a century, Alex finally spoke. "My name's Alexandra," Alex began, surprised at the strength of her voice.

"I know who you are," the woman responded. Her voice was low and soft, but hollow. The voice didn't sound real. It was kind of like a robot would sounds, Alex thought. It sounded sort of disembodied.

"I know why you're here, and I've been waiting for you. I knew you would come." The woman's voice was eerie; it seemed to come from somewhere else.

"Then you must know what I want. Will it stop?" Alex marveled at the strength in her voice.

"I don't know. It's not up to me. It is not my curse." The woman continued to stare at them without blinking, her face white and translucent. Alex could see pale blue blood vessels in the woman's neck and her lower face but she didn't believe she had blood in them. She looked like a corpse.

OMG, Alex thought. Maybe she is dead and all of this is

voice activated or something. I wonder if she feels as cold as she looks. Alex nearly jumped out of her skin when a black cat jumped on the counter from a nearby shelf. "Who's it up to? Who can remove the curse?" Alex challenged the woman. Once again she became mesmerized by the movements of the snake that she swore was looking directly at her. Her heart was beating so hard she was convinced it would burst through her chest wall.

The woman made no comment but started to hum, and continued to stroke her snake. The sound of her humming was like nothing Alex had ever heard. It unnerved her.

Alex spoke again, feeling a little braver, "What can I do to stop it? Many good people have been hurt. It must stop."

"It is not in my power to alter things. It is not my curse."

"Then where can I go? Who can take the curse away? Who can I talk to? You must know something else," Alex continued breathlessly, her body beginning to tremble in fear and frustration.

The woman continued to stroke both the cat and the snake for a few moments and said, "Go to the feast tomorrow, at midnight near the old Spanish fort by Bayou St. John."

The woman turned her back to them, and placed her cat and snake behind the counter. The cat meowed in protest.

Alex and Elizabeth continued to stand at the counter until the woman turned around and said, "Leave this place. Be gone, now. Don't return here, ever!" The woman left the counter and disappeared into the back room of the store.

Alex was about to follow the woman into the back room to get more information when Elizabeth suddenly seemed to wake up. She pulled her by the arm and said, "Let's get the hell out of here. Move! This place gives me the creeps."

Alex didn't argue. Outside the museum, her heart sank when she didn't see Martin's cab, and it was pitch black. She felt as though a dozen pairs of eyes were following her and staring through her, and she was scared to death.

As they stood helplessly on the curb, the partying people around them had taken on an ominous, evil look, and even the jazz music seemed to have an evil beat. The Mardi Gras masques of many partiers were grotesque, ominous and she was terribly frightened. Out of the corner of her eye, she saw a mean-looking man with a long pony tail coming toward her. He was about to touch her when Martin's big white cab pulled up to the curb. Alex and Elizabeth jumped in, just narrowly evading the grasp of the ponytailed stranger. Martin's cab felt like a safe oasis, a place where her heart beat and breathing could return to normal.

Alex felt mentally and physically exhausted. She was also numb all over. Her heart was racing and felt irregular. Very little conversation passed back and forth, as each was caught up in their personal thoughts. Even Martin was quiet for a change.

"Where can I take you ladies"? Martin ventured.

Alex checked her watch. It was seven but she felt like it was midnight. "Can you drop us at Copeland's on the Avenue? I think that we both need a good stiff drink. That place was really something, Martin. It was eerie, really spooky. I hope that woman who works there makes a good salary. She's pretty good, plays her part well."

Elizabeth stared at Alex. "I think she's a witch, no question.

I also think she's involved with voodoo. I understand why everyone's so afraid of this stuff. Scared the hell out of me. I can hardly believe what I just saw!"

Alex's voice was sharp and she replied hotly. "Get over it! She's dressed up like Halloween. She's not a witch just because she had on white face powder and black lipstick. She's playing a part. Her job is to sell all that stuff in the store." Alex's tone was condescending.

Elizabeth responded hotly, "Get real, Alex! Face it! You were just as scared as I was. Now I better understand what we are dealing with and you should too. How do you account for the fact that she knew who you were and what you wanted?" Elizabeth's pupils were wide and dilated, and her eyes were as defiant as her voice.

Alex squeezed Elizabeth's knee. "Shut up," she hissed under her breath. More loudly she said, "Let's talk about this over a drink. Martin, the traffic is lighter now. Can you hurry?"

"I still say she's a witch," Elizabeth retorted, not to be so abruptly silenced. "And, stop telling me what to do, Alex. You're pissing me off. I've had enough of your attitude."

"She's a witch. That she is, that she is. Don't mess with her," Martin replied as he pulled his cab in front of Copeland's restaurant. "See you gals later. Have a pleasant evening." Martin's voice was tense, his words were short. He'd made his point.

Alex tried to apologize. "Martin, Sorry I am in such a bad mood. I guess I am just tired. I have been so stressed over the stuff at CCMC. Forgive me?" she asked as she prepared to close the cab door.

"Sure, just be careful," he admonished before he pulled off.

An uneasy silence followed as Alex and Elizabeth entered the restaurant. After being seated and quickly consuming their first drink, white wine for Alex, and a bloody Mary for Elizabeth, both women had visibly relaxed. The atmosphere of Copeland's was a welcome relief after the museum. Alex glanced around at the happy couples and families enjoying dinner, once again assured that life was good and normal.

She began the conversation. "Liz, sorry I am such a bitch and sorry I was cross with you. I didn't know exactly what had happened in there. I wanted us to talk about this alone before we got too emotionally involved." Alex hesitated, as she surveyed her friend's body language. "Let's talk about it. Can we?"

"What the hell. I need another drink. I don't know what to think," Elizabeth began. "I didn't believe any of this before tonight. I thought all of these people were superstitious crackpots and ignorant assholes, but now… I don't know. There was a lot of power in that place and it was evil. Something very ugly and threatening is connected with this. That witch knows, and somehow she's involved. Who told her we were coming? Nobody knew but Martin, did they? You tell anybody we were going there 'cause I sure as hell didn't? We didn't even know about it 'til this morning." Elizabeth nervously tapped her fingers on the table as she sipped her drink.

Alex looked at Liz and watched as many emotions flickered over her face. Liz continued "I went there on a lark, thought it may be fun. Didn't expect to learn anything. I'd just planned to buy a book or something to help me understand voodoo better. Believe me, now I don't even want a book. I don't want to know anything else about it, or even to talk about it. I also believe that there is a curse against CCMC and I also believe that part about being vulnerable if you accept the curse."

Alex carefully considered Elizabeth's remarks before she answered. Her voice was uncertain. "I don't know. I don't know the answer to any of this. I think the woman, witch, whatever she is, is only peripherally involved. I don't think she really knows anything."

Elizabeth's voice was impatient. "Get real Alex! Lose the denial! She sure as hell knows something. Somebody's been talking to her. What about going to that feast, or whatever it is on the Lake? Surely you aren't going to go? Are you?" Elizabeth raised her eyebrows at Alex studying her responses.

Elizabeth watched her friend's face and became alarmed. "Don't even consider it. It's crazy, absolutely crazy to expose yourself to anymore of this nastiness. We're dealing with a lot of stuff we know nothing about. These people are probably mentally ill. Black magic, curses, magic powders. People who are native to New Orleans know about this stuff and stay away from it. Don't forget the behavior of our board members. Several of them were scared shitless. We, the hospital, and most specifically you, should do the same."

Alex pondered Elizabeth's comments for several moments. "Don't you see, Elizabeth? Fear's the voodoos greatest weapon. It's just like I said to the governor this morning. If we give up, it's like letting the evil, the Voodoos, the witches and warlocks and black magic win. That's bullshit. We've got to take the next step and confront this stuff head on." Alex's voice was firm with resolve.

"Promise you won't go to the feast. It's dangerous, I know

it. I can feel it. Someone may grab you or you could be hurt or killed and never be found."

"I promise I'll take a large, strong man for protection," Alex smiled at her friend. Alex was relieved that she and Liz had returned to their old banter, and that their friendship was back to normal.

Alex checked her watch. I have a date with Mitch. I have to go in a couple of minutes.

"Mitch Landry? He's so hot! I might even go to a black magic feast with him. Are you sleeping with him yet?" Elizabeth looked coyly at Alex.

Alex shook her head. "Nope, it hasn't gotten that far. Hasn't asked me to."

"What! He needs to ask you?" Liz's raised eyebrows conveyed her disbelief. "I'd have jumped his bones a dozen times by now." Both women laughed and paused to order a third round of drinks.

Elizabeth continued, "Ready for the Extravaganza? It's only a few days away. Did you get your dress from Yvonne? I can't wait to see it." Elizabeth rambled, obviously happy to be talking about more pleasant things.

Alex shook her head negatively. "I haven't even thought about the ball for days. Last week it was the most important thing in my life. I would go to sleep at night dreaming about the ball and a weekend with Mitch. Do you realize our entire lives have been turned upside down in less than four days? And to answer your questions, no, I'll get my gown tomorrow from Yvonne. I'm so excited about it. Speaking of Mitch, I've got to go call him. We have a dinner date later and I need to find out where to meet him. He won't want to come here. Thinks these places are too commercial and considers Copeland's and Shoney's equal in their cuisine. He likes the off the beaten tracks restaurants more. By the way, you're welcome to join us, but only if you promise not to horn in," Alex offered and smiled at her friend.

"Can't promise I wouldn't, so I'd better not." Elizabeth smiled mischievously. "You need a break from me and CCMC, and I need a break from you. Do you realize that the voodoo museum trip actually made me mad at you? But, I will have another drink and then take a cab home."

Alex removed her cell from her purse and looked around Copland's searching for a quiet area to make her call to Mitch. As she waited, Elizabeth mulled over the events of the day. The alcohol was working on her and her thoughts were a bit jumbled. In her heart Elizabeth knew the voodoo woman was involved in the events at CCMC. I know she knows a lot more than she was saying, Elizabeth said to herself. I'd give a week's pay to know exactly what, she mused as she studied the ice cubes in her drink. Then she remembered the morning meeting and the possibility of closing the hospital. Whoops, I better keep my money. I may not have a job in two weeks. That thought terrified her. Public relations jobs were hard to find in the current economy. She'd been lucky to find her job at CCMC. Gosh, I'd hate to lose it. Elizabeth continued to have fleeting thoughts of unemployment that terrified her. She was deep in thought when Alex returned.

"A penny for your thoughts, Liz." Alex was obviously much happier upon returning to the table. She had a faint blush to her cheeks.

"I'll need all the pennies I can get my hands on if the governor closes the hospital. I'm really scared, Alex. Do you realize that we may be unemployed in several weeks? That possibility just crossed my mind. I've saved a lot, but I can't be unemployed for very long."

"It's not going to come to that. We've got a week to figure out exactly what's going on and what we have to do. Besides, I just don't see how closing the hospital will solve anything. We'll get through this." Alex patted her hand and continued, "Just have faith. Somehow, it'll all work out." Alex hoped she sounded more convincing than she felt.

"Hope so. You look better and you're blushing. Your hot date going to meet you here?" Liz's eyes sparkled.

"And let you have a go at him? I think not. No, we're going to go to the Cafe Volange, in midtown. Mitch seems in a good mood, much better than he was this afternoon." Alex remembered back to their earlier conversation. "I think he thought I was calling to cancel our date. Not a chance. I need some fun after today. Want to share a cab?"

Elizabeth looked sheepish. "Think Martin'll pick us up? I think he was pretty miffed at you."

"Justifiably so. I was rude to him. He'll come. He's on retainer and besides, he really likes me. You call though, just to be safe. I have to hit the ladies room. I'll meet you outside."

As Alex caught up with Elizabeth outside the restaurant, Liz was looking dejected. "I'm a little jealous. My fun will come in the form of whatever's on HBO tonight. I'm envious. I think Mitch is a good guy - you all make a good pair, a good match. I hope all goes well this weekend. I'll be cheering for you." The friends smiled at each other.

"Thanks, Liz, I appreciate it. I really want this to work. Mitch means more to me than any other man I've been with since my divorce. I guess I really want to get married again soon and have children." Alex was astonished at her words. "I can't believe I said that. My grandmother would die if she heard me say those words. Matter of fact, I'm surprised that I said them myself," Alex shook her head. Must be the alcohol, she thought to herself.

"Well," Elizabeth replied, "I'm certainly not interested in getting married or having any children any time soon, but I'd sure like to have a date." Both women were laughing as one of Martin's cabs pulled up. Martin wasn't the driver, but his son-in-law, Henri was.

"Evening, ladies." Henri couldn't get out of the cab fast enough to open the door for Alex and Elizabeth. His deferential manner always irritated Alex a little bit, but she figured she'd better keep her mouth shut at this point. She's caused enough damage for one evening. I'd hate to lose Martin for good. He's dependable, and that's much more important than what it costs. Plus, she thought, I really like Martin and depend on him to teach me about the culture of New Orleans.

"Hi, Henri. Know Elizabeth Tippett? She works with me at CCMC." Henri nodded and smiled in greeting.

"How's the family doing?" Alex knew all about Henri's wife who was Martin's daughter, Violette. Martin was always entertaining her with stories about his family and his two year-old grandson.

"Fine, fine. Everything's just fine. Martin said he's sorry he couldn't come back and get you, but he and his wife's have a standing date on Wednesday nights. They go to Shoney's every Wednesday for the fish fry. You know, all you can eat. Then they go to the Casino in Kenner and gamble till late. You know, Martin, he plays them blackjack tables and his wife, she plays the slots. She was the big winner last week. Where to ladies?"

"I need to go to the Cafe Volange and Elizabeth needs to go home uptown. You can drop me off first. Okay with you, Liz?"

Elizabeth nodded.

"Okay. You've been having a terrible time over at the hospital, ain't you? I'm just so sorry. You know, that voodoo is some awful stuff, just awful bad when it catches you, ain't it?"

"Yeah. It's awful. It's been hard. I'm out of here," Alex said as they pulled up in front of the cafe. "See you Elizabeth. Get some rest. Really appreciate you coming, Henri," Alex said as she slipped him a tip.

CHAPTER 13

As Alex shut the door of the cab and moved toward the restaurant, she noticed two men standing in a doorway. One man had a ponytail, and the other man was short and stocky and was smoking a cigar. Something about the two of them gives me chill bumps, Alex thought. My imagination is certainly working overtime. I could swear that's the same man I saw earlier. Must be getting paranoid. She continued to feel uncomfortable as she felt the heat of their eyes following her as she passed. She could feel them tearing her body apart, limb by limb. Alex quickened her pace to the café.

Reaching for safety, Alex entered the restaurant and immediately forgot about the men when she spied Mitch sitting at a quiet table by a window. He looked startlingly handsome in a white open neck shirt and dark pants.

When he saw her, Mitch smiled broadly and rose from his chair. After clasping her hands and kissing her on the cheek, he said, "You're looking beautiful for a lady who's had a rough week. Sit, and let's have a drink. White wine?"

Alex warmed to the sigh of Mitch's smile. She already felt a million times better. "Of course. Mitch, you look just great. It feels like years since I've seen you, even though it's only been two days. This week seems like an eternity. I'm not sure it'll ever end."

Alex paused for a few moments while the waiter served their drinks. Then she continued, "I don't want to spend all evening talking about CCMC – I've been consumed with it for every waking hour. I'd rather hear what you've been doing. Any traveling?"

"Only back and forth to Lafayette and Baton Rouge. I've been researching some architectural designs for my project and had to travel back and forth to the historical library at the LSU campus." Mitch paused for a few moments and continued, "Actually, my week has been rather boring compared to yours. Research is a slow, tedious process but certainly useful. Sometimes I wish my work had a little more excitement."

Alex smiled, "Well, I wish mine had a lot less and that I could do my job."

"I bet," Mitch responded. "As a matter of fact I watched the ED shoot-out news report on a TV in the research library. The library staff in Baton Rouge heard about the ED disaster at CCMC and projected it onto a big screen via a video projector. And, this morning, I caught you on TV. That's some bad stuff going on over there. It never seems to let up. You guys need to catch a break."

"You got that right. How'd I do on TV?" Alex gave him a questioning look. "Did I look OK," she teased him.

"You were beautiful. Great. You and Elizabeth held your own. You both looked great as well. But, it seems like the plot at CCMC thickens. How're you dealing with it?" Mitch looked concerned and reached for Alex's hand.

Alex smiled wryly. "As best I can, I guess. It's really been incredible. Things have been crazy. Admissions are down, the staff isn't reporting to work; the patients are leaving in droves. We have some patients' leaving against medical advice, and Don is about to commit hari-kari. Physicians are admitting and transferring patients to other hospitals. Even the doctors who have exclusive contracts with us are scrambling to find reasons to admit their patients elsewhere. We are bleeding millions and I don't know when, or how, it'll end. In most respects, we're in a desperate situation."

Mitch gave her a concerned look and replied, "Can't last forever. It'll blow over soon. Heard on the evening news the governor's moving his wife to another hospital."

Alex interrupted him, "Oh no. That was on the news? Not good."

"It was the lead story. Reporter said it was the aftermath of the CCMC situation – particularly the medical center's inability to offer quality care and security for their patients. They showed a news clip of Andre Renou and the governor stating they were extremely concerned about CCMC and had offered the assistance of the Louisiana State Police to boost security. Of course, the feds are involved too. By the way, did hear about the *People* magazine story?"

Alex nodded. "Yep. Hell yes, I know all about it." She was very quiet after Mitch related the story. Deep in thought, she stared into her wine glass. She didn't understand why the governor had made a public statement about the situation at CCMC unless he wanted to go on record as being concerned about CCMC, perhaps even set the stage for closing CCMC. And, a bigger question was why he wanted to go on record. Of course, it had to be a political maneuver. Still, he'd agreed to give CCMC a week. While Alex knew that moving Grace Raccine to East Jeff was bound to get out, she hadn't expected it would already be on the local and national news. This information alone would further damage the credibility and finances of the struggling medical center, not even to mention tarnish a perfect image as well. These thoughts depressed her and she was beginning to believe Crescent City Medical Center was a done deal when Mitch interrupted her thoughts.

"You look so sad. It couldn't be all that bad. You're not going to lose your job, or anything. Do you think security's good at the hospital? Do you think it's safe? The hospital won't be harmed if people think it's a safe place."

Alex retorted hotly, "How in the hell do I know if the place is safe? It should be safer now than it was last week before any of these things happened but there are still a million things that can go wrong. I don't think anywhere is ever safe if someone wants to hurt you. It's like trying to keep the U.S. free from terrorists. There are plainclothes policemen all over, and the state police are at all outside doors, elevators, and stairways, like that's really going to keep someone out who wants to do harm. There are undercover DEA agents everywhere. The fact of the matter is that you and I know no place is really 'safe' if somebody wants to get at you. What do you think safe is?" Alex knew she was being sarcastic but she couldn't help it. Her fuse was very short and she didn't want to talk about CCMC on her date.

Mitch was hurt by Alex's words and manner. He held up his hands in a back-off gesture and said, "Sorry. You're really upset. Sorry if I'm prying. Didn't mean to upset you or cause more stress. Look at me. So sorry."

Alex felt her eyes burn with tears, and quickly reached for her pocketbook. As she dabbed her eyes, she started apologizing. "I'm sorry, I never should've spoken to you that way. I guess I'm as out of control as the rest of the CCMC staff. Excuse me." Alex abruptly left the table and headed for the ladies room.

Mitch played with his napkin and studied his menu as he waited for Alex to return. His thoughts were equally sad. He struggled with his conscious. I feel so bad for her. I really wish I could just take her away from all of this, but I can't because I am a big cause of it. Out of the corner of his eye he noticed the "hoods" or "lowlifes" as he preferred to think of them, loitering on the opposite side of the street. The short one with the cigar waved at him and winked. The other glared. Mitch felt the weight of the world on his shoulders without considering the guilt he felt as he returned to his menu. He ignored the lewd hand gestures of the men hiding in the shadows.

He began pondering his life, wondering how he'd become involved in such a desperate situation. He'd had everything, family connections, an education, plenty of money, power. But of course, that was all gone. Of course he knew where it went - he just didn't want to admit it to himself. He felt his greatest loss was his self-respect. He felt empty inside. His self-loathing depressed him. He looked up, Alex was returning, a bright smile on her face.

"I'm better Mitch. I'll see if I can't control myself and behave for a while. What looks good on the menu?"

"Never had a bad meal here. Let's have another drink and order. What d' you say?" Mitch's eyes were sparkling.

"Sounds great," Alex replied, smiling.

They concentrated on their food, carefully avoiding any further reference to the hospital. As they ate, they spoke at length about their plans for the weekend and discussed some options following Mardi Gras.

Over dessert, Mitch made a suggestion. "Come with me to Lafayette soon so you can have a before and after appreciation for the project. I'd like to get your opinion on some of the things I'm attempting to do."

Alex was pleased. "I'd love to see the project. It sounds great. Of course, you're just flattering me about helping you with ideas for the restoration. I don't know anything about architectural history."

"You amaze me. You underestimate yourself all of the time. You've got lots of talent in restoration, look at what you did to your home in the city. I'm not even mentioning your eye for antiques, quality and color. We'll make a weekend of it. I know a lovely bed and breakfast not far from the Arcadian project. We can stay there Saturday night and visit the antique shops in Lafayette on Sunday." Mitch felt momentary happiness and was animated, as he looked forward to spending more time with Alex.

Alex smiled happily. "Sounds perfect. Count me in." Her voice was light, and her heart was skipping at the possibility of spending two consecutive weekends with Mitch. The thought made Alex more cheerful than she'd been in days. It was a great break from recent events.

"You're looking mighty happy, young lady. Want to share your thoughts with me?" Mitch reached for her hand, and smiled warmly.

Alex could feel her cheeks burning. She knew she was blushing. "Oh, Mitch. I don't really know..."

Mitch's grasp tightened over her hand. "I know what you're trying to say. Alex, I care for you very much. Soon you'll know how much. I have some things to get straight first, but then you'll know." Mitch's voice faded a little as he looked at her across the candles.

"I'm looking forward to being together more and knowing each other better. In the meantime," she said briskly, "you'd better get me home so I can get my beauty rest so I can deal with the demons tomorrow."

Mitch leaned across the table and gave Alex a tender kiss. After a brief moment, they stood to leave.

***

The two men, hiding in the shadows, looked on while the gangster leered and made crude gestures. The evil one could have given a shit.

Frederico and the evil one continued to stare at the couple. "Well, well, well, look at our Mitchey boy. I do believe he's gonna nail the lawyer. About time. He's been playing around with the broad for months. Good thing we turned the heat up under him, ain't it. Otherwise he'd have gotten close to her. Strange boy, our Mitchey. What's wrong with him? He go both ways? Is he bi or queer?" Frederico looked at the evil one.

"I don't think Landry much cares who he's with, at least most of the time. Not particular about nobody or nothing once he hits the blackjack tables. He makes love to the roulette table. You give him enough time and enough credit and he's yours forever." Salvadal looked vaguely disgusted.

"Play's good part. He's a charmer. I don't give a shit who or what he screws, snorts, or gambles with as long as he gets me my land. Need that land. Boys in Chicago are losing patience. I need the deal finished soon. Need that casino on the river. It'll make us millions." Frederico's good humor was gone. His voice was ominous. "You get it, you bastard. That was the deal. I need that land soon." The gangster's small eyes glittered like those of a pig. His face was close to Salvadal's and he reeked of bad breath, rotten teeth and tobacco.

Salvadal pushed the gangster back against the wall. "Shut up, Frederico. Fuck you and get out of my face. Don't need any noise out of you. You and I both know what we want. You get close to me like that again and I'll kill you. I'm handling things." As he spoke, his voice was soft and melodious.

Frederico watched him quietly. A shiver came over him. Damn, he's a weird mother fucker the mobster thought. I've seen lots of spooks in my life, but there is something about this guy that just ain't right. He makes my blood run cold. Those were strange feelings for Frederico; fear wasn't a common emotion for him. He tried to remember what he'd had heard about the ponytail man. Not much. Only that he had international experience and was the best around. Frederico didn't know why the evil one was interested in CCMC or Bonnet. He just wanted the SOB out of his way. The gangster continued to think about the ponytailed man and became more and more uncomfortable. Be glad when this one's over, he thought, Must be getting old. He looked over at the ponytailed man and thought about killing him himself. He's a crazy bastard, Frederico thought. He kills just for the fun of it. I kill for money. That makes us different.

Frederico backed off. "Okay, Okay, I got you. Let's go to Impastata's for a pasta snack and then pay pretty boy Mitch a visit when he gets home from his fancy date." Frederico watched the couple leave. "Either he's the best actor I've ever seen, or he's fallen for her. He's such a sorry bastard. He better get us our info."

The evil one tightened his grip on the leather strap, and stretched it tautly from end to end. He said, "If he's not, he's dead." Frederico nodded and the two men headed for Impastata's.

As Alex and Mitch were leaving Cafe Volange, they looked like perfectly matched lovers. Both tall, well dressed and handsome, they were hugging and laughing as they made their way to Mitch's car.

As Mitch walked Alex to her door, she contemplated inviting him in for a night cap. She decided to wait. She was too tired. As Mitch departed, he whispered in her ear, "Know I care for you very much, Alex. No matter what happens, I care."

Alex smiled up at him and quietly closed the door.

CHAPTER 14

Mitch returned to his loft apartment in the warehouse district feeling guilty and fearful about his relationship with Alex. Most of all, he was depressed about what he'd done and what he still had to do. He hardly noticed the celebration and conviviality of his beloved neighborhood.

Mitch had lived in the warehouse district for about two years, and loved the neighborhood's "eclectic" flavor. The warehouse district, frequently called the South's own Soho, was just steps from the French Quarter. The district was the artsy part of NOLA. It was filled with galleries, restaurants, and residences. The ambiance of the area matched Mitch's love of historic restoration and art, good food and nightlife. The obvious downfall was its proximity to the New Orleans riverfront casinos that sang a siren song for Mitch.

Mitch's gambling had placed him in trouble before. His family, affluent in New Orleans for many years, had bailed him out of his gambling debts numerous times, but had finally drawn the line several years ago. He'd entered treatment for his gambling addiction three times, only to fail. His family had nearly disowned him, and he saw them only on holidays and at special family events.

He parked his car and entered the lobby of the renovated warehouse that housed his apartment. Frederico and the man with the ponytail he recognized from the Cafe Volange appeared out of an alcove in the rear of the building. Mitch casually reached to his belt and snapped on his tape recorder.

Frederico's voice was terse and ugly. "Talk us up Mitchy

boy; we need to do some serious talking."

It was obvious that Frederico had a gun, but the ponytailed stranger with the leather strap was more threatening. Mitch pressed the button for the antique brass elevator. The ride up to the top seemed endless since no one spoke. Frederico entered the loft and centered himself on the sofa. He relit his wet, slimy, cigar while the ponytailed man stood at the door.

"What do you got for us Mitchy? We've been real patient. Is the broad singing yet?" Frederico spoke in his best Chicago tough guy voice.

"Don't have much now, but I'll get it soon."

"You were supposed to have it by now; we gave you an extra week. Going to deliver or what?"

Mitch felt desperate. "It's been harder than I thought. Alex has a lot of ethics. She's also smart and doesn't talk as freely as I thought. I've been playing it kind of low, so she wouldn't be suspicious. Besides, you know what's happening over there. Things are in chaos. Things have to be going your way. You're responsible for all those 'accidents' at CCMC. Isn't this what you want? You guys are really low. Murder, for God's sake. You stop at nothing."

Frederico rose from the sofa and came within inches of Mitch's face. His face was ugly because his skin was greasy and porous. He had big red veins in his nose and small, dark glittering eyes. "Landry, you ain't got a clue about what we do. You ain't got no idea about what we've done. But to satisfy your curiosity, yeah, me and my buddy here been working the hospital over pretty good. Couple of dead nurses, a dead doctor. What the hell!

There's plenty of em! Got a new one in tonight. Betcha they don't even know it yet!" Frederico laughed as he thought about his escapades.

The gangster continued with his voice low and threatening. "But, Mitchy boy, more importantly, you don't know what we will do. Fantasize Mitchy; it'll be your worst nightmare. We need your info, got the picture?" At that point Frederico grabbed Mitch's right arm and held it in an iron grasp while he burned his forearm with his lit cigar. "Now, talk Mitchy. Tell Frederico what you know."

Mitch gasped as the hot cigar seared his arm. For a few moments he was unable to speak, as he was forced to concentrate on the pain.

"What's up, spill your guts, lover boy? Talk now or I'll match your other arm." You're an architect. You like things to match, right?" Frederico was threatening as he reached for Mitch's left arm.

Mitch pulled back, raising both arms in a reflexive posture. "Okay, okay. I know Bonnet's under a lot of pressure. All the patients that've been hurt are his. But, you know that," Mitch sneered at them. "The administration's messed up. None of them are getting along. They're also worried about media leaks. Seems like everybody else knows what's going on as soon as it happens. That's all I know." Out of the corner of his eye Mitch caught a secretive smile on the ponytail's face and noticed that he was stroking his strap more aggressively and seductively. This man's evil, like a demon he thought to himself. Wonder if he hurt Mrs. Raccine?

"You ain't told us nothing. You ain't delivering on the big

one, Mitchy. You gotta do better. Spill the dirt." Frederico took another menacing step towards Mitch. "Maybe a little pillow talk is what you need. Never know what you can learn from pillow talk. Wouldn't mind it myself." Frederico leered at him.

Mitch was frantic, and tried to buy some time. "I'm seeing Alex all weekend. We're going to the Endymion Extravaganza Ball Saturday night and staying the night at the Fairmont. The weekend after, we're going to an inn near my preservation project in Lafayette. I'll know more then. I promise!"

"Ain't good enough, Mitch. You told me you'd have what we needed two weeks ago. You got twenty-four hours and that's all. After that, it's over if you don't deliver. You and your girlfriend both'll be history. Get my drift?"

Mitch was both terrified and desperate. "Okay, you've got it."

"We'll meet tomorrow night so you can spill your guts. I'll call and tell you where."

Mitch nodded.

"Don't screw with me...bastard," the gangster threatened.

The ponytailed man spoke for the first time. His voice was quiet but cold. "Maybe you better get over there tonight and start that pillow talk. You're about out of time, pretty boy." Salvadal gestured menacingly towards Mitch's throat with his leather strap.

When Mitch was sure they were gone, he went to his bar and poured himself a double scotch. Thoughts crossed his mind and all ran together. He felt guilty about using his relationship with Alex, pumping her for information to repay his gambling debt to the mob. His love affair was the black box. I've fallen in love with her. I can't do this, he thought.

After about a half an hour of disjointed irrational thinking, only one thought became comforting to him. He picked up his coat, got in his Lexus, and drove out I-10 towards the Gulfport-Biloxi Casinos. I still have a credit line at Casino Magic and the Biloxi Belle. I can make enough to get out of New Orleans. Alex and I can escape to Switzerland or New Zealand, maybe even Australia where they'd never find us. Mitch continued to have these irrational thoughts throughout the hour drive to the coast.

***

The St. Charles Inn, a late night hot spot on St. Charles, was host to all walks of life. The Cajun food was good, cheap, and the coffee was usually fresh. Raoul DuPree had just gotten off work at Tujague's and saw the evil one and Frederico as they came in. They sat in a booth several down from his. Raoul was facing Frederico and slumped down in his chair and tried to avoid recognition.

Tonight the St. Charles Inn provided a watering hole for Frederico and Salvadal. Each was drinking heavily to offset their displeasure with Mitch. They were both obviously pissed.

"Don't like the pretty boy, Frederico. I don't think he's gonna come through for us. What're you going to do?"

"The son of a bitch will pull it off. He's scared. Just needs a good night with the broad. Don't worry," the gangster tried to lie to shrug off Salvadal's words.

"You stupid fucker. Do you think you can blow me off?

My bosses are getting restless and want to move. I'm sick of waiting for the Ivy League snitch to come through." Salvadal was impatient and becoming more and more agitated the longer he spoke. The liquor seemed to irritate and aggravate him rather than calm him. Frederico noticed his companion was again stroking his leather strap.

"Landry'll get us the goods, the shit on Bonnet and the hospital. Too scared not to. We'll know soon. He's only got 'til tomorrow night." Frederico spoke with more confidence than he felt. "Besides, what other choice do we have? The hit on Bonnet is already set up."

"I have lots of choices. I got freedom to make lotsa choices and one of those choices is to kill you if you don't deliver. Make sure your boy delivers what I need. You and the choir boy came to me, remember. I never would have sought out two assholes like you. No later than midnight tomorrow."

Salvadal took a last sip of his drink, slammed the glass on the table, and left abruptly.

Frederico sat and contemplated his dilemma, wishing over and over he had more information on Salvadal's connections. The more he drank the more paranoid he became. Bastard's crazy, he thought. You'd think that damn strap was his lover the way he rubs it all the time. Frederico's most constant and comforting thought was that Salvadal's connections couldn't be more powerful than those of the mob. Besides, he could always have his man snuff the ponytail. Hell, he was just one man, wasn't he? The mob had plenty of talent he could call to get the job done. After several more drinks, Frederico felt better, made a phone call and staggered drunkenly out of the St. Charles Inn.

Raoul DuPree watched him leaving, and searched his conscience about whether he should warn Dr. Bonnet.

***

Alex again slept fitfully, dreaming of Mitch, dark strangers with ponytails, and a Voodooist attacking Robert. Her phone ringing at six a.m. was almost a welcome respite from the nightmare. "Hello," she said sleepily.

"Get in here," bellowed Don Montgomery. "We have another one." Before she could ask any questions, Don hung up.

CHAPTER 15

It took Alex no time to reach her office at CCMC. She headed toward administration where Don and Dr. Ashley sat in Don's office. Both men were silent, and stared at the floor.

Alex walked in. "Well," she demanded, looking at them. They both just looked at her. "What's happened?" she asked again loudly.

Dr. Ashley was visibly upset. "Not sure about this one, Alex. This is different. It could be a tragic accident. At this time there's no evidence otherwise." John Ashley's voice was discouraged and he was grey with fatigue and stress. Alex was concerned about him and his ability to withstand much more chaos.

"For heaven's sake, John, tell me what happened." Alex's look conveyed her irritation.

"We have a patient in the cardiac care unit recovering from abdominal surgery. Last week she had a heart attack, probably the stress of surgery, I guess. Anyway, about two this morning, she started to have some heart irregularities and the nurses hooked her up to a twelve-lead EKG to get a printout of her heart's activity. It's not clear how it happened, but her EKG machine malfunctioned and she received severe burns at each contact site. I don't know how it could've happened. That equipment is absolutely safe."

"Bullshit it's safe!" Don screamed.

"She's alive?" Alex was afraid to hear the answer.

"Yes, at least for now. Although the electrical shock has

played havoc with her heart and may end up killing her. She's having serious arrhythmias now."

As Alex looked at them, a thought crossed her mind. Her eyes searched the room as she said, "Let's go over to the Cajun Cafe and have some coffee. I could use a little breakfast."

Both men looked at her like she was crazy. Alex put her finger on her lips to silence them, and gestured towards the ceiling as she walked out the door. They didn't understand but followed.

Alex said in a soft voice, "I think the executive offices and conference room could be bugged."

Don gave her a shocked look. "Are you crazy? What makes you say so?"

"We've had too many leaks. Why take the chance? How old is this woman?" Alex asked as they walked towards the cafe.

Dr. Ashley answered, "She's forty-seven. Bonnet's patient, once again. Apparently, Dr. Bonnet thought she may have some underlying malignant disease and did an exploratory. Anyway, she had rheumatic fever as a child, and developed heart valve disease that wasn't diagnosed until after her heart attack."

They reached the Cajun Cafe, a gaily decorated restaurant within the CCMC complex and were greeted by a yawning waiter. Alex asked him if they could use the private dining room. The waiter nodded and the three went into the small room.

"So, what's her prognosis?" Alex questioned, not really wanting to hear.

"Don't know. Pretty bad, I guess. Her hands are also badly

burned. Plus, she has long narrow burned areas on her body where the leads wires were attached to the contacts. There's the fear of infection, body fluid shifts, and so on."

"Especially when you factor in her heart problems. Dr. Bonnet know?"

"Haven't reached him yet. You have any idea where he could be?"

Don was livid. "Bonnet is the reason that all of this has happened here. He's the cause. He's the common denominator. Somebody's got a hardon for him. Probably somebody's surgery he's screwed up or something!"

Alex ignored Don's tirade. "No, of course not, no idea where Robert is," Alex replied. Boy, the CCMC grapevine is powerful, she thought to herself.

Don Montgomery glared at Alex and started again. "Bonnet's nothing but trouble. Have you noticed all of the patients that've had accidents or problems at Crescent City are his patients? Don't you think that's a little suspicious? Told you weeks ago Bonnet was trouble. I also told you to fix him." Montgomery was working himself in to a real rage and was glaring at her, and looked angrier than she had ever seen him.

Alex glared back and held her ground as she addressed Don's accusations. "You mean both patients don't you, Don? Overall, that's an insignificant number when you consider all the patients Dr. Bonnet admits to CCMC. Does the press know about this latest accident and have the NOPD been called yet?"

"No press that we know of. I called the NOPD, but they're

not here yet. Guess we'll have to put up with Francois again. What a week, and it's only Thursday." Dr. Ashley rolled his eyes.

"I'm going to the cardiac care unit," said Alex. "Ask hospital engineering to meet me there, along with the safety coordinator. We need to find out why this EKG machine malfunctioned. Most of all, we need to be sure this doesn't happen again. Don, have you talked with this patient's family?" Alex was in control but very worried.

"No, and I'm not going to. You do it. You and John do it. You're better at it than I am. I'm the CEO, not a babysitter." Don was sitting with his face in his hands. "Somebody's out to get us. It's beyond the realm of probability that all this could happen to one hospital in one week. Someone's deliberately trying to destroy us. Just wish that I knew who and why? Who, Who Who?"

Dr. Ashley shook his head at Don's accusations before Alex answered slowly. "I don't know. But I'm beginning to believe you. There's some sort of plot here."

"Damn right there's a plot to put us out of business, or force us to merge with someone. Robert Bonnet's heavily involved in it. Bastard has to be the center of all of this, there's no way that he couldn't be. Whoever's doing this is doing a good job. The hospital's only about thirty percent full now and most of our outpatient surgeries and diagnostic services have been cancelled. We're going to be history shortly."

Don stopped for a moment to catch his breath and continued, "Our competitors are doing well. Oh yeah, they're doing just fine. They've picked up our admissions and elective surgeries. Maybe they're plotting against us. Maybe that's who bugged our conference room. We're losing more physicians and patients each day while our competitors are picking them up and making those millions...our millions. I just don't understand. Why is this happening to us?" Don finished speaking, put his head on the table and started weeping. He knocked over his coffee cup in the process.

Dr. Ashley turned to Alex. "I'll go with you to the cardiac care. I want to see the patient myself."

Dr. Ashley and Alex left Don in the Cajun Cafe and ran smack into Captain Francois in the corridor outside. He was his normal, cocky self.

"Why're you all meeting here? Conference room bugged?" Dr. Ashley and Alex gave each other a funny look. The captain noticed but continued without commenting on it. "Think I'll open a satellite office here. May as well report here every morning and forget about going downtown. Secretarial support's probably better too." Francois winked at them.

"We're going up to cardiac care. Been up yet, Captain?"

"Nope. Tell me what you know. All I know is that you have a burned patient. Any other particulars I need to know?"

Dr. Ashley answered, "Apparently a patient's EKG machine malfunctioned and she was badly burned."

"Now, that's a change. That sounds like a normal hospital accident," Francois snorted.

Alex retorted hotly, "Being burned in your bed by routinely safe medical equipment is not a 'normal' hospital accident."

"Relax, I'm on your side. This business is getting out of

hand. Besides, I'm genuinely concerned about CCMC. If this accident is the work of the same group, their MO is taking a turn that'll hurt CCMC. If the public perceives a lack of expertise and safety, you'll be out of business in no time."

None of the group noticed Don Montgomery coming up behind them. They turned when he began to speak. "We're practically out of business now. Our admissions and surgeries are down, and patients are going to other hospitals. We're in serious trouble financially and professionally. Someone's trying to put us out of business. Can't you DO something," Don demanded of the captain.

"I'm working on it. Yeah. I agree. Somebody wants CCMC gone. Let's go check this out, then we'll talk over coffee." It was clear Francois wasn't saying anything else, so the trio proceeded toward the coronary care unit.

"I'll be in my office," said Don as he turned down a hallway and left the group.

The unit was quiet as the group approached. A plain clothes policeman sat in the lobby by the elevators. Alex saw Barton Browning, the hospital safety coordinator, sitting in the nursing station. She signaled for Barton to wait for her.

A nurse took Alex, John, and the captain to Blanche Henderson's room. The nurse reported that she was heavily sedated and the cardiac monitor indicated a stable rhythm. The nurse also mentioned that the malfunctioning machine was back in the equipment room.

Alex called to Barton when they left the patient's room, and the four talked in the hall. Alex begged for more information.

"What happened, Bart?" Alex asked.

"Don't know. All I can tell is the machine delivered more current than it should have. I'm on my way to check it out. Our electrical equipment is fitted with adapters which prevent this. They're permanently affixed to the machine plug. The monitor of the machine in question is an older one, so it may not have that safety feature. Still, it's been used many times before without incident. Can't tell you anything else until we check it out. I have checked all the product literature on the internet and there have been absolutely no incidences or accidents like this ever reported."

"Let's check the monitor," Francois suggested. The group entered the equipment room where several nurses were talking about the accident. There was an immediate hush as the group broke up and left the room.

When Francois, Dr. Ashley, Bart, and Alex bent down to examine the machine, it took only an instant for them to see what had happened. The adaptor had been neatly filed off, leaving the machine without any grounding at all.

Francois immediately called an officer to secure the room as a crime scene and suggested they find an empty room and discuss some things.

They found an empty patient room and quickly shut the door tightly. Alex and Dr. Ashley sat on the bed while Francois and Barton sat in the chairs.

Bart began, "This is unbelievable. This is more than an accident. It was done on purpose, and recently. We check this stuff all of the time."

Francois barked at the safety coordinator. "Who has access to your equipment when it's not in use? Where's it stored?"

Browning looked uncomfortable. "This monitor's stored in the room we were in. Each floor has its own equipment room, and the equipment is checked and tested periodically which is standard hospital policy and standard practice."

"So, you're telling me anybody can get to this equipment, whether they're staff, patients, or visitors. Is that what you're saying?"

Browning hesitated, "We don't keep equipment locked up unless it's dangerous equipment, like x-rays and other radioactive stuff. An EKG machine isn't dangerous or hazardous medical equipment." Barton thought for a moment and added, " Yes, anybody could've gotten to it and filed the adaptor off."

"When was the last time the machine was used or inspected?" Alex said.

"Several weeks ago. No service was done, and it worked perfectly. You'll have to ask the nurses when it was used last. I don't keep a record of that."

"I'll check with the nurses. Anything else you can tell us?" Captain Francois asked.

"I'll be glad to contact the sales rep and get all of the technical information for you. We may have some additional product information in the office. I'll check."

"Thanks Browning. You can go. Get that info ASAP. And keep your mouth shut about this, understand?"

"No problem. I'll get you the information." Browning left hurriedly.

"What can you tell me about him?" Francois said to Dr. Ashley and Alex.

"Not much. He's been here a little longer than me. He's a good employee, conscientious, seems to know his stuff," Alex said. "I hardly know him, seems to be a good worker, and he is very cooperative. We recruited him from Pennsylvania several years ago. I've never heard anything negative about him, ever. He is a medical design engineer. You don't think Barton Browning had anything to do with this?"

"I cover all bases," the captain retorted. "Anyway, you'd better have your safety team examine all equipment ASAP. You don't need any more accidents or deaths here. I'll have the crime unit investigate the monitor and dust for prints, but I'm sure they won't find anything."

Alex turned to Francois. "You mentioned you'd talk to us, that maybe you had some information."

"I said I'd talk over coffee. I need a caffeine fix and a jelly doughnut," Jack said, grinning at Alex. "I need it bad since I stopped smoking. Let's get coffee somewhere private where's there's no big ears."

"Back to the cafe. I'll call Don and have him meet us. He should hear whatever you have to say. That okay with you? They have good coffee there, and it's as private as it gets around here," Alex suggested.

"Yeah, let's get Montgomery, although I've about decided

both he and Bette Farve are useless." Francois rolled his eyes.

Alex was surprised to hear the captain vocalize this and smiled to herself while Dr. Ashley looked embarrassed as the group headed toward the elevator lobby. When the elevator came, Dr. Robert Bonnet flew out of the doors and raced down the hallway toward the cardiac unit. He didn't speak, but instead hurried to see his burned patient. Alex doubted that Robert even saw them.

"Wait for me," Alex said as she paused outside the elevator to call Don Montgomery. Alex pulled her cell phone from the pocket of her lab coat. The men watched her as she dialed. Francois had his finger on the 'Door Open' button. She said "Hello, this is Alex..." then she paused and listened. The men knew it was bad news by the look on her face. She walked slowly to the elevator, clearly upset.

She said sadly, tears in her eyes. "Diane Bradley just died. The unit called administration, and they just paged us. Robert was with her. I'm going to see him for a few minutes, and then I'll be down. Have a doughnut for me, Captain. I find sugar comforting at times like this."

"Yeah, me too. If I could, I'd spike the coffee." Francois' eyes lit up, and he grinned impishly. He was a handsome man when he wasn't being an asshole.

"Captain, I can handle you much better when you're rude and impossible." Alex smiled.

"Don't you worry, miss lawyer lady." the captain smirked. "You got precious little management around here. God forbid I corrupt what there is." The captain's voice resumed some of its old brusqueness and sarcasm.

"Thanks. See you shortly, John." Alex flashed them a brave smile as Dr. Ashley got on the elevator as Jack headed for the stairway.

CHAPTER 16

Robert was listening to Mrs. Henderson's heart when Alex entered her room. The patient was awake and in considerable pain.

"Dr. Bonnet, what happened? Why do I have these bandages?" Mrs. Henderson's voice was weak.

Robert touched her hand. "Something happened to your EKG machine and your hands and feet were burned." His voice was quiet and soft.

"Will they get well?"

"Yes, but it will take time. I'll give you some more pain medicine so you can rest. Your heart's doing well, but rest is important. Try to get some sleep." He stood beside her and continued to talk softly, offering comfort. Alex noticed his hand on her arm. She had always liked that about Robert when they were married. He was very touchy feely,

Blanche Henderson looked up and noticed Alex.

"Don't I know you?" Mrs. Henderson said weakly.

"I'm Alex, and I'm a colleague of Dr. Bonnet's."

"Yes, of course." Mrs. Henderson's eyes brightened with recognition. "I remember now. We worked together last year on the Charity Benefit for the Children's Center. I can't quite remember who you are or why you are here."

Alex replied softly. "I remember working with you. Rest so that you can get better. We'll take good care of you."

Alex remembered the energy and enthusiasm Mrs. Henderson had expended on the benefit that raised several million dollars for the children's oncology center at CCMC. Her own little boy had died from childhood leukemia several years ago, and ever since then, Mrs. Henderson had worked tirelessly to raise money for research. She'd also started support groups for families with similar situations.

"Thanks for stopping by. Come back and see me, Alex. We'll plan our next Charity Ball." Mrs. Henderson smiled weakly and closed her eyes.

"I will. I promise." Alex took Robert's hand and led him out of the room.

Alex walked into the private dining room at the Cajun Cafe. Don, Dr. Ashley, Elizabeth and Captain Francois were sipping coffee and sitting around the table. Francois asked Don to get him a copy of Barton Browning's personnel file, but Don objected, protesting an "inquisition". The meeting wasn't going well, but after an exchange of hostile words, Don agreed to supply the file.

"Captain Francois, you mentioned a report for us, based on your investigations. What do you know?" Dr. Ashley's voice was calm, but his body language suggested otherwise.

The captain cleared his throat. "It's safe to say there's a conspiracy against CCMC. My theory, but I can't yet prove it, is there's a group of powerful and evil people who want to injure and destroy you, in fact, put you out of business. They are working hard to do it. They're hiring thugs and killers and cloaking it in threats and black magic to further alienate people, making them too scared to come here for medical care. The Voodoos are simple instruments to do the dirty work."

Don Montgomery's animosity toward Jack Francois was intense, palpable. "Bingo, Francois, no shit. Go to the head of the class. Is this all you have for us? You're such an idiot Francois, I knew this three days ago. Why don't you get your son-of-a-bitching ass out there and find out who's responsible?" Don's face was distorted and ugly. A brief silence followed Don's outburst and Captain Francois, while angry, quietly responded.

"Listen, Montgomery. I'm not going to resort to your level, but once and for all, I'm on your side. I'm trying to find out who's behind this. We're working closely on this. Now, my advice to you is to shut up and give me the information I need. A little cooperation from you could go a long way."

The captain turned and addressed the entire group, his eyes moving from one to another of those seated at the table. "I need to know ASAP if the medical center has been approached by any corporation wanting a merger or take-over. Who are your pissed off patients? Who has an axe to grind at CCMC? I also want to know what kind of litigation there is against the medical center, and who the plaintiffs are. I'm particularly interested in knowing who has it out for Dr. Bonnet." Francois was eyeing each person as he spoke. "In fact, I want to know all of your dirty linen."

Don sneered at the captain. "There's no one trying to 'buy' CCMC. We're not for sale. We were approached several months ago by a Catholic hospital chain, which wanted to merge with us. Our board voted unanimously to stay independent." Don's face was red with anger and his response was riddled with sarcasm."

After a moment, he continued, "We were, up until this week, in excellent financial shape, completely solvent and our board had no desire to change our direction. I hardly think a group of nuns are out to get us," he said sarcastically, as he glared at Francois. "Of course, not knowing what Obamacare will do to us, or any hospitals for that matter, we have put away some money in discretionary funds. Try again, Francois, your theory stinks, just like your police work."

Francois glared at the CEO. "You know, your brain ain't no bigger than your nose. You're a stupid dumb ass and a dumb mother fucker! I can't believe you actually think you run this hospital!"

Fearing the worst and sensing this could easily get out of control, Alex interrupted the captain. "Do you think there's a separate plot against Dr. Bonnet?" You seem particularly interested in any actions against him."

Don jumped from his seat and went to Alex's chair and wagged his finger in her face, and shouted. "Shut up, Alex. I forbid you to talk to this idiot about this medical center's business, Bonnet or anything else. I want someone from the NOPD who's competent and knows what they are doing. I'm calling the police commissioner right now. The hell with you, you son of a bitch. Get out of my hospital, **NOW!**" As Montgomery got up to leave, Francois spoke quietly.

"The Commissioner and the governor are tight, very tight. I doubt the Commissioner would go out on a limb for you, especially since he knows the governor's planning to close this place. I'm the best thing you've got going, so you better sit yourself down and listen."

Don didn't move. Francois addressed Alex and Dr. Ashley. "What's the scoop on Bonnet?" Who wants him out of practice?"

Dr. Ashley immediately began, "Dr. Bonnet's an excellent surgeon, and his practice is impeccable. I see no reason why someone would sabotage him."

Don glared at Dr. Ashley, and then turned his rage on him. "You damn doctors are stuck so far up each other's asses, it's sickening. The way you cover for each other is criminal!"

Hoping to diffuse the situation with a little light humor, Alex intervened again. "Captain Francois, guess you can tell that administration and medicine don't necessarily agree all the time. Recent pressure's been too much. I can speak to Dr. Bonnet's practice and the current legal situations."

Don interrupted rudely. "Who're you to talk about Bonnet's practice?" He glowered at her. "You're his ex-wife, you are the scorned, pissed off, discarded ex-wife bitch who still wants to get in his pants. Bonnet could kill your mother on the table and you wouldn't say a word against him. That's the reason we're in this situation to begin with. I told you to control Bonnet, and you ignored my directives. You're fired, Destephano. I'm sick of you, your placating crap and your inability to perform. Get the hell out of here and don't come back." Don glared at her, his face suffused with anger.

Alex spoke, quietly, but firmly. "You can't fire me, Don. It's a board action and must come from the board of trustees. At this point, I'm not leaving. Get the picture?" Alex knew she was being rude, but it didn't seem to matter. She continued in the same vein, "As a matter of fact, I'm going to assist Captain Francois with his investigation and give him the info he needs on Dr. Bonnet," she said.

Just at the moment, Robert Bonnet entered the Cajun Cafe.

Don Montgomery stood up, scowled at the group, stalked around the table and gave threatening looks to all his colleagues who were seated. Apparently, Robert's presence was more than he could handle.

Francois said quietly, "Montgomery, you're interfering in an official police investigation. Keep that in mind. It wouldn't take two seconds for me to arrest you. I'd do it now but it would hurt the hospital even more." Captain Francois' voice was quiet, but his meaning was clear.

Don shot a hateful look at the Captain and left, and slammed the door behind him so loudly it caused the glass in the windows to rattle.

Robert sat down, looked around and gave everyone a lopsided grin. "What's going on, Don's not looking too happy." Robert's voice was light as he attempted to smooth the situation.

Alex looked sheepish but smiled. "To suggest Don's having a bad day would be an understatement. Captain Francois wants to know about any potential legal situations that concern both you and CCMC, and I was getting ready to tell him about our conversation earlier this week. Do you have any problems with that?" Alex gave Robert a hard look.

"No, no, of course not. I trust you on this. It's pretty clear that someone's trying to destroy my practice and my reputation. I think there's a conspiracy against me," Robert said glancing around at the others. "Tell him everything you need to." Robert looked resigned.

Captain Francois nodded and said, "Shoot, you got my attention."

Alex began, her voice formal. "Presently Dr. Bonnet has three complaints against him, filed in less than six months. One has resulted in a malpractice action. He operated on a patient with cancer who developed post-operative septicemia and died. The patient's family is suing Dr. Bonnet claiming wrongful death, suggesting that the surgery was inappropriate and caused his death. John Marigny's firm is handling that claim. Another complaint concerned what the patient perceives to be an unfavorable outcome of plastic surgery." Alex paused while Francois rolled his eyes. She continued, "The third complaint is internal. Several staff members have complained that Dr. Bonnet is 'erratic, unpredictable, and unsafe' in the operating room."

"Who're these staff members?" Francois asked as he broke off a piece of jelly doughnut.

"One nurse and several operating room techs. I haven't talked with them yet. That complaint is fairly new. After I interview them, I'll get back to you. That's all." Alex finished speaking.

Francois turned to Robert as he chewed the doughnut. "Is this lady with the bad boob job pissed enough to kill your patients?"

Robert looked bewildered at the thought. "I don't think so, although she's mentally unstable," he added.

"She may be unstable, but she's well-connected and not someone we want to alienate. Especially not now," Alex added.

"Who is she?" Francois asked.

"Elaine Logan. Her family's been treated at CCMC for

years, and are heavy contributors to the hospital's foundation," Alex said.

Francois laughed and his dark eyes sparkled. "I don't think she's smart enough to be responsible for this. Dr. Bonnet, is there anything else you want to tell me?" Francois looked carefully at Robert.

"No, not really," he hesitated, and eyed Dr. Ashley and Elizabeth.

Apparently taking the cue, Dr. Ashley said, "I need to make rounds. Let me know if you need me further, Captain." Formal, as always, Dr. Ashley shook hands with the captain and left. Elizabeth also made her excuses and left the Cafe.

Francois, Alex, and Robert were left in the private dining room. Francois looked at Robert. "Dr. Bonnet, you seemed to hesitate earlier. Is there something you think may be associated with all of this stuff?"

Robert threw up his hands. "For God's sake, Jack! Call me by my first name. We've known each other for years. Quit the formal stuff!"

"You got it," the captain replied.

"There is something else. I mentioned this to Alex earlier this week. I've gotten a lot of pressure, and some threats, about selling a piece of land I own jointly with my father. The caller insists that I sell. Each phone call becomes more and more threatening. They have even gotten hold of my cell phone and are calling that as well. Even if I wanted to sell, my father would never agree. He has other plans for the property."

"Where's the land?" Francois asked as he finished the doughnut.

"On the riverfront, near the Hilton Queen Riverboat Casino and the Riverwalk."

"That's some big money property. Prime real estate. Makes you wonder who wants it so bad. Any ideas?" Francois had a probing look on his face.

"No, not really, I don't. I really don't." Robert hesitated, an uncertain look on his handsome face. "A woman I was dating, a real estate agent, said she had a buyer for the property and suggested I consider selling. Told her to forget it, my father'd never sell. She really wasn't too happy to hear this."

"I can only imagine," Jack rolled his eyes. I bet it cost her a big commission."

Robert continued, "Yeah, huge. She was pissed. Soon after, the calls started coming, at all hours, day and night. 'They,' whoever 'they' are, even called me over at my house at Gulf Shores. They've been very persistent to say the least."

Robert paused for a moment and then continued, "I don't know enough about these internal complaints to even address them. Alex won't tell me who made them. Makes it hard for me to defend myself, wouldn't you say?" Robert said angrily as he shot Alex a rueful look.

"Robert, after I interview them, we'll talk. I'll tell you then. You know that." Alex responded, nonplussed.

Jack intervened. "Thanks, for telling me this stuff. I'll put a trace on your phone in case you get any more calls. My guess is that somebody, probably the mob, wants that land to build more casinos or hotels. Stay close and let me know if anything develops," Francois told him.

"Thanks, Jack. There's one more thing. I've gotten two other phone calls from a man. Sounds young and says he knows somebody's out to get me. Said he's warning me because I helped him once."

"Who? Any ideas?"

"No. His voice is vaguely familiar but I don't recognize it. Could be anybody. A patient, student, family-member.....who knows?"

"It's somebody who thinks enough of you to take a risk and call," Francois replied, his face serious.

"Yeah. Good point. I need your help, all of us do." Robert checked his watch. "Got to make rounds. Call me if you need anything else."

Francois and Alex were alone. Captain Francois broke the silence. "What do you think's coming down here?"

"Don't know. It seems like a conspiracy. Let me draw a picture of what we know, I think better that way."

Alex pulled out a piece of paper and made three columns. One column was labeled 'CCMC', the second 'Dr. Bonnet', and the third 'Events'. All of the items in the 'events' column related back to CCMC and Robert Bonnet. It was clear that most of the events involved Robert as a central focus. Except for Robert's land, there was a clear and distinct relationship.

"I guess," Alex mused, "that there're a number of questions. First of all, who'd want to destroy CCMC? Who'd benefit? Finally, who's powerful enough to destroy us?"

Alex and Jack, each caught up in their own thoughts, were silent for a few minutes. Seeing the events in black and white convinced Alex and Jack there was a plot against the hospital. The Voodoo curses were appearing and reappearing in the ED shootout and the burn injury.

Then Alex continued, "Another question is who has a big enough grudge against Robert to want to destroy him? Are the events at CCMC related to someone wanting to buy his land?"

"Yep", said Captain Francois. "Good question. Another is whether they want to destroy Dr. Bonnet and CCMC together. Are they the same people and are the events related?"

Alex thought for a few seconds. "Can't imagine why they're together unless they are related in some way. There's just too much happening too quickly. Maybe someone's just interested in destroying Robert and the fallout on CCMC is just that, a fallout. But then, Robert wasn't directly targeted in the ED shootout..."

"I doubt it. And, I think there's another rotten egg at the top." Francois glanced up in the air and looked even more disgusted.

"Montgomery? No way. That self-serving bastard would never sabotage his own hospital," Alex was adamant. Then noting Jack's face, she said, "What aren't you telling me?"

"I don't know. This is in confidence, of course. I got called into the chief's office late yesterday, and was told to play the

CCMC thing down. You know, the spiel to lay low. Just go slow on the investigation."

"Huh? What? That's unbelievable! Why would anyone want to stop us from finding out what is going on here? People are getting killed and injured every day, and the whole city's reeling from this bogus voodoo scare. I'd think the chief would want these crimes solved. Could you have misunderstood?" Alex's voice was loud, her eyebrows raised and her face revealed the incredibility of the Captain's confidence.

"Be quiet, for God's sake, Alex. I shouldn't have told you. No, I'm not wrong, and I got a clear read on this stuff from the brass, and the word was to back off. I think this thing's rotten to the core. There must be some really heavy hitters involved, corruption at the top. That's all I'm saying. Well, almost all. I have a couple of questions for you."

Alex nodded, still smarting from the news that someone high up in the NOPD wanted to 'sit' on the problems at CCNC.

Captain Francois continued. "Don said no one was interested in buying the hospital and that the trustees had voted to stay independent. Right?"

Alex nodded affirmatively. "To the best of my knowledge that's correct."

"Have there been any changes in the trustees recently?"

"Well, no, not really."

Suddenly she remembered the new member at the board meeting this week, the man with the ordinary face. "Wait a minute, yes, we do. There's a new member. I'd never seen him until this week. I haven't been introduced to him, and I can't remember his name."

Then it dawned on Alex, "But you know what, Captain? He hates Robert. You should've seen the look of hatred cross his face when Robert appeared at the meeting. It gave me the shivers. I'll call Latetia, Don's secretary, for his name and address."

Alex grabbed her cell to phone Don's secretary.

Francois was still staring at the piece of paper they'd composed when Alex clicked off. "She's at lunch. I'll track her down later and call you."

"Okay. Here are my numbers. The first one is a beeper, then cell and home. The cell is the best number. I'm never in my office. I'll call you right back." Francois prepared to go but looked as if he had something else to say. His face was concerned.

Alex pressed him. "What? Is there something else?"

Jack was silent.

"Ask me. We're on a roll. I'm actually beginning to like you." Alex gave him a playful smile.

"It's a little harder, Alex. Hope you won't take this wrong." He hesitated. There was an uncomfortable pause and Francoise stared at the floor and played with his car keys.

"Stop staring at the floor. Tell me Francois, let me have it." Alex couldn't imagine what could be so difficult.

Francois began slowly. "Understand you've been seeing Mitchell Landry. How well do you know him?"

Alex felt a knot in her stomach. "I've been seeing him about three months. Why? What does Mitch have to do with anything?"

Francois ignored her question. "Sorry to question you like this, but I have a good reason. How well d' you know Landry?"

"Mitch and I see each other socially. It's a perfectly respectful relationship, Captain. Why'd you ask?" Alex could feel increasing stress and tension in her neck, headed towards her temple.

Francois seemed distinctly uncomfortable with Alex's anger, but wasn't going to give up. "You know anything about his habits?"

"What habits? I know all about his passion for art and nineteenth century literature. I know he loves opera and theater. Is that what you mean?" Alex's voice was caustic and she was pissed as she scrutinized the police captain. She noticed Jack's discomfort.

"Landry's a compulsive gambler. Gets him into big trouble. Guess you didn't know."

Alex gasped and her face paled. "What, you're crazy."

Jack Francois averted his eyes and looked apologetic.

"Mitch is a gambler?" Alex's voice was sharp. "I've never ever seen play board games? You have got to be wrong!" Alex was shocked and unbelieving.

"He's been in trouble before because of his gambling. Has unscrupulous, nasty friends that show up when he's overspent his credit line."

Alex was quiet for a few minutes as she thought about the implications of what the captain had said. She remembered the man who'd approached Mitch outside her apartment, and the two men she'd noticed outside Cafe Volange last night. Finally she spoke.

"I know nothing about Mitch's gambling. He's been a good companion and a friend to me." Alex was visibly upset because she had tears in her eyes.

"Sure you're okay?"

"Yeah, thanks for telling me, Captain Francois."

"It's Jack. Take care Alex, and be careful. I'll be back around later this afternoon." The captain's voice was gruff, but his look was gentle as he touched her shoulder on his way out.

Alex felt like crying the moment that Francois left. Mitch'd been the only positive thing in her life, and now, even he was suspect. She was developing a terrible headache. Wish I could go home, she thought as she left the Cajun Cafe.

CHAPTER 17

Alex returned to her office and became more depressed as the hours passed. She continued to think about what Francois had said. I had no idea that Mitch gambled, she thought. I can't imagine he's involved in this. I'd never get over it. I had no clue. There has got to be something wrong with me. What have I told him about CCMC? Alex's brain was trying to replay the tapes of her recent conversations with Mitch as she tried to remember what she said or had not said to him about CCMC in last few weeks. Had she betrayed the hospital or any confidentiality? I probably haven't told him anything of substance, but I probably shouldn't have told him anything. Why am I so stupid, such a loser? A nagging voice reminded her she'd talked about some of the situations at the hospital. She'd voiced her concerns about the press coverage.

The more she thought about things, the more anxious Alex became about her relationship with Mitch. Of course Mitch knows I've seen Robert...he left my house on Tuesday so Robert could stop by.

The more Alex concentrated, the more jumbled her thoughts became and the more her head ached. After several hours of reviewing things in her mind, Alex was convinced that it was preposterous to think Mitch could be involved in the mess here. If he's a compulsive gambler, I'll find out myself. I'll ask him. Nevertheless, Alex couldn't put the images of the stout man with the cigar and the man with the ponytail out of her mind.

It was clear to Bridgett that her boss was having a bad day. After several attempts to cheer her up, she finally said, "What gives, Alex? I've never seen you so down. Is it Diane's death or the accident with Mrs. Henderson, or what?" Bridgett's blue eyes reflected her concern.

Alex looked up at Bridgett. "Don't know, Bridge. I guess I'm just tired. It's been a rough week."

"No, that's not it. Don't look so sad, Alex. The weekend is coming up. You've been waiting for this weekend for months. Try to put this CCMC stuff behind you and have some fun. After all, you *do* have a date with a hunk."

Alex groaned inwardly, yeah, a compulsive gambler hunk that I'm not sure I know or trust anymore, Alex thought to herself.

"I'm going home. I have a bad headache and I don't have any appointments for the rest of the day, do I?"

Bridgett shook her head no. "Get some rest. You need it."

"I'm just tired. I haven't been sleeping well this week. Nobody has. By the way, did Latetia give Captain Francois the name of that new board member? Do you know his name?"

"Nope, don't know, but I'll handle it. Get out of here. I'll take care of things for the rest of the day and I'll call you only if absolutely necessary. I promise."

"I've been called three days this week because of extreme emergencies. You'll need a better excuse than that." Alex was laughing as she got up from her desk. "See you tomorrow."

"Don't forget your ball gown. You need to pick it up Yvonne's," Bridgett reminded her on the way out.

"Got you. I'm out of here. Take care." Alex went straight

home, not caring to stop at Yvonne LaFleur for her ball gown.

**

Mitch woke up at eleven o'clock that morning. He had a terrible headache, and little recall of the previous evening, at least the latter part. He remembered his dinner with Alex and his late night visit from Frederico and the stranger. His burned forearm confirmed that visit. He also remembered his quick trip to Gulf Shores to gamble. He'd played blackjack at the Casino Magic, lost a bundle of money and his credit line. He recalled two men approaching him at the Biloxi Belle Casino, closing in on him while he was drinking Scotch. The men, gangsters no doubt, had "reminded him to deliver the goods by tomorrow night." After their threat, they'd become friendly and had a drink with him.

Mitch couldn't remember anything after that. I don't even remember getting in my car and driving home. God, I feel terrible, he thought as he staggered out of his bed to the nearby bathroom. He was repulsed at what he saw in the mirror. His left eye was purple and swollen shut. The right side of his face had a long jagged scratch down the side. Mitch became ill as he thought he must have been drugged not to remember getting beaten. It terrified him not to remember.

When he recovered several minutes later, he rushed to the window to look for his Lexus. It wasn't there. No wonder I don't remember driving home. He returned to his bed and remembered he had no car, no money, no info for Frederico and his gangster friends, and no means of escape. After dismally surveying his situation and seeing no plausible way out, he went to his bureau and pulled out his forty-five semi-automatic.

As he fingered his gun, he decided he really didn't have

many options. I'm going to be dead tonight anyway, he thought. They're going to kill me if I don't get some information from Alex. Mitch held his gun for a few minutes as he felt the cold steely barrel and fingered the etching of the serial number. Then he made his decision.

CHAPTER 18

Sunlight was streaming through her windows as the staccato ring of her house phone jolted Alex out of a deep sleep. As she grabbed for the receiver, her clock radio indicated it was after five. She'd been sleeping for over three hours. The unmistakable voice of Jack Francois greeted her groggy hello.

"You sleep? It's Happy Hour!" Francois joked.

"I left work a little early. I had a terrible headache, came home, took some aspirin and fell asleep. Feel much better now." Alex was surprised but she really did.

"Good. Listen up. I got the name of your newest board member, Jonathan Mercier. He's from somewhere in the Midwest, and now lives in Slidell. The interesting part of it is that he spent a fair amount of time in Virginia a few years back. He oversaw some kind of huge commercial real estate venture and made a ton of money. He bills himself as a venture capitalist"

Alex said, "What commercial development?"

"Damned if I know what development. I ain't no Forbes rep reporting on the lifestyles of the rich and famous. Anyway, that's all I know. He seems to be on the up and up, at least no rap sheet. I'm going to talk to some people at his office. As far as I'm concerned, this guy's too clean a package for my jaded brain. The fact he lived in Virginia when Bonnet was in medical school is interesting to me, especially since you said he looked like he hated Robert."

"Good. Let me know what you find and get some rest, Captain. It makes you feel much better," Alex yawned loudly, not meaning too, right in Jack's face. "Whoops, 'scuse me."

"Can't and Can't. Got a hot date with the voodoo Queen."

"Huh?? What're you talking about?"

"Late tonight there's a voodoo gathering out at the Lake near the Bayou St. John. Voodoos been hanging there since the beginning of time. I'm gonna look up a few old friends; see if they got a handle on CCMC. Should be real fun."

Alex immediately remembered the gathering. "Can I go with you? I think they know something about CCMC."

Francois' voice was curt. "Hell no. You out of your mind? These meetings aren't for the faint hearted. They're pretty ugly, sometimes gory, kill animals and run around naked. No way in hell." Francois' voice was firm. "But, what makes you think they know something?"

Alex hesitated, and then decided to tell him. "I went to the voodoo museum last night, and the woman there told me they did. I was thinking about going myself, but to be honest, I forgot about it after everything today. Take me."

"No way. I'll talk to you in the morning." Jack's voice was gruff and he clicked off the phone.

Alex spent a restless evening. She kept hoping Mitch would call, and then prayed he wouldn't. She vacillated between wanting to see him and never wanting to see him again. After thumbing through several magazines and toying with her TV remote, she took a long hot bath. She was just beginning to relax when the phone rang.

She answered it quickly, thinking it was Mitch.

"It's Robert. Nothing new has happened. I just wanted to check on you. Do you know anything?"

"Do you remember our new board member? He gave you some pretty angry looks while you were talking. He looks like he hates you."

"Jonathan Mercier? I know him, and does he hate me. Why?" Robert said curiously.

"Well, Francois said Mercier spent some time in Virginia, and the captain thought you may know him. He's checking all possible leads to figure out who's after you. How do you know Mercier and why does he hate you?"

Robert sighed into the phone before answering. "He thinks I killed his wife and baby."

"What?" Alex nearly jumped out of the tub and got water all over the bathroom.

"When I was a surgical resident in Virginia, his wife was in a terrible auto accident on I-64 near Charlottesville. She was eight months pregnant. She had massive internal injuries and a ruptured spleen. The steering wheel had crushed her chest and her trachea. She couldn't breathe. I did an emergency trach and surgery, but she didn't make it. She really never had a chance. Neither did her baby."

Alex was jolted back seven years. "Never mind, Robert. I remember this now. It was awful. You were upset for weeks afterward."

"It's one of those cases that have haunted me for years. I felt like a failure for a long, long time. Mercier still blames me for his wife's death. For months he wrote me letters, which threatened to sue me and have my license revoked, anything to cause me pain and difficulty. He tried to sue me, but it was thrown out as being frivolous. He tried to take me before the Board of Medicine in Virginia, but they would not hear the case. That made him angrier. He was in a rage for months."

"Could he still be in a rage after all of this time because of the accidents that happened to your patients?"

"I don't know. I certainly wouldn't think so. It's been almost seven years." Robert paused as he considered the possibility. Alex could picture him, thinking hard, his forehead wrinkled up. "I almost panicked when I saw him at the trustees meeting. I knew trouble could come from it, but I forgot about it until now."

"We need to talk to Jack." Alex could feel her heart thudding.

"Yeah, we will. First thing in the morning. If you need anything else, call me. Have a good night." Robert's voice was warm as he said good-bye.

After her talk with Robert, Alex became more restless. I'm going to the voodoo gathering, she decided. The heck with what Francois says. He'll never know I'm there. She considered calling Martin, but decided against it since she knew he'd try to talk her out of it. He'd already told her it wasn't safe. What the hell, she thought, I'll drive myself.

At eleven-thirty, dressed in black jeans, a black hooded

sweatshirt sweater and black boots, Alex drove her silver BMW down to the Bayou St. John near where it intersected Lake Pontchartrain. On the way, it occurred to her that she had no idea what she was going to do or how to talk to the Voodoos or any way to get to the person or persons who might know something about the CCMC incidents. I'll just have to play it by ear, she thought. It couldn't be but so bad, she admonished herself.

When Alex rounded the bend in the road, she immediately heard the sound of drums. She parked her car in a grove of trees next to a new Lexus. She convinced herself that anyone owning a Lexus couldn't possibly believe in voodoo. Alex walked towards the lake where she noticed a group of about two hundred people congregated around several bonfires.

She stayed hidden in the shadows under a tree and peered through the mist at the water. Between two fires stood a table, covered with a black cloth. A round white cloth covered the ground below the table.

It was cold and damp. Alex pulled her hooded sweatshirt closer around her body, and she stretched the hood to cover her face. The chill of the night air and the icy fear racing through her veins made her shiver.

She strained her eyes and peered through the mist on the lake and thought she saw a boat approaching. Whatever was in the water was illuminated by candlelight. Suddenly, people rushed to the shoreline where loud chanting erupted and numerous pots of fire were lit by a group of cloaked figures. The raft came closer. Alex was so intent on watching the scene in the fog and mist below; she didn't notice the huge black man approach her from behind. Suddenly, a quiet voice spoke directly into her ear.

"Who are you, and why are you here?" The voice was lilting, and the man spoke in a dialect she thought was Gumbo French.

Alex almost jumped out of her skin at the sounds of his voice. She was unable to speak as she looked at the huge man. She was terrified and afraid that she was going to pass out. She struggled for control and gawked at the big man. He wore a white billowing poet's shirt and tight, dark breeches. His skin was the darkest black she had ever seen, and his hair reached nearly to his knees. He had much of his hair tied up in a number of knots and braids secured by bones. The pupils of his eyes were dilated and glassy. The more Alex gazed at him, the more frightened she became. She was sure he man could hear her heart thudding in harmony with the drums.

The man eyed her steadily. "I asked you who you are. Speak or leave." His voice sounded foreboding, threatening.

"My name is Alexandra Destephano. I work at the Medical Center, and I have to find someone who knows about the voodoo that's been happening at the hospital. Can you tell me?"

"I know nothing. Leave here. You're not welcome. You're not one of us." The man, his pronouncement ominously final, pointed towards the cars.

"The lady from the voodoo museum told me to come." Alex persisted as she shook so hard her teeth chattered. "She said I could learn more about the voodoo curse at the medical center from the people who were here. Who are you?" Alex was shocked that she was even able to speak. She couldn't figure out if she was shaking from fear or the cold air.

The man just stared at her. His eyes were enormous. The whites of them almost blinded her in the darkness. "I'm a witch doctor. My name's Dr. John. I serve the High Priestess. Leave here at once. I demand it. If you do not leave immediately, we will kill you."

Alex watched Dr. John move steadily towards the lakefront. She hid behind the tree when he turned to look for her. She watched until he disappeared into the crowd and breathed a sigh of relief when he was gone. She turned her attention to the crowd. Suddenly the tempo of the music increased, the drums beat faster. A group of women stripped off their clothing and began to dance naked. Several of them donned white camisoles and circled the bonfire, their movements undulating in the firelight. Alex was mesmerized by the female dancers. The dancers escalated their movements to the driving drum beat. Alex could hear them panting and could clearly see the rising and falling of their breasts as they moved around the bonfires.

Suddenly, the music stopped. Alex moved closer and hid as best she could. The barge on the river had reached the shore. Alex could vaguely make out some activity aboard the barge. It was difficult to see through the mist. She then noticed an old black man sitting on a cylinder made of thin cypress staves hooped with brass and headed by a sheepskin. Alex thought it was a makeshift drum. With two sticks the old man beat a monotonous ra-ta-ta, ra-ta-ta, ra-ta-ta. On his left, a large black woman sat on a low stool beating another tone with two long bones. A third mulatto woman accompanied them on the other side of the drum. She began beating a higher, faster beat on some sort of steel instrument. It was an eerie sight, almost supernatural, to see the trio banging on drums with animal bones. The sounds that emanated from the drums were queer and frightening and unlike any Alex had ever heard. It was spine-chilling. Alex stared, beyond belief, at the sight, as she became captivated by the music and sounds. It sounded like a movie build-up in a horror film. The women in white had formed a semi-circle around the altar table and continued to undulate suggestively to the rhythm. Alex did not know who the women were, but they were obviously important. She remembered the camera in her cell phone and snapped several pictures of the sights. The sounds continued, ra-ta-ta, ra-ta-ta, ra-ta-ta, while a woman and two men descended from the barge and walked toward the altar. The crowd, in rapt silence, paid homage to their Queen. The crowd swayed back and forth to the ra-ta-ta, ra-ta-ta beat. The scene was frightening and sinister.

It was impossible to guess the age of the voodoo Queen. She was ageless. Alex, struck by the immensity of the power the Queen commanded, was also awed by her magnificent presence. She was regal, majestic. The Queen wore a full cotton skirt of many colors and a bright green blouse. She had gold hoop earrings in her ears and numerous gold chains around her neck and waist. Her hair was bound up under a brightly colored turban which added height to her statuesque beauty. The voodoo Queen was royal, stately and beautiful in her presence. Her skin was a cross between the color of honey and cafe au lait. Alex was awestruck and could hardly look away from the Queen's face. She was captivated in the moment.

Sounds of exultation broke from the crowd as the woman, the High Priestess of New Orleans, mumbled something and threw powders and liquid at the crowd from a calabash in her hand. As she continued to mutter and gestured upward with her arms, the crowd became more and more frenzied, ecstatic and euphoric.

The Queen raised her hand to the drummer as he dismounted from his drum and withdrew an immense snake from the basket at his feet. He wildly brandished the snake above his head. The crowd roared with pleasure and began to chant. He handed the snake to the Queen. She talked and whispered to it. At every word the reptile, with an undulating body and darting tongue, seemed to acknowledge and relish the power the Queen asserted over it. The crowd crossed their hands on their chests and began to moan, a long, sonorous, lament, and moved in unison from left to right. It was without a doubt the most fearsome sound Alex had ever heard. She felt as if her face would burn up but her body was frozen in place The crowd chanted, "Voudou. Voudou Magnian," over and over again. The Queen continued to flaunt the snake, finally compelling the reptile to stand upright exposing ten inches of its body. The snake danced alone for several minutes.

Alex was fascinated and awestruck. The crowd continued to moan and chant as the Queen began to twirl the snake around her head and over the crowd. She forced the snake to wiggle and writhe over and over, around the circle. The crowd uttered the words, "Voudou, Voudou," repeatedly. Suddenly, and without warning, the Queen twirled the snake around by its head and with great skill cast it into the blazing fire. A yell, that no words could truly describe, arose from the crowd. It was inhuman... feral... fearful. The drums began again, and crude musical instruments played by the Voodoos contributed to the bedlam. The sounds became louder and louder until Alex could hardly think. It was as if her brain and her body had been taken over. Chaos reigned. Alex thought she'd entered the chorus of Dante's Hell in the heart of darkness in deepest Africa but for the life of her, she could not move.

Suddenly, up sprang a magnificent specimen of human flesh - a beautiful, lithe, tall black woman with a body which waved and undulated like the snake - a perfect goddess from the jungles of Africa. The woman confined herself to a spot not more than two feet in space and began to sway on one and the other side. Gradually, the undulating motion controlled her body from the ankles to the hips. She tore a white handkerchief from her head, apparently a cue for the huge witch doctor to join her in the circle. The two undulated together, in pure passion and ecstasy. Both were naked but Alex didn't think that any of it was about sex, it was more about possession. Maybe evil possession. Nevertheless Alex remained spellbound. She couldn't have moved if she'd willed herself. She was so engrossed she didn't feel the chill bumps all over her body. The dance continued for what seemed an infinite length of time. Finally, the Queen raised her hand. The dancers disappeared.

The only sound was the continuous ra-ta-ta, ra-ta-ta, ra-ta-ta of the drums. The Queen moved herself into position behind the altar. Alex watched, fascinated, as a large cauldron was put into the fire; it was filled with water and powders which were put in by an old man, who jabbered something in a strange dialogue Alex couldn't understand. A young quadroon girl moved to the center of the altar behind the cauldron and sang a mournful song in an unknown tongue while she put seasonings in the cauldron. Then a box was placed on the table from which a black snake was removed and immediately cut in three pieces to represent the black Trinity. The Queen, the old man, and the young quadroon girl each threw a piece of the snake, still writhing, into the pot. Steam, or the snake, made a horrific hissing sound.

Immediately a new chant began: "Mamzelle, la Queen

chauff ez ca." The crowd continued the chant until the Queen brought forth a cat whose throat she immediately slit. Blood spurted out from its neck arteries over the white cloth on the table and on the ground. Blood also spurted onto the watchers. The crowd went wild with the sight of blood, and they reached out to touch it and spread it over their naked bodies. The queen cast the cat into the cauldron. Again there was a terrible cry and a great hissing sound. Next a white woman, dressed in white, danced towards the altar. She carried a black rooster. The black rooster was dazzling against her white gown. The woman danced with the rooster in the firelight. The crowd, chanting, continued to sway back and forth. After another repetition of the chorus, the Queen tied the feet and head of the rooster together and tossed it alive into the pot. Another hissing sound. A second rooster was bought forward and immediately beheaded - its headless body moved awkwardly as it bled profusely on the white cloth. The rooster's awkward body movements gave the illusion of a dance and it seemed to keep time to the chant. The crowd continued to sing until the rooster finally died. Sounds of exultation emanated from the crowd. The voodoos raised their hands to the heavens as the rooster, too, was cast into the pot by the witch doctor.

The Queen then ordered the remaining crowd to undress. Her followers stripped off their clothes. Some of the women danced with large white handkerchiefs which they raised towards the sky as they moved from head to toe like snakes. A select group joined hands and danced around the cauldron. They began singing and chanting the chorus, "C'est l'amour, oui Maman c'est l'amour," over and over and over. The sight wasn't human. The music, the drums, the blood, and the chanting created a macabre sight as two hundred bodies, men and woman of every color writhed erotically and gestured to each other. Alex was gruesomely fascinated. She couldn't tear her eyes away from the sight below her.

Finally the chant slowed and the dancing ceased. The crowd formed a semi-circle around the cauldron and again began to moan and hum simultaneously and watched the approach of the witch doctor with his final gift to the Queen. He came dancing naked into the firelight, the light from the flames glistening over his body. Firelight danced off his gold chains and reflected his ebony color. He was carrying a white sack. His hair hung to his buttocks, and his enormous erect phallus was clearly visible as he raised the sack toward the heavens in ultimate sacrifice. The crowd continued to chant and moan incessantly in rhythm with the drums. After a period of time, the witch doctor placed the white sack on the altar for his Queen. She unwrapped it, and held up a new born baby. The crowd went wild with ecstasy. The Queen smiled in approval and held the infant up for all to see while the little old man handed her a clean, glistening knife.

That was it. Alex was jerked back into reality. She screamed in terror and started running toward the altar to save the infant.

As she made her way through the dancing bodies, a hard arm grabbed her around her neck, stifled her screams, and caused her to lose consciousness for a few moments. The man was large, his body completely covered in black. His grip paralyzed her. She couldn't breathe. Alex gasped for air. She tried to fight him, but his intense strength made her efforts useless. She kicked at his legs and grabbed at his head as she thought briefly that he had a ponytail under his hood. As her assailant continued to drag her up the hill toward the clearing, Alex fought frantically. The man never said a word, but increased his grip around her neck. After what seemed to be an interminable length of time, the grip on her neck relaxed. Another man, also dressed in dark clothes, had attacked her assailant from behind, and knocked him down with a large tree limb. Alex felt a severe blow to her shoulder and arm as she was tossed down. She heard a long string of curse words as the two men began to fight. She watched, dazed, as the men circled each other repeatedly. Finally, her assailant fled, with two other men in pursuit. Only then did Alex turn to her rescuer. She was incoherent with fear. Her rescuer also wore a long cloak and his face was hooded. Was she to be exchanged as a gift? All sort of ludicrous possibilities ran through Alex's mind. Was she to be the next ritualistic sacrifice? The hooded man came toward her, grabbed her, and hurled her forward.

As Alex's eyes adjusted to the darkness and mist, she saw the small, furious eyes of Jack Francois.

"What in the fuck are you doing here?" Francois hissed at her. His face was livid. "This place is dangerous, a hell hole. You almost got yourself killed. You were stupid to come out here alone. These people are all drugged up and crazy, not to mention that man who's been eyeing you all night -- You are a dumb, crazy bitch," he uttered under his breath.

Even though Alex was angry at Francois for talking to her like that, she was so glad to see him she almost kissed him. Instead, she said as best she could, "Captain, they were going to kill that baby. Oh my God, that's murder. We have to go back, we have to. Can we go back and get it?" Alex's voice was scratchy and her throat was sore.

"The baby's fine. My men rescued her. Let's get out of here before they cook us in that damn pot." Alex needed no encouragement. She bolted, her right arm sagging at her side.

After they had gotten near the cars, Jack asked, "How are you feeling? You don't look so good." Francois examined Alex critically as he opened the car door. As the light from the car blanketed her, it was obvious she was injured. She was pale and sweating.

Indeed, Alex's shoulder was on fire with pain. "I think my shoulder may be broken. It hurts like crazy." She was sweating profusely even though the air around her was cool.

"Give me your car keys. I'll have one of my men drive your car home. I'm taking you to the emergency department at CCMC."

Alex started to protest, but seeing the look in the captain's eyes, she decided to save her energy. "Okay," she relented meekly.

The Captain assisted Alex to his unmarked silver Cadillac, outfitted with the very latest in police technology. Jack was obviously proud of his wheels. He looked at her carefully and said, "Would it be better if I called an ambulance?"

"Heavens, no. If anybody knew I was out here at a voodoo meeting, I'd get fired - again - twice in one day is more than I can handle. I'll be okay." In truth Alex's shoulder was killing her and she was feeling woozy and afraid she might vomit. She couldn't wait to get to the emergency department.

"Jack, who was that man who assaulted me? He had a killer grip around my neck. Think he was trying to strangle me?" Alex barely recognized the sound of her own voice, it was so scratchy.

"I don't know. I don't know if my men caught up with him or not. He was a big SOB and strong as hell. The man's a physical monster. Do you remember anything else about him?"

"No, not really. I think he was white and had a ponytail and I think I'm going to pass out." Alex stopped talking.

When the captain looked over at her, he noticed that she was sweating profusely and had passed out. He checked her pulse and it was racing. She's going into shock. I got to get her there fast. He pulled his siren out and sped towards CCMC. Damn her, he thought. Just like a dumb woman but, of course, he had to admire her spunk, even if what she had done was stupid.

The care at CCMC in the emergency department was prompt. There were no other patients. Her shoulder was broken, separated actually. It was after 4:00 a.m. when Francois dropped Alex off at her house. He walked her to the door and made her a pot of tea. He even waited until she was in the bed before he left.

"Jack," she murmured quietly. "Are there any messages on my voice mail or my cell?"

"Nope, not a one. That's good news. CCMC must be quiet tonight."

"Of course it is. We were just there. Yes, that's good. But you know Captain, I haven't heard from Mitch today. That's unusual." Alex drifted off to sleep.

Before Jack Francois left Alex's home, he looked around and was impressed at the beauty and elegance of the furnishings. He called her office and left Bridgett a voice mail message, saying Alex would check in at noon. He left Alex a note telling her he had called Bridgett. He also called the station and arranged for a unit to sit outside her apartment for the rest of the night. The ponytailed stranger could come after her again, a recurring thought that concerned Jack. He racked his brain to figure out why the ponytail was after Alex.

On the way home, his heart thudded with fear with what had almost happened. Francois had eyed Alex earlier in the evening, and had almost missed her abduction by the stranger. I'd like to know who that bastard is and how he fits into this puzzle. It's a shame the bastard got away from my men. Francois was frustrated and scared as he drove through the cool, New Orleans night. Who in the hell was the huge SOB with the ponytail?

CHAPTER 19

Alex awakened at eleven in the morning to a furious pounding on her door. As she staggered out of bed, pain seared through her arm and shoulder. She gritted her teeth as she attempted to put on her robe. The pounding continued until she opened the door. Robert stood in the alcove.

His face flooded with relief as he saw her. He pulled her into his arms and hugged her.

"You're crushing my shoulder. It hurts bad enough without you squeezing me to death," Alex attempted to joke while trying to hide her pain, but felt she was unsuccessful.

"I've been worried about you. I saw Francois several hours ago, and he told me what happened. Called you, but there wasn't an answer so I decided to just come over here. How're you feeling?"

Alex yawned. "I must have been really knocked out not to hear the phone. Truthfully, Robert, it hurts like hell. I'm going to have a hard time wearing my ball gown with this sling on." Alex panicked as she realized she still hadn't heard from Mitch.

Robert noticed the look on her face. "What? You look worried."

"I haven't heard from a friend for a couple of days. Let me check my voice mail and cell. Maybe he left a message this morning."

Alex listened to her answering service and checked her voice mail, but Mitch hadn't called. She felt herself becoming increasingly agitated as her concern for him increased.

Robert was aware of her increasing anxiety as she paced around her dining room. "Maybe we should talk about it a bit."

Alex wasn't sure she wanted to discuss her weekend date with her ex-husband and said instead, "How 'bout some coffee? I need to get up and get going."

"I'll make coffee and some breakfast for you while you start getting ready, but let me catch you up on this morning. You missed the board of trustees meeting, but not much happened. They're supportive of the hospital and don't understand Governor Raccine's actions or behavior. Several of them expressed overt anger with the Governor. By the way, you'll be happy to know Don didn't suggest the board fire you."

Alex gave him a wry smile, and her eyes lit up. "Terrific. I'm pleased to hear that. Anything else happen?"

"No, not really. Today is Ron Davis' funeral. It's at 1:30 at Saint Anne's Church and Diane's funeral follows at 3:30 at Saint Bartholomew Parish. Ron's burial is at Lafayette Cemetery, but Diane's is in Old Metairie. Can you make it?"

Alex sighed and shook her head, her face reflected the misery of the week. "Have to make it. Why's Diane's funeral so soon?"

Robert's face was sad and he said slowly, "I think her husband just wanted to get it over with. I don't think he ever thought she had a chance of surviving. Besides, I'm sure that both families want them buried before the weekend when Mardi Gras is in full swing. The traffic will be even more horrendous then."

"I suppose so. It's so distressing, all of it. It's going to be even sadder when we actually bury them." Alex had tears in her eyes. It was a poignant moment for both of them. "Do you know if Don Montgomery is going?"

"I would certainly hope so. I know Dr. Ashley and Elizabeth are planning on coming together. Would you like to go with me? If you hurry up and get dressed, we can grab a bite for lunch on the way. Better still, I'll make us an omelet while you get dressed. Do you need any help because of your shoulder? I'm available." He looked a little embarrassed.

Alex looked sharply at him to see if he was serious. He apparently was. She was a bit chagrined. Before she could respond, he said, "You know, I'm a doctor." He was blushing by this time and his tone was officious.

"And, I'm a nurse. I can manage. If I need you, I'll call, though."

After her shower, a painful ordeal at best, Alex decided on a black loosely-fitting linen dress. It was simple in design and a strand of pearls was all the jewelry she needed to complete it. She selected some black heels and critically checked herself in the mirror. She decided she looked OK, not great. She was pale from the pain and her normally glorious reddish-blonde hair had lost its normal luster. After several attempts which caused agonizing pain, Alex realized she was unable to button her dress. She went to her closet to try and find a simpler outfit to wear, but all her clothes seemed to have similar fastenings. Finally, she went for help.

When Alex reached the kitchen, Robert was pouring orange juice into two crystal juice glasses. Two fresh mushroom and Andouille sausage omelets were waiting in the pan beside some grits on the stove. Rich New Orleans coffee with chicory completed the menu and it smelled great.

"Grits are for you," Robert quipped cheerfully. "I still can't eat them."

Alex shook her head at him and said woefully, "Guess I'll never make a Virginian out of you. Eating grits and going to the rivah are fundamental social requirements. Do you think you could help me button my dress?"

"Oh, I see, so you do need some help." Robert's eyes were twinkling at her. "I'll be glad to assist. Let me check that dressing as well. It looks a bit crooked to me. I may need to adjust it."

Alex grinned at him. "Just keep it professional, please!"

There was little conversation as they ate. Both seemed caught up in each other's presence so they only exchanged polite conversation. She felt comfortable and awkward with Robert. It seemed strange, but she sort of liked it. She decided to take a risk and talk about Mitch.

"Do you know Mitch Landry?"

Robert looked surprised at her question. "Sure. I knew him when we were kids. Haven't seen him much since undergrad LSU. Why?"

Alex was silent for a few minutes as she debated whether she should confide her fears about Mitch.

Robert continued and tried to make it easier for her. "I know you've been seeing Mitch. Is that what you wanted to tell me?"

"No, not really. Do you know whether he gambles?"

Robert looked at her strangely. "Gambles? You mean like at the casinos?"

"Yes, I guess. Francois told me yesterday Mitch was a compulsive gambler. I've been seeing him for a few months, and I've never seen evidence to suggest that, and it threw me for a loop. Anyway, Francois thinks he may be in trouble with the mob, or somebody for a bunch of money. What concerns me is that I've noticed several men loitering around when we've been out. I haven't heard from him for a while, and I am a little nervous about it."

Robert thoughtfully scratched his chin and said, "Well, I've heard rumors, but I don't know for sure about the gambling." Robert stopped speaking for a moment and seemed to be remembering something.

"What?"

"Oh, nothing really. It seems like I did hear a couple of years ago that he'd been treated for compulsive gambling. Tell me more about the men that you have noticed hanging around. What are they like?"

Alex could picture them vividly in her mind. "One's short, stocky and smokes a cigar. The other's tall and has a ponytail."

She dropped her fork in recognition. "I'm sure the man that grabbed me last night had a ponytail also. If there's a connection, then Mitch's somehow involved in the CCMC events. We've got to call Jack."

She ran out of the kitchen to get Francois' numbers . He

was out of his office and his cell phone said, "the party you are trying to reach is unavailable." She left her number on his beeper and cell. As she returned to the kitchen to finish her coffee, Alex continued to think back over her conversations with Mitch and became more convinced that he was involved in the events at the hospital. It was an upsetting thought, for many reasons.

She finally said to Robert, who'd been watching her carefully. "I left my number with 911 on Jack's cell.

"I'm sure he'll call soon," said Robert as he took a forkful of omelet.

Within seconds the phone rang. It was Francois. Alex didn't give him time to speak.

"Francois...Jack. Thanks for calling me back so soon. I think you're right about Mitch. I'm so worried. I haven't heard from him in two days. That's not like him....."

"Slow down, Alex," he said in a hint of his old self.

"Sorry, I'm just so worried. It just hit me. I think something might have happened..."

"I'll send a car over to his place. How's the shoulder?"

"Hurts like hell!"

"Lucky you didn't get killed! Listen, I got to go. I'll get back with you."

CHAPTER 20

At 1:20 p.m. Robert and Alex arrived at Saint Ann's Parish Church for Ron Davis' funeral. The church was jammed with hordes of people. Alex recognized ten or so staff members from CCMC as well as several board members. She suspected much of the crowd were curious onlookers, most likely thrill-seekers. Alex also spotted Francois and recognized several of his staff who had worked the nursing units for the past few days. She continued to survey the crowd and felt certain there were other state police as well as DEA staff about.

Alex and Robert seated themselves in the same pew with Dr. Ashley, Elizabeth, and several other CCMC physicians and administrators. Elizabeth was stunning in a black suit which set off her dark hair and startling green eyes. Dr. Ashley looked impeccable in a dark suit. He smiled and acknowledged both of them as they were seated.

Don Montgomery was conspicuously absent. Out of the corner of her eye, Alex noticed Jonathan Mercier seated several rows behind them. His eyes looked like cold grey steel and were focused directly on the back of Robert's head. Alex shivered a little after noticing his gaze, but said nothing to Robert about his presence.

Ron's widow, Sarah, was very sad but seemed to be doing well as she followed the casket down the aisle in the knave of the church. She had each of her small children by a hand. The little boy looked solemn; his dark eyes enormous while his little sister, probably about three, brought smiles to the mourners' faces as she waved to them while she walked down the church aisle. The funeral mass proceeded without mishap. Alex and Robert followed the mourners out of Saint Ann's Church into the bright sunshine. They joined the CCMC group who were talking quietly while they waited to speak with Ron's widow.

Sarah had just approached Robert when they were accosted by reporters. A female reporter approached Robert Bonnet and extended her microphone to him.

"Dr. Bonnet, how do you feel about Dr. Davis' death? Do you feel responsible? Word has it that all the accidents at CCMC are related to you and involved your patients. Was Dr. Davis an unplanned event?"

Robert was speechless, stunned as were the others from CCMC. No one spoke.

Suddenly, out of nowhere, Jonathan Mercier appeared. "I'm a member of the board of trustees at Crescent Center Medical Center."

Immediately the reporters focused on him.

Mercier continued. "I can officially say, on the record, that I'm concerned with Dr. Bonnet's practice, and the 'accidents' or whatever they are, that've occurred to his patients. I plan to have his practice investigated immediately by the Louisiana State Board of Medicine and would suggest that those affected pursue legal actions, if not malpractice, then civil suits against Dr. Bonnet."

Suddenly, Sarah's gentle voice interrupted Mercier. The reporters turned quickly. Mrs. Davis said quietly, "Dr. Bonnet's not responsible for Ron's death. As a matter of fact, Robert was Ron's mentor, and taught him many things about medicine. It is because of Dr. Bonnet that we moved to Louisiana and CCMC. Dr. Bonnet was my husband's valued and dear friend. My husband's death was a tragic accident and nothing more. Now, if you wouldn't mind, I'd like all of you to leave so we can continue on with the burial. Thank you." Sarah turned to Robert and hugged him. She said, "Ron loved and valued you as his friend and colleague." Robert returned her hug, and Alex watched as Francois approached the press group.

Francois was livid, his face bright red, and he was gesturing wildly. Alex could swear she saw smoke billowing from his ears. "You heard the lady, get out of her. For God's sake, this is a funeral. Get outta here or I'll arrest you for unlawful assembly."

Alex watched as the press scattered and Jack murmured, "What a bunch of nosy bastards."

She smiled brightly at Francois. "Thanks. Where'd Mercier go?"

"To hell, I hope." Francois blurted and abruptly left.

Robert was quiet and withdrawn on the way to Diane Bradley's funeral. His face was somber. As they crossed Tulane Avenue, on the way to St. Bart's Church, Alex said quietly, "Don't let Mercier bother you. He doesn't have any authority, and he's only speaking as an individual. As soon as it's known he's carrying a torch of destruction and out to get you, all of his complaints will be dismissed."

Robert's voice was forlorn. "I'm not so sure. These things are always damaging. Even if the Board of Medicine finds no fault with my practice, I'll be suspect. I'll lose face with my patients and colleagues. Anyway, I don't want to talk about it now." He dismissed her reply with a wave of his hand. Alex touched his hand as a gesture of comfort.

***

St. Bartholomew's Church was also filled to capacity. Many CCMC nurses were present. Diane's husband, parents, and young 'tween daughter were consumed with grief and were escorted down the aisle for the funeral mass.

The priest had been Diane's priest all of her life, had heard her first confession, and had officiated at her marriage. He knew her very well. He was more personal than Father Henry had been and told several amusing anecdotes about Diane, her childhood, and her family. The service, while personal, seemed sadder to Alex, and she felt an enormous lump in her throat the entire time. At times she wasn't sure she could even breath, the service was so emotional, so tearful. It all seemed so unfair, so useless, and for what? That was the question that plagued her and seemed to eat away at her insides.

After Diane's interment, Alex and Robert stopped for coffee at a small coffee house near Alex's house. She listened patiently while Robert reviewed the recent events at CCMC. Eventually, Robert looked sadly at Alex and said, "Maybe that reporter was right, who knows? Maybe I am responsible and maybe I should give up medicine."

"That's ridiculous, Robert. We know you're involved because you're being singled out. Remember, though, the emergency department incidents, when Ron and Diane died, were specifically directed at CCMC. Ron and Diane were not your patients."

Robert's face was grave, his eyes tearful as he responded,

"No, they were my friends. Which is worse?"

"I don't know," Alex responded dismally. "Want to come over for a while?"

"No, I need to go see Sarah Davis and her children. You know I'm her son's godfather?"

"No." Alex's voice was quiet. "Would you like me to go with you?"

Robert's practiced medical eye searched her face. "You look a bit pale. You're having a lot of pain? You are moving as though you are."

Alex replied bravely. "Not that much."

"I'll drop you at home and call you later."

CHAPTER 21

Alex checked her voice mail as soon as she got home. There was only one message from her grandfather, but there was nothing from Mitch. She checked her face in the mirror and groaned and then changed into her bathrobe as best she could. Then, one armed, she went into the kitchen where she made herself soup and a sandwich. The phone rang as she was sitting down to eat, so she went to answer it. It was Francois.

"How're you feeling? You weren't looking too good at the funeral."

"Okay, Jack. More emotionally drained than anything. The funerals were just so sad, sad beyond all belief." She paused, then said, her voice hesitant, "I still haven't heard from Mitch."

"Can't find him either. He's not at home and I've had my men outside his place all day long. Any ideas where he could be?"

"Did you check his work sites at Lafayette and little Arcadia? Sometimes he spends the night up there."

"Nah, I'll have the locals check it out. Is it unusual for you not to hear from him?"

"We talk every day. I'd expect to hear from him now, since the Extravaganza is tomorrow night. If he calls, I'll find out where he is. I'm worried about him."

"Yeah. I'd like to talk to him. I've assigned a unit to sit outside your house. Don't want your buddy to come back for you tonight."

"What? You think he would?" Alex's heart began to beat

quickly. She hadn't thought of another visit from the ponytailed stranger.

"Don't know, not taking any chances, though."

Alex had never thought she could be in danger. The thought of the man coming back just creeped her out and scared her to death. She was sure he would kill her this time. She could hardly breathe or speak from the fear.

"Alex, are you still there"

"Jack, what do you think the chances are he would come back?"

"I don't know. He might be involved with Mitch. The fact he went after you last night, assuming it's the same man, makes me think he's after you now. If we can't find Mitch, he probably can't either, and maybe he thinks he can get from you whatever he wanted from Mitch. Am I making sense?"

Alex was silent for several moments, thinking. "Unfortunately, yes. Think the ponytail man was using Mitch to get information about CCMC?"

"Maybe, possibly. I think the ponytail's involved with what's happening at CCMC and we know Mercier's after Robert. The dumbass made that pretty clear today. What an asshole. Been trying to connect the two, but I can't. I don't know who the ponytail is, at least not yet... what I do know if that he is a strong son of a bitch."

"What about the short fat man with the cigar? Know how he fits in?"

"Got an idea it's Frederico Petrelli, a gang boss from Chicago. Runs the gambling operation here. I'm not positive though. It's just my theory."

"You sound pretty certain. This is getting more complex." Alex's felt her senses were dulled and doubted her brain was as quick as usual.

Francois hesitated for a moment and then responded. "Well, I got some other theories. Need to find Mitch though to test 'em out, that is, if Mitch's to be found."

"Do you think Mitch's okay?" Her chest felt heavy with fear.

"I think he's running. If he's smart, he's running. You sit tight and stay safe. My man's outside."

"I promise. I'll talk to you later. Keep in touch. Let me know if you hear from Mitch."

"OK. Ciao."

Alex ate her supper while she thought about her conversation with Francois. She began to worry incessantly about Mitch and wondered for the first time if he was dead. It seemed strange no one could find him. She kept trying to figure out the relationship between Mitch, Ponytail, the fat man, and Robert until she thought she would scream, but nothing came. Alex knew there was a connection, but she needed the missing pieces. She cleaned up the kitchen and looked at the clock. It was 8:00 p.m. in New Orleans, 7:00 in Virginia. She decided to phone her grandparents. Her grandmother answered.

Alex almost cried when she heard her grandmother's voice.

It seemed so long since she had talked to her, although she routinely called her once a week.

"Grand it's so good to hear your voice. Seems like forever since I talked to you. How're you feeling?" Alex's voice was choked up.

"I'm fine, Alex. But you certainly aren't. You sound down."

Alex couldn't reply as she blinked back her tears. She knew her grandmother would be upset if she knew how badly Alex felt.

"We've been keeping up with the New Orleans news. Sounds like the medical center's having a bad run of it. Have the police tracked down who's responsible?"

"No. They've some theories, but to tell you the truth, everything here's pretty chaotic. This voodoo business is unbelievable. Can you imagine using some religion to cloak a bunch of crimes?"

"Pretty smart, if you ask me. Of course, it'd only work in New Orleans. Somebody really wants to ruin CCMC." Just hearing Kathryn Lee's sympathetic voice brought tears to Alex's eyes.

"It's been terrible. Today Robert and I attended the funerals of two of the people shot in the emergency room. I've wanted to cry so hard all day."

Kathryn Lee listened quietly and allowed her granddaughter to vent her emotions, then she said gently, "I'm sure you did. Maybe you should. Why not come home for a few days?"

"I'm going to, soon. As soon as things settle down here. I'm coming for at least a week. How are the horses?"

"Beautiful, great, healthy. Did you say you went to the funeral with Robert?" Grand was a sharp as ever.

"Yeah, he's had a rough time. You know Grace Raccine's his patient?" Alex began.

"How's Grace?"

"About the same. She's still not responding, but what happened was so traumatic, it may take her a few weeks to come out"

"How's her cancer?"

"Don't know for sure, but they can't start any chemo or radiation until she's alert. It'd be too hard to monitor her."

"I'm sure the Governor's beside himself."

"He is, but seems to be handling it well. You know he moved her from CCMC to East Jefferson, don't you?"

Kathryn replied, "News covered that pretty well. Did it cause any hard feelings between him and Robert?"

"No, Robert was completely understanding. Things at CCMC are pretty bad, Grand. It seems like a conspiracy against us and the physicians are jumping ship as fast as they can and taking their patients with them. Meanwhile, other patients are afraid to come for care because of the Voodoo. Can you believe we are cursed or hexed or whatever it is?"

Grand was pensive as she thought for a moment and said, "Yes, I believe it because it is happening. I guess we should never discount people's culture and heritage, you know?"

"Yeah, I know. I guess I can't blame them. Finances are plummeting and Don Montgomery's afraid we'll go out of business."

"That's exactly what whoever's behind this want to happen. Clear as a bell to me. What about this woman who was burned by her EKG machine. How'd that happen?"

Alex was stunned. "Was that on the news?"

"CNN at six this evening, along with the clip of their reporter hassling Robert at the funeral. You think Robert's involved with these accidents?" Her voice was fraught with concern. Grand had always had a special place for Robert and had been very sad when he and Alex had divorced. She had often said they were the perfect couple, a match made in heaven.

"I don't, yet there are too many coincidences for me to remain comfortable. Both of the patients are Robert's. Plus, Ron Davis and Diane Bradley were good friends. Robert's the godfather of Ron Davis' seven year old son. He feels responsible for the children now and he's down, depressed and sad about everything."

Kathryn Lee didn't speak for a few moments, and then said, "Knowing Robert, he will take his godfather responsibilities very seriously. Do you think there's a plot against him? Is someone using him to put CCMC out of business?"

"I don't understand it all, but I do think there's a plot or at least a connection. But who would use Voodoo to sabotage a huge medical center?"

"I would say someone who is pretty smart and had planned well. Probably have some inside help somewhere," Grand responded.

"Yep, you are probably right. Just hope it's solved quickly. Do you remember the man whose pregnant wife died in Virginia a few years ago? She was Robert's patient, and her car skidded and wrecked on Afton Mountain?"

"I vaguely remember it. She died during surgery, didn't she? I remember that Robert was devastated."

"Yes. Her husband, Jonathan Mercier, is the man you saw on the news tonight making threats against Robert. Still blames Robert for her death. He could be out to ruin him."

"So you think Mercier is part of this conspiracy against Robert and CCMC?"

"I can't prove it, but I think so. The police don't have enough information to question him yet."

"Why's Mercier in Louisiana, for heaven's sakes?"

"I don't really know. He is wealthy, a venture capitalist or something. He was doing business in Virginia when his wife was killed. To top it all off, he's on the CCMC board of trustees." Alex's voice broke in exasperation.

"The plot thickens, as they say. You okay, Alex? You're safe, aren't you?" Alex could hear suspicion in her grandmother's voice.

"I'm fine, just in emotional overdrive after this week, and today. But, I'll be fine. How's my mother doing?" Alex could barely talk over the lump in her throat.

"She's the same. No change. Sure you're not keeping something from me?" Her grandmother's instinct seemed to be working overtime.

"I'm really okay. Is Granddad there? He left me a message."

"I'm right here, darling. Been listening in so I have a fewer questions for you. Hang up, Kathryn, so I can hear Alex better."

"You old goat, Alex teased." "How dare you listen to my conversations?"

As Kathryn Lee hung up the phone, she said, "Take care, Alex, and come home soon. We miss you. Besides, now I'm worried about you."

"I'll be fine. I love you, too, Grand. Take care of yourself. See you soon."

After Kathryn Lee hung up, her grandfather exploded. "Alexandra, what in hell's going on there? Something sounds rotten. This shit is getting worse and worse," her grandfather demanded, his voice gruff and demanding.

Alex laughed. "Yep, Adam, we got some real rotten stuff. Worse part is, I don't have anything solid on what's happening, and neither does anybody else."

"Tell me everything," Adam Patrick Lee demanded, "from the top."

Alex could see her grandfather in his study as he lounged in his green recliner, his favorite dog Beau at his feet and his Jack Daniels in a glass next to him. Piles of legislation stacked everywhere around the handsomely appointed room. She shook her head as she remembered her grandmother's tirades every time she entered the room. It brought a much needed smile to her face.

"Alex, would you talk, what's the hold up?" Her grandfather voice was impatient and demanding.

Alex related the entire story to her grandfather and included the part about Frederico and the ponytailed man, but excluded the attack on her, and Francois' concern about her safety. She also didn't mention Mitch or any part he might play.

Her grandfather listened carefully, without interruption. When she mentioned that Governor Raccine was planning to close the medical center, her grandfather exploded again with a blast of fiery expletives. "That's the dumbest damned thing I've ever heard. A governor closing the finest medical care facility in the State, not to mention it's a world-class medical center. The loss of revenues would kill him and cut deeply into budget!"

Adam paused for a moment and then continued, "Yep, you got something really bad going on, maybe even crooked. What motive could Raccine possibly have for closing CCMC?"

"Well, he claimed it was affecting tourism, and, of course, it's Mardi Gras, the biggest tourism season on the year. He suggested that people were finding New Orleans an unsafe place to visit based on the voodoo scare at the medical center. Apparently, his tourism office reported substantial cancellations for Mardi Gras festivities."

"That is unadulterated bullshit. You know it, and so do I.

That would make more people come to New Orleans, especially all of the sickos and perverts. This story is selling hotel rooms. It will draw tourists, especially at Mardi Gras, particularly if you threw a few ghosts in there There's something bigger here. Is he just upset because of Grace?" Congressman Lee asked.

Alex could see her grandfather's furrowed face as he contemplated the situation. "I'm sure he's concerned. It's especially bad for us since the Raccine's usually go to East Jeff anyway. First time they've come to CCMC, so moving her gave us a vote of no confidence."

"For sure. Why'd they come this time?" Congressman Lee's voice was suspicious.

"Well, Grace has cancer and CCMC has the best cancer treatment program. Besides, Robert only operates at CCMC and he's Grace's surgeon. Why?"

"Nothing really. Robert still Grace's doctor?"

Alex responded, "Yes, he is. I know he applied for special privileges to treat her at Jeff. I haven't heard anything different. But, to be honest, I don't know for sure."

"Find out. Just a little bit of information I'm going to throw your way. Don't know that it means anything, but it's worth repeating.

"Some weeks ago, your Grandmother and I ran into George and Grace at the Washington Club. They were dining with some corporate hospital group. Their conversation seemed pretty intense. I wasn't listening, but when they mentioned New Orleans hospitals, I did listen a little harder."

Alex smiled a little as she visualized her grandfather eavesdropping for bits and pieces of communication that could affect him.

"Anyway," her grandfather continued, "I heard CCMC mentioned several times throughout the conversation, so Kathryn and I invited George and Grace for Sunday dinner at Wyndley. I tried to pigeonhole George into spilling the beans, but all he said was that this hospital conglomerate was planning to buy up some smaller hospitals in south Louisiana. He played it off as a small deal, you know, no political thing. Claimed that he was trying to get himself educated on health care reform. Isn't that some bull shit since none of us, not even Obama, know what's in that 1,000 page healthcare bill. I asked him about CCMC, feigning interest because of your position there. Raccine said CCMC had been approached, but wasn't for sale. He led me to believe that CCMC was so financially solvent that a merger or acquisition weren't even a possibility. Anyway, that's my story."

Alex thought for a second before she answered, "Well, CCMC *was* approached by a hospital conglomerate. I assume this group you're talking about is HealthTrust. They've bought up most of the hospitals in Louisiana, and they're pretty powerful with a lot of international connections. I suppose that's why they wanted CCMC. We have an enormous international patient base for transplants, orthopedics, cancer and even plastic surgery. I don't really think it means a lot, but I'll keep it in mind."

"I still think something's rotten. I'm gonna put my aide on it tomorrow. I'll let him look into it. I need this kind of information anyway. I'll let you know if there's anything interesting that comes out of it. You're sure you're okay?"

Alex hesitated too long. "Sure, I'm fine. I'm really okay."

"The hell you are. I can tell from your voice. What the hell else is happening down there? Speak up, or I'm coming back down."

"It's really nothing."

Briefly, Alex outlined her visit to the voodoo museum and her visit to the voodoo meeting the evening before. She casually mentioned her injured shoulder.

"Shit, why are they after you? Something ain't right. Speak up, damn you! Tell me everything, Alex. Now, or I'll charter a friggin' jet and come there to serve as your personal bodyguard...and...I may bring the Virginia National Guard with me. How'd you like that?"

Alex grimaced at her grandfather's tone of voice. Consequently, she told him about Mitch and their relationship. When she mentioned that Mitch was missing, her grandfather became absolutely livid. Alex could feel his anger jumping through the phone wires. She knew he'd keep her grandmother up all night long now. She could kick herself for hesitating.

"Alex, this man was pumping you for information. Don't you see that? If he's missing or dead, they'll come after you. I'm coming down. What information could you have that they possibly could want?"

"I don't know, I have no idea at all. For all we know, they have Mitch somewhere. Anyway, Captain Francois has an officer sitting outside my house as we speak. I'm perfectly safe. When Robert calls later, I may ask him to come over for a while." She pleaded, "Please don't worry, I'm okay." Alex knew she was unsuccessful in convincing her grandfather.

"Shit, sounds to me like Bonnet would be the bait, the cherry on top of the pudding. I wouldn't have him over. Call me first thing in the morning. I'm going to make a few calls on my own. I do have some connections, you know."

"Really Granddad, keep this to yourself and don't tell Grand. She'll just worry and become upset," Alex pleaded, probably to no avail.

"Hell, maybe I'll send her down there with that sawed-off shotgun of hers. She'd kill anybody that came within ten feet of your door. How'd you like that? Woman's scary ...unstoppable!"

"Both of you stay in Virginia. This'll blow over. I promise I'll call you in the morning."

"One more thing, Alex. Is George Raccine up for re-election? How popular is he now?"

Alex thought a minute. "Yeah, he's up for election. He's reasonably popular, but he's vulnerable. Many people don't think he's done anything."

"That's what I picked up earlier this week. Very interesting. Man doesn't have a platform anymore. Soft on everything. Call me tomorrow." Her grandfather's voice became gentle as he said, "I love you."

"Love you too, Granddad. I'll talk to you in the morning. Sleep tight."

Alex hung up feeling very homesick wishing she could get

a jet out of New Orleans straight to the family farm.

She spent the next hour thumbing through magazines and hoped that Mitch would call. Then went into her bedroom to take some pain medicine. She reconsidered and instead took two extra-strength Tylenol. At eleven, she called it a night and went into her bedroom. She peered out her bedroom door and saw the unmarked police car in front of her house. Taking some comfort in that, she changed into her gown and went to bed.

***

At two in the morning, she was awakened from a fitful sleep by the phone. She answered just as her answering machine picked up. It was Mitch.

"Alex," Mitch began breathlessly, "Sorry to call so late. I'm out of town, but I'll meet you tomorrow at the Fairmount. If I don't see you there, I'll meet you at the ball. I'm so sorry to call and awaken you, but some things have come up. And, please don't tell anyone, I mean anyone, you've talked to me. I've got a lot to tell you, a lot to explain. I love you and I'm ashamed for whatever you may now think about me."

"Where are you," Alex asked, but it was useless. The phone was dead.

Alex went to the kitchen for a glass of water so she could take more Tylenol. The pain in her shoulder was excruciating.

She was jerked into reality and almost passed out when she saw the dark shadow of a man lurking at her back door. As she opened her mouth to scream, the intruder broke through the glass, turned the knob, and stared at her, face to face.

***

At precisely midnight, Governor Raccine was reading in his recliner in the library of the make-shift executive mansion in New Orleans. He was in desperate need of sleep due to his travel between Baton Rouge and New Orleans. Keeping up with state business had worn him out, not to mention his concerns about his wife and CCMC.

He dozed for several moments and awoke, startled at the sight of a tall, swarthy man entering his library through the glass doors from the courtyard.

"What the hell," he began, but he was immediately silenced by the dark, evil look of the man standing in front of him.

The stranger stared at the governor for several seconds before he said, "Evening, Governor. Late night?" The stranger's was soft and menacing. "Getting your business in order?"

"Who the hell're you," the governor blustered as he frantically searched the room for a weapon. It was useless because there weren't any. The governor had always felt safe in Baton Rouge, but this was New Orleans and he'd forgotten his gun. Damn, he thought to himself. I'm really slipping. No weapon, no security, little chance of defending himself. "Who're you and what d' you want," he said, his voice angry.

The dark man said nothing and continued to stare at him, a half smile on his swarthy face.

The governor watched in awe as the intruder sat on a footstool in front of his chair. The stranger was silent as he stroked his leather belt.

The governor felt his fear mount. If I had a gun, I'd blow his fucking head off, he thought to himself. The stranger outweighed him by at least forty pounds and was at least 25 years younger. He appeared rather strong. George Raccine was trying to guess his age when he noticed he had a ponytail. By God, he thought to himself, I'm being accosted by a fairy. The governor, empowered by false security, stood up and looked down at the dark stranger. The man didn't move and continued to look at him with disgust.

"What the hell d' you want", the Governor blustered. "You know, if I make any noise, I'll have ten security guards in here in a second."

"No," the stranger said softly. "You'd only have eight and they are not immediately available. Two have been unavoidably detained. You see, they didn't want me here, visiting you so late at night, especially without an appointment."

"What the hell d' you want, money, what?"

"I want Crescent City Medical Center, immediately. You know some of my partners. I believe you had a nice dinner in Washington a while back and you promised them CCMC. Remember? Remember the arrangements set at that meeting?"

The governor laughed. "You couldn't possibly represent HealthTrust. They're a corporation which happens to be on the up and up."

The man smiled slightly. "Of course they're very reputable, on the up and up as you say, and I help them stay up by making sure they get what they need."

There was a long silence and the Governor began to feel a scary feeling permeate his body. The hairs stood up on his arms and neck. Both men glared at each other. The ponytailed stranger continued, "You're a politician, a smart man, I hear. You know how to get the things you need..."

"I don't need anything you SOB. I have everything I want."

The dark stranger just stared at him and said, "I understand you have some rather unique tastes for young people, isn't it?" The ponytailed stranger smiled broadly at the governor's discomfort.

As the evil one's insinuations sunk in, the governor paled. "You son of a bitch. You're a dead man. I can have you killed."

"Ah, but you won't, you can't. Your taste runs a little towards Latina young people, doesn't it? Pubescent, I believe. You and I both know about your 'specials needs'. We both have special ways of getting what we need."

Governor Raccine listened helplessly as the stranger caressed his leather belt at an accelerated pace.

The stranger's voice became stronger. "Governor, as a matter of face I know lots of people who would stand in line to kill you...people you have lied to and deceived over the years."

The Governor, his fear mounting, continued to listen to him.

"I want Crescent City Medical Center, tomorrow. I want a write up in the *Times Picayune* on Sunday explaining why it is necessary for CCMC to join the HealthTrust network. Think of it as sort of a Mardi Gras gift to the group who've financed you in the past, and, who may finance you in the future if you give us what we want. Of course, they may kill you as well. Besides, if you do what we say, we won't tell the good people of Louisiana about your sexual proclivities."

"I don't want a dammed thing your group has to offer. I was dealing with a reputable group, or so I thought. Get the hell out of here." Raccine was strong, but not nearly as strong as he needed to be to overpower the stranger. He could feel himself shaking as he realized what the stakes were.

"It's not going to happen, Governor. You see, my people control CCMC now. We could control East Jefferson if we wanted to, maybe we will. By the way, how's Grace?" The evil one's voice remained soft as he continued to look up at the governor. "Haven't seen her for a few days."

The impact of the stranger's words hit the governor like a wave of cold water. "Get the fuck out of here. I'll expose you as you are - a band of thugs!"

The ponytailed stranger stood up, facing the governor. "Go ahead, do it, but I can guarantee that your betrayal to the people of Louisiana will be a bigger story. You'd be history, rotting in jail while the cops look for us forever. They'll never find us."

Raccine continued to stare at the stranger, unable to speak.

The ponytailed man continued, "Governor, where is your political reason? Your astuteness?" Salvadal egged him on, his voice terrifying the chief Executive. "You have no bargaining power, nothing. You failed with the paroles. You failed with the prisons, you failed with everything we asked you to do. I am not sure why you are still alive. Each day, sometimes each hour, I sit and wait for the order to kill you. "

Raccine said nothing, his eyes wide open. He was paralyzed with fear.

The stranger continued, "Some of our best people are still in prison because you screwed us. Didn't you also fail some Latin children? One young girl, in particular, as I remember? She's grown up now but remembers everything you did to her, and she is ready to talk."

The color began to drain from the Governor's face.

The ponytail continued. "We want CCMC tomorrow. You understand?" You disgust me. Raping children on a missionary trip. What kind of low life bastard are you? I should kill you now."

With that, the ponytailed stranger lunged at the governor. He moved behind him in an instant, wrapping the leather strap around his neck and making him gasp for breath. His eyes bulged wildly, as he anticipated his death.

The stranger held the strap for just the right amount of time, and then released the strap just seconds before the governor lost consciousness. He said, "CCMC tomorrow. No excuses or Grace dies. It won't be a painless death, and neither will yours."

The evil one left quietly through the terrace door of the library and headed towards the French Quarter.

CHAPTER 22

Robert and Alex stood gaping at each other in her kitchen.

"Robert, you scared the hell out of me. I thought you were an intruder, someone coming to kill me. Why didn't you call?" Alex was so frightened her voice was shaking, and her breath was little gasps. She thought her lungs would burst.

"We've got to get out of here. You're in danger. Right now. Hurry, my car's out front!"

"I have on my nightgown. Besides, there's a New Orleans cop guarding my house." Alex hesitated for a second, and then added, "He's obviously not doing a good job since you got in."

Robert shook his head and said in a terse voice, "He's dead. Got a fresh bullet hole in his head. Grab a coat, we're leaving!"

"Call Francois while I get dressed. His numbers are on the table by the phone. Tell him we're coming to the station, to meet us there." Robert nodded, and Alex ran into her bedroom to grab some clothes.

Robert had just dialed Francois' cell when he heard Alex scream. Robert dropped the phone and ran into Alex's bedroom where a tall, ponytailed man was attempting to break through the glass doors. The double dead bolt was the only reason he hadn't entered.

"Hurry, Alex." Robert grabbed her and pulled her out of the bedroom. They were leaving through the front when they heard the sounds of breaking glass.

The two made a dash for Robert's Mercedes parked in front

of the NOPD police car. Alex heard several dogs barking as Robert tried repeatedly to start the car. "Damn, it won't start. He must've pulled the coil wire."

"We've got to run, Robert! It's the only way!"

They ran down the street, aware the stranger was following. Alex thought he was gaining on them. She could almost feel his hot breath on her neck. At any moment she expected to be shot in the back. Why doesn't he kill us, she wondered. Alex's muscles were burning in her legs, and she was weak and tiring. Her heart felt like it would burst in her chest. The pain in her shoulder was excruciating. She knew they were losing the battle when suddenly, luck intervened. Alex heard a loud snarl and a curse. She looked back and saw two Siberian Huskies attacking the ponytailed man. Thank goodness for those dogs, she thought. They belonged to her neighbor down the street, a sculptor who stayed up at night working.

The dog fight gave Alex and Robert an edge. They crossed Saint Charles and headed towards the Vieux Carre where they lost themselves in the thinning crowds of the French Quarter. They sat on a bench in Jackson Square for a moment to catch their breath. All around them drunks, street people, and masked tourists looked at them strangely. At any other time Alex would have been petrified to be in the Quarter at two in the morning, much less in her nightgown. But now, this motley group was friendlier than the ponytailed stranger. A slightly worn, weary clown sat down beside them and asked if they were okay.

Robert answered quickly. "No, we're not. A tall man with a ponytail is chasing us. We've got to go somewhere and hide, at least until we can get the police. "Uh-oh. Got to go, Alex!" Robert gestured toward the man two hundred feet away at the corner. Alex and Robert ran up Saint Peter's to Bourbon, hoping to get lost in the crowd.

The evil one saw them take off. He figured they'd head toward Bourbon, so he cut through some alleys and courtyards to meet them. He wasn't even winded from the dog attack or the run. One of the dogs had bitten him, although it didn't hurt at all.

Alex's breath was again coming in short, small gasps as she and Robert approached Bourbon Street, and she had a terrible pain in her shoulder. She knew that she couldn't go much further.

Suddenly, they were face to face with the ponytailed man. She was paralyzed with fear. He looked at them both and smiled. As he reached toward Alex, he grimaced, then crumpled to the ground, unconscious. Behind him stood the clown, wielding a large pink club in his hand. On the side of the club was printed the word "BONK" in large green letters.

"Call Alex at CCMC next week. I'll reward you. You saved our lives," Alex, breathing heavily, managed to say.

The clown smiled broadly, his make-up thin and running. "Mind if I hit him again when he wakes up?"

"Be my guest. Do what you want, but call Captain Francois at the NOPD before he gets away. Thanks. You saved our lives." Robert shook the clown's hand before he and Alex moved off. Alex wanted to hug him but there was no time.

They ducked into the Maison Bourbon where Robert's friend, Steve, the owner, was stacking chairs on tables. Several of the jazz musicians drank coffee as they sat in the corner of the store. They looked startled when the tall man and the beautiful lady in her nightgown entered the bar after hours.

"Steve, you've got to hide us. There's a man down the street trying to kill us. Can we go upstairs?"

One look at Robert and Steve didn't hesitate. "Sure. Want me to call the police?"

Steve looked nonplussed, calm and collected as if half dressed women entered his bar after hours every evening. Of course, this is New Orleans, they probably do, Alex thought to herself.

"Take us up and we'll talk. No police. They'll lead him to us." Robert knew he wasn't making sense.

Steve looked at Robert strangely. "Let's go."

Taking a circuitous route, the three of them headed through the kitchen and passed cases of wine and kegs of beer. They headed toward the back room where Steve summoned an ancient brass elevator. With considerable grunting and groaning, squeaking and screaming, the monstrosity pulled to a screeching halt and the three got on. In a normal situation, Alex would never have boarded the old brass elevator but at this point, there was no choice. Her uncertainty showed on her face and Steve noted it.

"Here goes. Cross your fingers." Steve pressed the big black button marked three. "It usually makes it." Steve's nonchalance was relaxing to Alex as he looked at her and said, "I promise!"

Alex gaped back at him, her blue eyes huge as she viewed her new brass prison.

"So…..Robert, what'cha been up to," Steve bantered and grinned at the bewildered couple as the elevator attempted to climb upwards. Alex decided she really liked Steve and admired his casualness and insouciance.

Robert picked up Steve's cue and responded dispassionately, "Not much really, just fighting voodoo, hexes and curses and running away from ponytailed strangers who are trying to kill us."

Steve nodded, "Yeah, I see that. Hang loose, we'll almost there." The ancient elevator finally reached its destination and the elevator opened into a studio apartment with a window wall that offered a panoramic view of the Quarter. The furnishings were art nouveau with Italian leather sofas. Antique juke boxes and pin ball machines lined the walls. From the exposed rafters hung numerous Tiffany light fixtures that colored the room with a romantic light.

"What a cool place," Alex stammered, stunned as she looked around the old building.

Steve gave her a crafty smile as he walked toward an antique walnut cabinet and removed a stainless Smith and Wesson 45 semi-automatic from the drawer. After making sure it was loaded, he handed it to Robert and took a 357 revolver for himself. Alex watched him with bewilderment, a dazed expression on her face. "Yeah, most people expect a warehouse with large rats and cockroaches. Now, what in the hell's going on with you two? By the way, who in the hell are you?" Steve asked, looking at Alex.

"It's crazy and tied together with the problems at CCMC," Robert began to explain.

Alex was shocked back into reality and interrupted. "I'm Alex. I must have lost my cell while we were running. Can I use your phone? I need to call Captain Francois at the NOPD." Alex was searching the apartment for a phone.

Steve handed her his black iPhone. Alex looked at Robert. "Do you remember the numbers?" Robert shook his head.

"I don't want to call 911 because they'll send a bunch of units here, and if the ponytail got away, you can bet he's looking for us." Robert thought out loud.

"Would you guys speak English? What ponytail?" Steve's voice was insistent as he became aggravated.

Alex tried to explain. "A man with a ponytail was chasing us. He broke into my home and was going to kill me. Anyway, he killed the policeman who was guarding my house. He chased us into the Quarter and had just caught us when he was hit in the head with a club by a clown." Alex finished breathlessly and realized how ridiculous her story sounded.

Steve started laughing. "I feel like I'm on an acid trip back in the seventies. You must mean old Frank."

"Who?" Robert and Alex said together.

"Old Frank. He's sort of a self-prescribed one man vigilante who spends his evenings and nights protecting unassuming tourists from danger in the Quarter. Usually he dresses as a clown although he has other disguises, too. Next favorite costume is a pirate. He hangs around Jackson Square and tells tourists about the safe boundaries of the Quarter. You know, don't go north of Bourbon, east and west of whatever. He's a good man." Steve looked particularly pleased at Frank's latest triumph since he had saved his old friend Robert.

"He sure saved us. Do you have that phonebook, Steve?"

"I haven't had a phonebook for ten years but I do have the internet. Be my guest. Steve directed Robert toward a computer where he quickly located the number for the NOPD. He left his name and an emergency message for Francois.

"Might as well have a nightcap," Steve said and handed them each an Irish coffee with lots of whipped cream.

***

Jack Francois was wild with worry. He'd recognized Alex's number on his cell but hadn't gotten an answer when he'd called. When he had arrived at her house, he found his officer dead and knew immediately Alex was on the run. He'd become even more concerned when her neighbor, Peter, verified Alex had been running down the street with one man, and another man in pursuit. Peter admitted setting his dogs loose to help protect Alex. He had sobbed uncontrollably when Francois had told him that both of his huskies were dead.

The death of the dogs disturbed Francois the most. Both dogs had been strangled, simultaneously. Francois couldn't imagine what kind of man had the strength to strangle two Siberian huskies at the same time. It was inhuman that one man could have overcome two such powerful dogs at the same time. His thoughts returned to the man he'd tussled with at the voodoo gathering. He was convinced it was the man with the ponytail. But, that was all he knew. He had no idea who the stranger was, or how he was involved with Alex and CCMC. Francois still hadn't been able to locate Mitch, but he didn't think Landry was dead - just well hidden. As he sat in his car, he was wondering where to look next when his phone rang. It was the watch officer at the precinct.

"I got a man here calling from a pay phone in Jackson Square. Says he helped a man and a woman get away from a man with a ponytail. You want to talk?" The watch officer added, "The man said the couple asked him to call you."

"Hell, yes, get his location."

"He's at Cafe du Monde. Says you can recognize him easily. He's a clown."

"A what?" Francois' voice was incredulous.

"A clown, sir." The watch commander's voice was deferential, without emotion.

"What the fuck. Tell him I'll be there in ten minutes. Tell him not to leave."

"Done. Ten-four."

Francois pulled out his siren and raced towards Jackson Square. He made record time and soon pulled up to the curb next to the Cafe. The clown was there all right. He sat at a table as he drank cafe au lait and ate a beignet.

"Who the hell are you?" Francois demanded after sitting down at the clown's table.

"Who are you?" the clown mimicked. "Got any ID?"

Francois felt a grudging respect and pulled out his badge

and ID. The clown read it carefully and matched the picture ID with the Captain's face. He seemed satisfied and said, "They told me to call you. So I did. I hit the man in the head."

"Wait a minute, one thing at a time. Who are 'they'? Let's take this nice and slow so I understand." Francois' heart was beating fast.

"Alex and her man friend. She said her name was Alex and told me to come to CCMC next week so she could reward me for saving her. The man was nice too. He shook my hand."

"What'd the man look like?"

"Oh, sort of tall, slender, had light colored hair. Talked like a native."

"What did the other man look like, the bad one?" Even though Francois was pretty sure who it was, he wanted confirmation.

"Tall, real big, and powerful. Dark hair with a ponytail. Mean face, real cold looking. I hit him in the head with the club I usually carry. He was lying in the gutter, and I was going to hit him again before I called you. He must've come to without me knowing it. I turned my head, just for a second to see if I could see Alex, and he kicked me in my privates. Knocked me over with pain. Bastard. That's when he took off."

"Where'd Alex and her friend go?"

"Don't know, just headed down Bourbon. Must've gone in somewhere, 'cause when I looked up they were gone."

Francois sat for a few minutes and looked at the clown.

"What's your name?" Somewhere, in the back of his mind, Francois could remember stories about a man who roamed the French Quarter. He was dressed as a clown or a pirate, a good Samaritan of sorts. He wondered if this could be the man. "I asked your name." Francois's voice was brusque.

"I'm Frank. I live over on Dauphine."

"Have a last name?"

"Nope. Never have. Wouldn't tell you if I did. You can find me through Steve at the Maison Bourbon."

"Okay, Frank. Listen, here's my card. If you see this man again, call me. You'll be able to recognize him, right?"

"Sure. Nice to meet an honest New Orleans cop. Thanks for coming."

Francois smiled at the weary clown, "Thanks, Frank. This man with the pony tail is really bad. Better go home and change to your pirate's outfit. I don't doubt he'd come back for you. He'd love to kill you. I'd lay low for a while."

"Yeah, OK. Thanks for the tip. I'll do just that." The men shook hands as they parted.

As Francois returned to his vehicle, his cell rang and as he grabbed it he felt a flood of relief when he heard Alex's voice on the other end. "I'll be right there. Sit tight."

Francois displayed his badge for Steve, who motioned for him to come into the back room. When Steve pushed the button for the ancient elevator, Francois broke out into a sweat.

"There's got to be another way to get up there. Don't you have some steps or something. These old things give me the creeps. Ain't you violating the fire code?"

"Nope, sorry. Building's been like this for years. Predates the building code. This old baby looks worse than it is. She usually makes it." Steve was studying the captain carefully.

Francois continued to sweat as the elevator came to a screeching halt in the back room. His heart almost stopped when he noticed that the elevator had lodged almost a foot below the entry level. Steve opened the door and urged the Captain to jump on. Francois felt his knees buckle as Steve punched the button for the third floor. "Are you okay, Captain?"

They started their slow ascent. "How long before we get there?" Francois said as he unbuttoned his collar.

"Just a few seconds. Sure you're okay, Captain? You don't have any chest pain or anything, do you? Are you breathing okay?"

"No, I'm okay', Jack gasped. "I just have a phobia about these things. Got shut in one when I was a kid. Never have worked through it."

In an effort to divert Jack's anxiety, Steve started an idle conversation.

"Sure seems like a busy Mardi Gras. This place's been packed. These people are drinking like fish. I've never seen so much booze go down people's throats so quickly. Should be a profitable weekend for me. Any special activities planned for crowd control?"

"Nah, just the same old thing. No glass, weapons. Anything and everything else goes. Business is good?"

"You bet. I'm busier now than last year on Fat Tuesday. Wish I'd raised prices. Every taxi driver I've talked to has turned down at least four loads tonight. Every hotel's filled. I, for one, am a happy man." Steve was smiling.

"Are Alex and Bonnet okay?"

"Yep. They're a little shook up, had a real nasty go of it with that bastard. Chased them all the way from Alex's house. Sounds like he was going to kill them."

"No question about it in my book. Shit, is this thing close to getting us to the third floor?" Jack broke out in a fresh sweat.

"Almost there, another minute or so. Relax, I ride this sucker two, three times a day. I get it serviced every six months. Those guys over at Otis Elevator swear it's the best elevator in all New Orleans." The elevator groaned and came to a grinding halt. Steve opened the door.

Francois hopped out in a flash, his eyes sweeping the room. "I'm sure glad to see you both," the captain's voice boomed as he relished the open space.

"Jack, he almost got us. The ponytailed man. We were saved by two dogs and a clown." Alex couldn't believe how ridiculous she sounded.

"I know. Just talked with Frank. You all right?"

"Yes," Alex replied, "Thanks to Steve for hiding us. You two met?"

"Yeah, on the forty minute ride up on that albatross of an elevator. Bonnet, you okay?" Francois extended his hand.

Robert clasped Francois' hand. "Sure am glad to see you. You look a little winded though." Robert's practiced physician's eye was scanning Francois disheveled, sweaty appearance. His face was beet red, and he was a little short of breath.

"I thought he was gonna stroke out on the way up," Steve reported.

"Yeah, I feel like I just tangled with an iron monster."

Steve interrupted. "The good captain doesn't like my elevator. Broke into a sweat while we were coming up and he was short of breath. I told him we'd be okay, but he acted like he'd rather tangle with your ponytailed buddy. I was afraid he was going to pass out."

"Oh shit, I'm fine. I just hate elevators. You don't need to do that, Robert."

Bonnet had grabbed the captain's wrist and was counting his pulse. "Just sit down a minute and rest, Jack. Your pulse is racing. Thank goodness I don't have a blood pressure cuff. When this is over, you're coming to my office for a physical."

"Yeah, yeah, yeah. Sure I am. When this is all over, we'll talk. Tell me everything that happened, from the top."

Alex and Robert took turns telling the story. Between the two of them, no detail was overlooked. The Captain asked numerous questions and took notes. Alex almost cried when he told her that both dogs were dead.

"Oh, no. Peter'll be so sad. He let them go to help us. Did he call 911?"

"Peter knows and he is heartbroken. Don't know who called 911. Your house is pretty wrecked. Is there something in your apartment he could've been looking for? It looks like he went through a pile of papers in your office and beside your chaise lounge, and he also pulled out some drawers in your kitchen. Any idea what he wanted?" The Captain looked at Alex directly.

Alex searched her mind and tried to visualize her home office. "I can't think of a thing. I have some files from the hospital, but I don't think any of them would interest him. Let me think about it. There's an address book by the phone in the kitchen."

"I don't remember seeing it, but I left the uniforms to dust for prints. I'll call in and ask." Captain Francois reached for the phone.

"Wait a minute, I think I know. Mitch called me at two. Was the tape in the answering machine?"

Jack shrugged his shoulders. "Don't know Alex. I was intent on finding you, so I didn't stay too long. What'd Mitch say?"

"He said he was out of town, but he'll see me at the Extravaganza tonight. He also said not to tell anyone I'd heard from him. Do you think the ponytail's after Mitch?"

"I'm sure he is. Was Mitch's conversation recorded on the tape?"

"Yes. I didn't pick up until the third ring and the machine picked up, too. It's all there."

"Let me call in." Francois called the crime team, while Alex and Robert sat on the sofa. Steve had retreated into the kitchen to make more coffee. Robert and Alex could tell from the captain's conversation that both the address book and the answering machine tape were missing.

After Captain Francois hung up the phone, Alex and Robert pressed him for details. "Your address book and answering machine tape are both gone. They couldn't get any prints, he probably wore gloves."

"Damn, my address book had everything in it. Numbers for my grandparents, family, friends." Alex had risen from the sofa. "Do you think he'll try to get at any of my family or my friends? I couldn't live with myself if something happened...."

Francois' voice was curt because he knew the ponytailed guy would do anything and go to any length to get what he wanted. "You've got to calm down. This isn't helping."

"My phone book's my life line."

Francois held up his hands. "Alex, I think it's okay. He doesn't have a lot of time to hassle people. I don't think he's going to bother your family or friends, unless it's to find you. Who's in the book locally?" Your family isn't local, is it?"

"No, they're in Virginia. Robert, I have to call my grandfather in the morning. He threatened to come out here if he didn't hear from me. Jack, everybody's in there. Elizabeth from work, Bridgett my secretary. I couldn't live with myself if anything happened to them." Alex was interrupted by the phone ringing.

Steve answered the phone. "Who is it," he said into the receiver. "It's for you." Steve handed the phone to Francois who looked embarrassed.

"Sorry. I gave out the number on the phone."

"It's okay. I don't mind. I'll change it again next week."

Francois smiled and picked up the phone. "Yeah, yeah, that's good. What, who was it? Yeah. Interesting. I'll check back shortly. I'll need a place to hide two people out for today. Check it out. Sounds pretty safe." Francois slowly hung up the phone while Alex paced impatiently wanting to know the other end of the conversation.

"Good news. They found your address book, near the dogs. Apparently he lost it in the bushes, and was so eager to get you, he didn't notice. So, your friends and family are safe. No cell, though. They didn't find your cell."

Alex was not mollified. My cell? All of my personal information is in my cell. That's even worse than my phone book. Oh my God. He can even access my email."

The captain glared at Alex and said, "Chill out. We don't even know if he has it!"

Alex heaved an audible sigh of relief.

Robert said, "What else?"

"Well, seems there was an attack on the governor tonight, here in New Orleans in his temporary residence. Some son of a bitch broke in through the glass doors about midnight and tried to strangle him. Killed two state troopers assigned to guard the governor. Strangled them."

"Is George okay?" Robert asked, as he wondered once again about his part in these events.

"Yeah, seems to be. He's resting under strict guard. There was a long silence as the three thought about the attack on Governor Raccine.

Alex broke the silence. "It's tied together. The ponytail must have done it. He was at my house at two this morning, right after Mitch called." Alex stopped to think, and continued, "He strangled the dogs. He strangled the state police. That's why he didn't shoot us, Robert. This man strangles people. I can still feel that killer grip he had on my neck at the voodoo feast. It must be the same man who attacked Governor Raccine."

Robert and Francois nodded, then Francois spoke. "Yeah, but he didn't want the Governor dead. Must still need him alive for some reason, or he'd have killed him, too. Just don't know his motive. We are missing that piece and it's a big one."

"Do you know who he is? If we knew that, we could probably put it together." Robert directed his question to Jack.

"No, but I gave a description to the local agent who was working out of the emergency department situation, and he sent it to the FBI at Quantico. I was hoping we'd get fingerprints from Alex's house to speed things up but no such luck. It could take weeks to get a match on a description only."

"Yes, but since he's attacked the governor, maybe they'd

give it priority," Robert said.

"Yeah, maybe, but we've got to get the governor's permission, though. I'm not sure he'll cooperate."

Robert gave a short laugh. "Ridiculous. Raccine's a law and order man. I'd stake my life on his cooperation."

"Hope you're right, Robert. I think Raccine's knee-deep in shit at this point. I doubt he'd be willing to push it."

"Raccine's been a good governor. You know the excuses we've had for governors. Besides, I know him. He's like my second father. He'll cooperate."

"Well, we'll see. In the meantime, I've got to get you guys to a safe place so we can all make it to the Extravaganza tonight. You two mind spending the day together?" Francois looked at Robert and Alex happily grinning from ear to ear.

"None of you leave before breakfast," Steve hollered from the kitchen. "Then you can all get the hell out of here, so I can go to bed." Steve came into the living room with four omelets accompanied by link sausages, tomato juice, and a pot of coffee.

"I'll eat. No problem for me." Francois said. "Smells delicious." Jack reached for a plate. The other three laughed and followed.

Jack pushed back his plate, looked at his watch, and said, "Well, it's six. Got to move you guys before daylight. Don't want to run into any trouble. I'm saving up my energy for tonight. Any way to get out of here other than riding that damn albatross elevator?" Francois asked as he eyed Steve.

"Not unless you jump through the window. Bourbon Street is three stories down. Could be a hard landing," Steve laughed at the police captain.

"What comes up must go down. I'll make it. Thanks for letting us hang out."

"My pleasure. You can return the sweats later. Robert, next time settle for a drink on the house instead of an escape from death? You guys be careful. Take care of them."

Francois nodded and moaned as he stepped gingerly into the elevator. "Wake me up when we land."

After an uneventful couple of minutes, Jack said, "Humph, guess I must have beaten this thing," obviously pleased with himself for not panicking.

"Maybe, but the true test is riding it every week for three months. Then you're cured," Alex said definitively.

"Not a chance. I pick my battles," Francois said.

After the three of them got in the captain's car, Alex said, "Where're you taking us? Is this really necessary?"

"No lip. It sure as hell is if you want to live. Besides, we have a ball to attend tonight. You're going. You've got to rest up for tonight."

CHAPTER 23

The safe house was a pit. The apartment was a third-story walk-up on Constance Street, in the outskirts of the Warehouse District. It looked as though it'd seen its last renovation in the early 1970s. The living room had gold shag carpeting. The appliances in the closet-sized kitchenette were avocado, as were the fixtures in the small bath. The half bath even had a pink toilet.

Alex was intrigued as she surveyed her surroundings. "This place is incredible, it looks like a hippie movie set. At any moment I expect to see Jerry Rubin, Abbie Hoffman or anyone else in the Chicago Seven come bounding in here", Alex said as she glanced around the living room. "Maybe even Martin Luther King Jr. or Peter, Paul and Mary...."

"Yeah, it sure is. That ancient TV could come on any minute and report the Kent State Shootings or the Viet Nam war. I'm glad we're only going to be here today," Robert agreed, as he smiled at Alex who was checking out the kitchen.

"At least it's neat and clean, and the kitchen's stocked. We'll make out. Besides, Retro is really in now," she said cheerfully, "You know, the new pop-up culture!"

Robert had opened up the cabinet of the old hi-fi. "Yep, I feel like I'm caught in a time warp, too. Look at this record collection. Some of these album covers are collector's items." As he sorted through the record cabinet he continued, "Some good tunes here. Want to play some?" Robert smiled at Alex and eyed albums on top of the ancient hi-fi player.

"You mean play a record? I'm not sure I could figure out how to work it. Sure, put a stack on but not too loud, though.

We're supposed to be hiding you know." Alex laughed as she poured each of them a glass of orange juice.

Without talking, they sat on the couch and listened to music. Robert was dropping off to sleep when Alex exclaimed, "How can I go to the ball tonight? I don't have any clothes, neither do you. I've got to call Yvonne to ask her to deliver my gown and everything else I'll need. I'm sure she'd bring it here."

Robert raised his hand in objection. "Call Francois first. We can't give anyone our location. He told us to not even use our cell phones unless it was an emergency."

"This is an emergency! I'm going to the biggest Mardi Gras ball in New Orleans and I have nothing to wear, except this sweat suit. You're not looking too spiffy yourself. Call him," Alex demanded as she pointed at his phone.

Robert reached for the cellular phone and entered their number in Jack's pager and Francois returned their call immediately. They talked for a few minutes while Alex tried to decipher the conversation from her end. Finally, Robert handed the phone to her.

Francois' speech was rapid. "Order everything you need from whats-her-name and I'll have someone pick it up. I'll bring it to you around five this afternoon. I'm getting Robert a tux, too. We'll go to the ball together." He sounded almost jovial- probably punch drunk Alex thought to herself.

"Jack, you need to get some rest. You've got to be at your best tonight." Alex's voice was reprimanding but earnest.

"I'm okay. Running on pure adrenalin. Listen, this is

important. Your phone kept ringing this morning so my men put a new trace on your voicemail just to see who was trying so hard to get in touch with you."

Alex looked puzzled. "I can't imagine."

"Your grandfather was the persistent caller."

Alex laughed and said, "On second thought, I can imagine."

"First he told your voice mail to go to hell, that he had important information for you. He hung up and called back fifteen minutes later. He was obviously agitated because it was six in the morning and you weren't at home. Sounds like a real character," Francois added.

Alex laughed, as she could imagine what he grandfather had said to her machine. "That is an enormous understatement. Yep, he's quite a man. He doesn't mince a lot of words. Don't let him fool you, Jack. He's a political genius and always gets what he wants."

"What's he do?" Francois was intrigued.

"He's the Senior Congressman from Virginia, Adam Patrick Lee."

Francois had heard of Adam Patrick Lee, and knew that he was a law-and-order politician. He'd had no idea Lee was Alex's grandfather.

"Well, I called Virginia and talked to your grandmother. She said your grandfather was a wild man and that he was so upset about you that he'd hopped a jet to New Orleans. He'd already left for Dulles International Airport, and he's due to arrive at three-fifty this afternoon. I'll have one of my men pick him up and we'll be there about five."

"You'd better get my grandfather a tux, too. I can assure you he'll attend the Ball as well. He's never missed a good party!"

"But, I don't have his measurements." Jack Francois began, pissed because he'd become everyone's personal valet.

"You can handle the 'buts' with him personally, Captain. In the meantime, I suggest you order him a tux. You can call my grandmother for his measurements, or still better, call Nathan's Clothier on Main Street in Richmond. That's his tailor."

"OK, OK, OK. If you insist." Francois was resigned. What the hell Jack thought to himself. The last thing he needed was a rift with a senior politician from Virginia about a damn tuxedo.

"Do you mind if I call my grandmother from this phone? I think she'd feel better if she heard from me."

"Sure, what's your grandfather know about things here?"

"I talked with him last night. You need to know that my grandfather can squeeze blood out of a turnip so I had no choice but to tell him everything. He knows all about CCMC and about Mitch. I told him about the voodoo meeting and the man trying to grab me from the meeting. He's also a close friend of Governor Raccine and suggested that Raccine's probably in some kind of trouble. He may have some information for us."

"Now I know why he's coming. Can't say I wouldn't be doing the same if you were my granddaughter. What kind of info do you think he has?"

"No telling. Adam's great at bending political arms. You know, Jack, I meant to tell you earlier this morning. Granddad saw the Raccine's at the Washington Club recently. The governor was meeting with some people from Health Trust and quite frankly, my grandfather was eavesdropping. "Anyway," Alex shrugged her shoulders and continued, "he heard CCMC come up in conversation and he listened even more carefully. Later he and my grandmother went over and invited the Raccine's to dinner the next day."

"And, then what?"

"The Raccine's accepted, and Adam tried to pigeonhole the governor into talking about his dinner meeting. They had a lively meeting about the perils of Obama Care which almost lead to a brawl. According to my grandmother, neither the Raccine's nor Adam got anywhere with their banter. The governor just said that Health Trust was buying up several smaller hospitals in Louisiana and that they'd approached CCMC and we weren't interested. That's common knowledge."

"Yeah, I guess it is. Anything else?"

"No, not really. Said Raccine seemed uncomfortable with the conversation and he'd felt he was preoccupied earlier this week. My grandfather was appalled when I told him about the governor threatening to close CCMC. Said it was the most ridiculous thing he'd ever heard. He swears that something's rotten with Raccine. Granddad is also pissed because Raccine is going soft on parole at the federal and state level." Alex finished.

"I think your grandfather's a wise man. I'm looking forward to meeting him and hearing what he's got. You and Robert get some sleep. We've got a big night ahead. I'll see you at five with your grandfather in tow. Go to bed and rest."

"You do the same, Captain." Alex yawned. "Granddad seems to think someone is blackmailing Raccine."

"Could be," Jack rubbed his forehead. "Certainly not out of the question."

"I'm turning in as soon as I call Grand. See you soon," Alex said as she pressed down the phone hook.

Alex dialed her grandmother at Wyndley. She could picture her grandmother sitting in her checkered green chair in the great room at the family farm watching her prized horses in the pasture through the huge double window wall that lined the back of the house. Her grandmother answered immediately.

"Alex, what in the hell's going on? Your grandfather's been trying to reach you since dawn. Where are you?"

Alex recognized the fear and strain in her grandmother's voice and immediately felt guilty for all the grief and anxiety she had caused her aging grandparents. The fact that Grand had cursed was indicative of her stress. Kathryn believed that points could be made without using profanity, reserving its use for the only the most serious and dire occasions.

"I'm fine. I'm in a safe place with Robert. Captain Francois of the NOPD is watching us."

Kathryn Lee wasn't placated. "Why can't you stay at home?" Not waiting for an answer, she continued, "Your grandfather received some sort of priority call at three this morning from his Congressional aide who'd been checking up on the Raccine's since yesterday afternoon. I don't know what's going on, but your grandfather left here in a big hurry. Tried to charter a flight to New Orleans, but a commercial jet was faster. What's happening? I'm worried to death about you both." Alex had never heard her stoic grandmother sound so worried.

"There was an attempt on the governor's life last night, and you know about this conspiracy against CCMC. To be honest, I don't know what's happening. I only know that someone wants to put Robert and CCMC out of business, and Granddad thinks that Governor Raccine's somehow involved. Anyway, I'm fine, Robert's fine, and if you really love me, you'll let me hang up and go to bed. I haven't slept much lately, and I'm taking Granddad to the Endymion Extravaganza tonight," Alex finished brightly.

"How's George Raccine?"

"He's fine and resting comfortably. Promise I'll call you late this afternoon after Granddad gets here and I get up."

"Okay. You win. You're the only person I know as stubborn as your grandfather. I know you're holding back on me, but I also know that's all I am going to get." Kathryn Lee sighed heavily and said, "Call me later. I love you."

Once again Alex felt a pang of guilt for upsetting the people she loved most in the world. She responded, "Love you too, Grand. I'll call you later. Bye."

Alex took several moments to work through her guilt and then consoled herself, firm in the belief there was nothing else that she could tell her. Grand knew the gist of the matter.

Alex looked at Robert sleeping, and on impulse, kissed him on his forehead. She could've sworn he smiled, but she was so tired she wasn't sure. She covered him with a quilt, and decided to sleep in the bedroom with the lime green shag carpeting. Alex set the antique alarm clock for four-thirty p.m. so she could get up, shower, and wait for her gown and her grandfather. Her lingering thoughts as she fell asleep were whether Yvonne Le'Fleur would include a hair dryer and a curling iron with her gown....and to think she had planned to have her hair done in an updo for tonight.

* * *

Alex woke, disoriented and startled to see Robert at her bedside. Then she recognized the lime green carpeting and remembered that they were in the safe house.

Alex, still groggy from sleep, said, "What time is it? Has Francois gotten here?" She nearly jumped from the bed to see the clock.

"It's four. We should start getting dressed." Robert continued, "Rest a little while longer and I'll jump in our vintage shower."

Alex smiled at Robert. "I think I'd better make some coffee and bagels. It's going to be a long evening."

While Robert showered, Alex went to the kitchenette and made fresh coffee. She found sugar and cream in the cupboard and heated bagels in the oven. As she was sitting down to eat, there was a loud pounding at the door. Alex peered through the keyhole and saw Francois and her grandfather at the door, their hands full of packages and bundles. She opened the door with a big smile.

"Granddad, why are you here? You didn't need to come. Anyway, I'm glad to see you." Alex hugged her grandfather and felt secure in his welcoming arms.

"I'm going to be your date to the ball. The Good Captain here got me a tailor-made tux, and you and I are going partying with NOPDs finest....and probably some crooks and murderers. God knows, there are plenty of them in New Orleans."

Alex kissed her grandfather and hugged Francois. They settled down in the living room for coffee and bagels, a poor substitute for hors d'oeuvres.

"Sorry the appetizers are so bad. The captain didn't provide us with room service or gourmet treats," Alex said as she gave Jack a sideways grin.

"I promised you a safe house, not a five-star resort. Your grandfather needs to talk with you and Robert, Alex. Where's Robert anyway?" Francois was looking around the flat.

"He's in the shower for heaven's sake, Jack. Where the hell do you think he is?

"Tell him to hurry up. Where's the bathroom?" Alex nodded her head towards the hallway.

As Francois headed towards the bathroom to get Robert, Adam looked around and said, "This place looks like shit. How'd they manage to find a place this bad?"

Before Alex could respond, Jack returned with a clean, but embarrassed Robert who felt he'd been caught in a love nest with the Congressman's granddaughter.

Adam stood and offered Robert his hand. "It's been a long time. Kathryn sends her best. Said I was to give you a kiss for her, but if you don't mind, I'll pass."

"I'd prefer to forego the kiss, too. It's good to see you too, Congressman. Perhaps I'll get to Virginia soon and she can give me one personally."

Francois cleared his throat and looked around impatiently. "OK, OK, enough. Your grandfather has some information about Raccine."

Adam glared at Captain Francois and said, "First of all, every bit of information I have, for the most part, is unsubstantiated rumor. Whatever I say here now is completely off the record." The Congressman gave all of them a hard, penetrating look. It was his serious and "don't push you luck" look that Alex remembered from her childhood.

"Anyway, the governor appears to have some dirty linen. I had my aide up all night doing some investigating and initially, he turned up nothing. Finally, in the wee hours of the morning he called and told me that Raccine recently had a million dollar campaign debt mysteriously paid off by a hospital holding group. He traced the known members of the group, and found some had significant, actually huge holdings in international health care conglomerates in Central and South American as well as the United States. Plush hospitals where the rich go for plastic surgery and hip replacements and such, you know, hospitals like we're gonna need after Obama Care in phased in."

Congressman Lee continued, "Anyway, the plan and mission of Health Trust is to buy up large, prestigious hospitals in the US so they can in essence control all hospital and health care services in the U.S. That would give them the ability to reduce costs through economies of scale and let them deliver efficient health care while they wipe out any competition around."

Alex was dying to speak, but held back and waited for her grandfather to finish. She noticed that Robert looked pensive and Francois' face was impassive as he continued to listen.

"There's also a rumor from one of the Louisiana Senators that Raccine had been in cahoots with the mob and had pushed legalized gambling here in Louisiana in return for some sort of favor. I literally had to beat this information out of a colleague at four this morning."

Congressman Lee turned his face toward Robert, "Do you want to say something? I know your families go back a long way?"

Robert shook his head.

"Well," Lee continued, "the only other bit of information I have is that Raccine was involved in some sort of politically damaging scandal in Central America a few years back. No one knows the particulars, at least no one's telling. Apparently used some international connections to shut the incident up. His enemies now want him to pay up or else."

"Are you suggesting these attacks are all connected to this international holding group?" Alex asked incredulously.

"I am not suggesting anything, Alex. I'm presenting information that's been given me. There are two critical pieces here."

Alex interrupted her grandfather. "What you are saying is that Health Trust wants complete control of the healthcare system in the US. That is unthinkable!"

"Jack, what d' you make of all of this?" Robert asked cautiously.

Jack shook his head as he said, "You ain't going to like it, but I think Raccine's dirty and I think he promised CCMC as payback. I think the Congressman is correct and there are many health care facilities and hospitals being pushed and bullied by these people."

Robert replied in a low, barely audible voice. "It's just hard for me to believe. George is like my father and I can't believe he'd stoop to this."

Alex reached out to touch Robert's hand as a gesture of comfort but she was still preoccupied with what a complete monopoly would mean for healthcare in American. "If these people are successful they would be able to control everything about acute care...who is admitted, who gets surgery, who gets paid...everything... the whole nine yards. They could control physician salaries, payers, and insurance companies. It's just unthinkable!"

Congressman Lee interrupted, "More importantly, Alex, they would control the largest financial sector in the U.S. Can you imagine the devastation that would cause for all of us? Can you imagine the decision-making power they would have? Who lives, who doesn't, and that is just the beginning!"

As the realization dawned on the group, they all sat and stared at each other mutely before the Congressman added, "This is massive...I am contacting the FBI."

The group sat staring at one another for what seemed like an eternity.

Francois broke the long silence. "Okay folks, look lively, the carriage for the Endymion Extravaganza leaves in forty-five minutes. I certainly wouldn't want to miss the Tableaux. The Extravaganza's theme is Saga of the Sea. Tonight I think we'll see the sea monster."

"Or monsters," the Congressmen added.

CHAPTER 24

Alex retreated to the bathroom to dress, while Robert, Adam, and Francois changed in the bedrooms. As they left the safe house, Adam Lee held Alex back for a moment.

"Alex darling, slip this into your evening bag. Hope you don't need it, but it's better to be safe than sorry. It won't kill quickly, but it sure will slow 'em down."

Adam slipped her a pearl handled derringer. Her grandmother's gun. "Remember how to use it?"

"Of course. I still target practice. How did you manage to smuggled this aboard a commercial flight?" Alex smiled and tucked it into her evening purse. It was a perfect fit.

"Didn't. Had is sent FedEx. It was waiting for me at the airport."

"Thanks for thinking of it, Granddad."

The traffic going down Poydras was maddening. It took over an hour to make the normally fifteen minute trip to the Super Dome. As they approached the Dome, Alex was struck by its magnificence and also taken back to the tragedy that had occurred at the Dome in post Katrina New Orleans.

Outside the Super Dome were hundreds of Endymion Krewe members and guests milling around and watching the crowd. As the limo stopped at the Extravaganza entrance, Alex craned her neck, frantically searching for Mitch, or the ponytailed stranger.

Her heart sunk when she realized how difficult it was going

to be to find anyone. Of course, she reasoned with herself, it'll be equally difficult for them to find us.

"I've never been to the Endymion Extravaganza," said Robert. "Most of the balls are much smaller. I went to Comus several weeks ago and there were only five hundred people."

"Are you a member of this group?" Adam asked of Robert.

"No, I'm a member of Comus and Rex, old-line New Orleans Krewes. Endymion's a newer Krewe and almost anyone can be a member." As Robert realized how stuck up he sounded, he started to apologize.

Francois spoke up. "Forget it, Robert. After tonight, you may never want to go to a ball again. This is going to be tough. You all keep your eyes peeled for our friends. I know they're here. We've about a dozen NOPD undercover officers with us, and Super Dome security is cooperating completely. They've descriptions of the ponytail and Mitch. We're hooked up with headpieces for sound, so if anybody spots anything, we'll know immediately.

"How'd you manage such cooperation?" Alex said.

"The attack on Raccine helped me get additional help from the NOPD, and your grandfather made a few select phone calls. Surveillance is in good shape."

Adam, Alex, Robert and Jack made their way through the glittering array of sequined ball gowns, masked figures, and tuxedoed men to their table. They seated themselves as a waiter approached them with a bottle of Virginia Chardonnay.

"This is for Miss Alexandra Destephano," he said. He

placed the bottle on the table and left.

"It's from Mitch. He must be here," Alex looked around frantically. Her grandfather stared at her.

Robert broke the uncomfortable silence by proposing a toast, and the group drank accordingly. Alex looked up and saw Donald Montgomery headed their way. Oh my God, she thought. Could this day get any better? Before she could warn anyone, he was at their table.

"What a surprise to see the three of you together. Something special going on?" Don glanced around suspiciously. "Oh, are you two dating? How sweet." he smirked as he looked from Alex to Robert.

"Hi, Don. No. We're just waiting for the Tableaux to begin. Would you like to join us?" Alex asked.

"No. I'm with friends. Just stopped by to say hello. I thought something might be happening since you were all together." He looked back and forth between them.

Alex said, "I don't believe you've met my grandfather, Congressman Lee from Virginia. He loves New Orleans and wanted to be a part of the festivities tonight." Alex turned to Mr. Lee. "This is Don Montgomery, CEO at CCMC."

The Congressman and Don shook hands and were exchanging pleasantries when a thunderous roar arose. The King and Queen of Endymion were entering. Their costumes were resplendent and glittered in the low lights. The couple glistened and sparkled like characters from a fantasy world.

"Got to go. Nice meeting you, Congressman." Don smiled

briefly before he disappeared into the crowd.

Alex's eyes followed as Don returned to his own table. She paled as she saw Montgomery sit down at a large table directly across from Jonathan Mercier.

Alex leaned toward Francois and said, "OMG, look who Don's with. I can't believe it. He hates Mardi Gras. Think it means anything?"

Francois shrugged his shoulders. "Could, although I think Montgomery's too stupid to be a part of a plot against his own hospital. Course, Mercier's another question. He could be using Don. What do you think, Robert?" Jack looked at Bonnet.

"I'm no good judging people. I thought George Raccine was spun gold until two hours ago. All I know is Mercier hates me and is out to get me." Robert looked so despondent that Alex squeezed his hand.

She said softly, "It's all speculation. It could simply be that Don's entertaining his newest board member."

Robert's expression was bitter, sarcastic. "Yeah, sure. Raccine's a crook, and Mercier's part of the conspiracy. We just don't know Montgomery's part."

Robert was interrupted by the roll of drums as the orchestra began playing the soundtrack for the ball. Alex watched, enthralled as the curtains opened to reveal a beautiful underwater, ocean scene. The backdrop of teal water, pink coral and hundreds of sparkling starfish provided an awesome sight. On the left stage was a horrific swamp creature, fifteen feet tall, covered with green seaweed. The monster's face was covered with Spanish moss. Red fluid oozed down his face as his eyes feasted on a dead dolphin at his feet.

The ball proceeded as the Master of Ceremonies began telling the tale of the Saga of the Sea. As the story unfolded, the Tableaux began.

Ten women, maids to the Queen of Endymion, represented the characters in the story. The first maid wore a gown of iridescent gold lame' trimmed with sequins. Across the gown's bodice were shells, oysters and fish that sparkled in the light. The maid's headpiece was a pink conch shell at least a foot tall. Alex knew the woman would have neck pain for days following the ball as she struggled to hold her head up under the weight.

One by one the maids were presented by the Master of Ceremonies. Each was spectacularly dressed as a sea creature. The third maid was an octopus. Her headpiece was the head of an octopus, and her gown wound around as the legs wind around an octopus. Her arms were outstretched in a "T" fashion, and she was carrying two ocean lanterns.

Another maid's headpiece was a treasure chest overflowing with diamonds, rubies, and other gems cascading from the trunk.

Alex was spellbound by the Tableaux. As the maids were presented, it was difficult to decide which gown was the most creative and lavish. The array of fabrics, colors, sequins, rhinestones, and feathers were outstanding. Even Congressman Lee appeared impressed. He whispered to her that he'd like to bring her Grand next year. Alex nodded in approval. She'd never seen such creativity in her life.

The show continued without interruption. Each maid and

her escort paid homage to the King and Queen of Endymion. The costumes, backdrop, and participants in the Tableaux were a testimony to the glitz, opulence and fantasy of the Mardi Gras season. Alex was sure the Tableaux had cost at least a million dollars... but it was worth it, she thought. A true testament to the rebuilding and rebirth of the Crescent City after the devastation of Katrina.

At last, the finale. The crowd gasped at the roar of the sea monster on stage. He began to move toward the maids leaving a wake of slime, moss, and silt. The maids cowed as he moved toward them. The monster was intent on their destruction. The crowd was spellbound as they waited for the sea monster to attack the maids.

Out of the corner of her eye, Alex saw another masked sea monster emerge from the right wing of the stage. This sea monster was carrying a black AR-15 assault rifle with an enormous magazine clip hanging from its underside. The gunman could kill dozens without reloading.

Alex screamed and pointed before she reached for her grandfather to pull him under the table. Francois pulled his gun and dove into the crowd, upsetting tables and chairs as he headed towards the masked man. Robert followed.

Shots sounded in the huge auditorium and high-pitched screams rose from the crowd. A unit of police officers rushed toward the right stage exit.

Alex ran forward, her derringer pointed towards the floor as she vaguely noticed Mercier just ahead, his gun raised and pointed directly at Robert.

Robert, who was unaware of Mercier, had seen Mitch just to the side of the shooter. As Mitch ran toward Alex, the monster aimed his rifle directly at Francois. Robert raised his arm in a defensive posture to protect Francois. At the same time, Mercier fired at Robert, the bullet deflected off the bone of Robert's upraised arm and into Mitch's neck.

The sea monster turned quickly in time to see Mitch fall. He aimed again at Francois, getting off two quick shots. One shot hit Francois as he dove toward the man. Jack landed on the floor, blood oozing from a chest wound.

Robert was bending over Francois and ignoring his own wound as he attempted to see if the captain was alive. There was bedlam in the right corner of the ballroom as people screamed and climbed under tables.

The monster with the rifle began to back out of the ballroom through the stage door. Alex finally made it within four feet of him. She raised her derringer and fired into the grotesque mask of seaweed and moss. He wavered a little as he frantically searched the crowd for his assailant. He saw Alex and raised his gun. She fired again, this time hitting him directly in the head. He fell backwards against the wall. The blow knocked off his mask to revealed dark hair pulled back in a ponytail.

Mercier ran toward Robert Bonnet, who was still bending over Francois. He stood over them and waved his gun. "I'm going to kill you, Bonnet, you son of a bitch, just like you killed my wife and baby."

The seconds seemed endless while Robert looked up at Mercier. Robert's voice was quiet and he said simply, "I didn't kill your wife and unborn child. I did all I could to save them."

Mercier's shouted back, "You're a fucking liar! You killed them! I've been waiting a long time to do this."

Alex watched as she saw Mercier's finger start to compress the trigger. Suddenly, in front of her eyes, Mercier's head exploded and he slumped forward onto Francois. Alex had no idea where the shot came from. No one saw Frederico Petrelli shoulder his weapon and leave the ballroom quietly.

Two men pulled Mercier's body off Francois who wasn't breathing. The paramedics were at the door when Robert started CPR. Robert, since his arm was useless, was doing the breathing and someone else did the chest compressions. Finally, the paramedics took over.

"Take him to CCMC and I'll follow to operate. Get my operating room team in." Robert barked at the paramedics.

Alex touched Robert's elbow gently. "You can't operate, your arms injured."

"I'll assist and I'm going in the ambulance." Robert said as he left with the paramedics.

Alex looked around and saw members of the NOPD covering Mitch and preparing to remove his body. Even from where she stood, she could see that Mitch looked peaceful in death. She went over to kneel by him and kissed him on his cheek. I loved him, she thought. I really loved him. She looked up from Mitch's still body and searched blindly for a friend. Someone who cared for her, someone who loved her. Someone she loved but there was no one. Then, turning to leave, she found the comforting arms of her grandfather.

EPILOGUE

It took Alex and Adam several hours to reach CCMC because of traffic. Upon arrival, they learned both Jack and Robert were being operated on. Doctors Ashley and Monique Desmonde joined them in the waiting room.

Both doctors hugged Alex and shook hands with Adam. Alex was quiet as they discussed the events at the ball. Her shoulder was hurting dreadfully and pains were shooting down her arm into her back. She could hardly sit up.

"Alex, you okay?" Monique looked hard at her.

"My arm hurts!" Alex said angrily. She looked at the psychiatrist and said, "I loved Mitch. He was my friend and now he's dead. Hell no, I'm not OK."

Monique's voice was matter-of-fact. "Someone from NOPD's coming to question you. Do you need anything?"

"Maybe some Tylenol for my arm. It's killing me and causing a spasm in my back. I need some clean clothes. Are there some scrubs I can wear? This ball gown has had it and all this blood all over it is creeping me out."

Dr. Ashley gave Alex a muscle relaxer and a pair of green scrubs from the supply room.

"How're Robert and Jack doing?" Alex asked.

Dr. Ashley responded. "The Captain's doing pretty well. The bullet missed his heart and lodged in his left side. He's a lucky man. The surgeon said he'd be okay in a few days."

"What about Robert's arm?"

The impact for a surgeon with a bullet in his arm had just occurred to Alex. Her eyes had a panicked look in them.

Dr. Ashley sighed. "We don't know. The bullet went through his arm after hitting the bone, but it damaged the medial nerve. Anyway, he'll live, that's the important thing."

"Maybe Mercier did get his wish. Perhaps Robert will be out of practice. He'll never adjust to not being able to operate. Even worse than death for him." Alex was so despondent that Dr. Ashley reached for her hand.

"Alex," her grandfather said, "it's too early to know that. Keep your chin up."

"Who killed Mercier? He was going to shoot Robert." Alex began to shudder.

"Don't know yet. Police're working on it. They'll be questioning you about shooting the monster. You up to it?" Congressman Lee carefully looked at his granddaughter.

"Does anybody know his name yet?" Alex looked around quickly.

"No," replied Doctor Desmonde, "but the name monster suits him well."

Several hours passed while Alex and her grandfather gave a report to a police officer. The surgeon reported that Francois, was out of recovery. Alex and her grandfather went to see him.

***

Alex could not believe her eyes. She was expecting the police captain to be asleep, recovering from the anesthesia but instead, Francois was proving to be a difficult patient. He was bellowing for coffee and running the nurses ragged demanding that they fax letters and bring him responses immediately. He'd set up a mini-police station in his room by having hospital engineering hook up a portable fax and a multiple-line phone and wireless internet. Jack was on the phone to the FBI branch in Quantico when Alex and Adam entered his suite.

He waved them both toward the sofa. They looked at each other with their eyebrows raised. Alex couldn't believe he'd just gone undergone major surgery and yet, was sitting up working.

Francois' voice was weak. "Glad to see you. Need you to fill me in on the details. My men aren't here yet, and I can't remember everything. Where's Robert?"

His voice was low, and a little hoarse from the endotracheal tube. Nevertheless, it was remarkable he was even alert.

Alex immediately knew he was unaware Robert had been shot. She said gently, "He's in surgery, Jack. He took a bullet in his arm - he had it raised to protect you. The bullet hit the bone and ricocheted off. It hit Mitch in the neck. Mitch is dead," Alex said with a tear in her eye.

"I don't remember seeing Landry." Francois was confused. "Tell me what happened? I thought I knew but now I'm not sure." Jack was hesitant.

Alex looked at her grandfather. "Want me to tell?" Adam

nodded.

Then Alex started, "It all happened so fast. The man, the sea monster, appeared in the doorway and you and Robert went after him. I followed with my derringer."

"Shit, you had a gun?" Francois was incredulous.

"Yep." Alex smiled. "Anyway, Robert held up his arm, and Mercier's bullet went through his arm into Mitch's neck, killing him instantly." Alex paused, a big lump in her throat. She glanced at the captain who was listening intently, and continued, "At that point, you got shot."

"Yeah, yeah, *that part* I know. Who killed the shooter?"

Alex and her grandfather looked at each other. Adam nodded at Alex.

"I did. I had my grandmother's derringer and I shot him twice."

Francois's face was shocked. "Huh? You killed the Ponytail with a derringer? Wow, you go girl." Jack leaned over attempting to give Alex a high five, but quickly fell back onto the bed groaning with pain. Gasping, he said, "Good job. Who killed Mercier?"

"No idea. I don't think the police know either. Mercier was getting ready to shoot Robert, when, all of a sudden, someone out of nowhere, shot him in the head. Guess it was the police." Alex looked perplexed.

"Wasn't the police. That much we know for sure." His voice was weak, tired.

"Jack, you've got to rest. We've got a lot of work to do to put this case to bed, and I need you alive."

Francois nodded his head feebly.

Congressman Lee grasped his hand. "Alex is right, Captain. We'll figure the rest out tomorrow."

Alex and her grandfather left Francois in the care of a nurse and headed toward the recovery room to see Robert. He was in relatively good spirits, but was concerned about his arm. Alex offered him as much reassurance as she could, but both knew that nerve damage would be fatal to his career.

It was after midnight when they arrived home. Alex was so tired, and in so much pain, she took two pain pills before she went to bed. She slept for twelve straight hours.

Alex staggered out of bed to the smell of coffee. Her grandfather was in the den watching TV and reading the Sunday paper.

She joined him with a cup of coffee. Her grandfather said,

"Francois called. Wants us to join him for lunch at CCMC so he can give us some new information. You feel up to going?"

"Sure. I'm much better today. How's he's feeling?"

"Pretty good, but he sounded a little weak on the phone. You know, I'm impressed by him. Like to have more police like him in Virginia."

Alex smiled at the Congressman. "Forget it. He's committed. This is his home."

"You know better than that. I could use him in Washington, maybe at the Federal level."

Alex couldn't control her laughter. "Jack Francois would never make it with a bunch of Washington bureaucrats. He'd either die or kill them."

Her grandfather smiled. "We'll see. Get dressed."

Alex and her grandfather entered Francois' VIP suite and were greeted by Doctor Ashley, Elizabeth, and Don Montgomery.

Francois was sitting up in the bed. "By the way, I like these digs. You arrange for them?" The captain gestured around the VIP suite.

Don immediately stepped forward. "I arranged it. How can we ever repay all you've done for us."

Don was interrupted as a nurse rolled Robert into the room followed by Andre Renou, who was looking stricken and sad. Robert was pale and wan.

Uh oh, Alex thought. Something's wrong. Her gut knotted up.

Francois began saying, "It's been a long week for all of us but I think we've got some answers. First of all, the Ponytail or sea monster has been identified by the FBI as Monte Salvadal. He's a paid assassin, suspected in a number of international corporate hits in recent years. His favorite method of killing was strangulation. Raccine confirmed that Salvadal was responsible for the voodoo attack on the first lady and identified him as the man who forced entry into his home several days ago."

Andre Renou interrupted Francois. "Before we go any further, I'd like to read a statement from the governor. First of all, he's unable to be here today but he's happy to report that his wife is now awake and doing well at East Jefferson."

Everyone applauded, delighted with the news.

"I also have a written statement from Governor Raccine."

The group waited expectantly while Renou unfolded a piece of official stationary, his hands shaking and read, "I'm pleased to hear things at CCMC are resolved. My congratulations to its leadership and staff. CCMC is, and has always been, the finest hospital in Louisiana. On another note, I wanted you to know that I've resigned as the Executive Officer of the State of Louisiana. I wish to be with my wife as she proceeds towards a complete recovery. Godspeed to you in the rebuilding process."

Alex spoke and broke the silence. "Please tell the governor we wish him and Mrs. Raccine the very best."

"Thank you, Ms. Destephano. I'll relay that message. If there are no questions, I need to go. Feel free to contact me if you need anything at all."

Robert looked devastated after Renou left. Don, Elizabeth, and Doctor Ashley looked surprised.

"Well, let me continue," Francois said after several moments. "We think Salvadal was working for Health Trust, and was in effect, assisting in the takeover of CCMC and other large health conglomerates."

Don smiling broadly in his vindication, interrupted. "I told you it was a conspiracy against us. Knew these couldn't be accidents."

Robert interrupted, "Jack, we know that Salvadal was responsible for the attack on Grace Raccine. What about the shootout in the emergency department and the lady that was burned by her EKG machine?"

"Don't know for sure, as I said it's speculation." Francois poured a cup of water from his bedside pitcher, and then continued, "Raccine told us Salvadal admitted working for Health Trust, and said he'd been hired to deliver CCMC to them. Of course, Health Trust denies this. Salvadal also claimed the attack on Mrs. Raccine. We can't yet prove that Salvadal was responsible for the other attacks."

"Of course, he was! He was trying to ruin our image and credibility. Any moron can see that," Don, red faced and blustering, said.

Francois looked placatingly at Don. "Proving it is another story. We will, at some point. We do know that Salvadal, Frederico Petrelli, and Jonathan Mercier had been seen together several times over the past few weeks, mostly in local restaurants. Of course Mercier is dead, and Frederico is hiding behind the mob lawyers out of Chicago. He denies knowing either man or anything about a conspiracy to ruin CCMC."

Alex said, "Why do you think they were together? What's in it for this Frederico? Who is he?"

"Don't know for sure. Frederico heads the mob here and is interested in gambling, drugs, and prostitution." Francois turned toward Robert and said, "Jonathan Mercier's motive was to get you. We figure the three shared common interests and were working together, but we don't know how they met or Frederico's motives. That's it for now." Francois took a sip of water.

"Who murdered Mercier? Do you know yet," Alex said quietly.

"Nope. Trying to put it together. None of the bullet trajectories for the NOPD match up. From the location of Mercier's wound, the shot had to have been fired from behind him. The bullet was from a .308 Winchester - a high-powered hunting rifle cartridge. We're not sure of the make of the gun. Nobody saw the rifle, so the shooter must not have been close. We're questioning people, but so far, nothing." Francois looked around. "Any other questions?"

"You know how Mitch Landry was involved?" Alex uttered this question in a small voice. Her grandfather reached to put his arm around her.

Francoise looked sadly at Alex. "Not really. Mitch was a good person from a fine family. Unfortunately, he had some problems with gambling. Our snitches tell us he was in debt to the mob for over a hundred grand. We suspect his part was somehow related to his debt, and whatever Frederico's motive was. I'm sorry he died."

"Thanks, he was a good man and was very talented." Alex brushed away her tears.

There was a knock at the door of the VIP suite and lunch was delivered. The group ate quietly and talked more about rebuilding CCMC's reputation than recent events. Shortly after lunch, the crowd broke up. Elizabeth went to handle the reporters, and Don gleefully returned to his office where he wrote a press release. Doctor Ashley went to make rounds and Alex made an excuse to go to her office to look over her mail.

Adam Lee stayed with Francoise and they continued to discuss the case and receive new information. Several hours later the Congressman and the police Captain sent out for a fifth of Jack Daniels after realizing how enormous, well-connected and well-monied Health Trust was. The criminal underpinnings had become clear. Both knew it would prove to be an international conspiracy and would take months to unravel. They only hoped there would be minimal retribution lodged against the events of the day.

It was strange to be in the office over the weekend, Alex thought. It was so quiet and there were no phones, no chattering Bridgett, and no interruptions. Alex reviewed correspondence as she sat at her desk. After a few minutes, she sat back in her chair and thought about the past week. Things were better, but she knew it would be a long time before she'd get over Mitch, if ever. She felt betrayed, cheated again. She wasn't sure if she'd ever trust a man again. She'd trusted Robert, and he'd divorced her. She'd trusted Mitch, and he'd used her. There were so many unknowns about Mitch and his motives. Had he deliberately used her? Looking through her open office door she noticed an overnight mail package on Bridgett's desk.

Alex sighed as she rose from her desk to retrieve the package. She picked up the parcel and when she read the return address, her heart started beating furiously. It was from Mitch but had been mailed from Biloxi on Friday. Alex removed the letter with shaking hands, and a tape recorder fell out of the envelope. Mitch's big, bold handwriting stared up at her as she read aloud. "Dear Alex, by the time you receive this, you'll either know everything because I've told you, or you'll know nothing because

I'm dead. This letter explains everything.

First of all, I was dishonest with you at the beginning of our relationship. I sought you out because I owed a large sum of money to a mobster named Frederico Petrelli. It was a gambling debt. He approached me four months ago demanding that I get the dirt on CCMC because his friends wanted to buy it. I arranged to meet you, with the intent of learning ways in which Frederico could ruin the hospital. As time went by, I began to care for you and detest myself. Later, when I didn't deliver, Frederico told me he wanted the land owned by Bonnet's family so his associates could expand their casinos on the Riverfront. Of course, there was no way I could do that. I think it was just another threat to make me deliver on the CCMC information. Anyway, Frederico and a large man with a ponytail came to my house after we had dinner at Cafe Volange and told me I had until five o'clock the next day to deliver. To prove his point, Frederico burned my forearm. I left immediately and went to Biloxi to gamble. I lost heavily at the casino, and after that, I have no recollection of what happened. I returned for the Endymion Extravaganza so I could again see you and explain what had happened.

The recorder holds a tape I recorded the night Frederico and the man with the ponytail came to my apartment. They admit their part in the CCMC crimes, at least the shoot-out and the attack on the heart patient. It's enough information to implicate them both. You almost caught me one night when my recorder fell out of my pocket. Forgive me for being so deceitful. I love you, Alex. Mitch.

Alex finished reading Mitch's letter and sobbed uncontrollably. A little later she called Robert and told him to meet her in Francois' suite. As Alex took the elevator to Jack's room, she was comforted with the knowledge that Mitch had loved her, and had tried to do the right thing. In reality, Mitch's letter would close the case.

Robert, his arm casted and in a sling, Adam and Jack were waiting for her when she entered the suite.

Alex said, "Sit down. There was a package from Mitch in my office. Mailed Friday from Biloxi. He also sent me a tape recording, which I think will answer all your questions. Jack, will you read the letter. I'm too emotional." Alex handed the letter to Francois.

Jack read the letter slowly. The letter was the missive of a doomed man.

"Turn on that damn recorder," Adam Patrick Lee growled. "Let's see what we've got!"

The recording implicated Frederico and Salvadal easily. In less than a minute Francois called for a warrant for Frederico's arrest. Within an hour Frederico was picked up and charged with the murder of Jonathan Mercier, the crime team reporting that the ballistics were a perfect match.

"Why'd Frederico kill Mercier?" Robert said.

"Frederico knew Mercier was the weak link. Knew he'd implicate him later on. The mob leaves no witnesses."

Robert nodded in understanding.

Francois turned to Alex. "We got them. All tied up in a nice little package, at least for now."

"Yep, we did. But, you owe me one and payback's going to be tough." Alex, her eyes hard and unsmiling, eyed the captain.

"What the hell, what payback?" Captain Francois was actually stammering. "What are you talking about, Alex." A light of realization paled the captain's already white face as he reviewed the possibilities. His thoughts returned to his recent elevator ride. He said, "Oh no, no way. No elevators, no damn elevators. I'm a sick man." Francois looked around frantically.

Alex smiled. Now she knew his weakness, his Achilles heel. She thought about it and said, "Hmm. Elevators, that's a new twist. I'll have to work on the elevator." She paused to allow the fear to sink in. Then she looked at Jack and Robert and smiled. "You're both sick men and you're both leaving for Virginia on Tuesday to recuperate at Wyndley." Alex winked at her grandfather.

"Absolutely, we've got reservations to leave New Orleans on Tuesday morning. No excuses allowed." The Congressman looked pleased with the plan.

Francois was so relieved that no elevators were involved, he said quickly, "Count me in, I'm coming."

Alex turned to Robert, "And you?"

The surgeon gave Alex a tender smile. "You bet. I want to see Grand."

ABOUT THE AUTHOR

Judith Townsend Rocchiccioli is a native Virginian and holds graduate and doctoral degrees from Virginia Commonwealth University and the University of Virginia. She has been a practicing clinical nurse for over 25 years and is currently a professor of Nursing at James Madison University and the author of numerous academic and health-related articles and documents. Her first novel is based on her experiences living and teaching in New Orleans. When not teaching or writing, Judith is an avid silk painter and multi-media artist. She lives in the Shenandoah Valley of Virginia with her family and six dogs.